Bodies
in
Motion

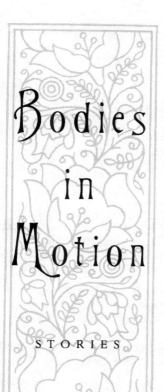

Bodies in Motion

STORIES

Mary Anne Mohanraj

Visiting Professor,
Asts + Science

HarperCollins*Publishers*

BODIES IN MOTION. Copyright © 2005 by Mary Anne Mohanraj. All rights reserved. Printed in the United States of America. No part of this book may be used or reproduced in any manner whatsoever without written permission except in the case of brief quotations embodied in critical articles and reviews. For information, address HarperCollins Publishers, 10 East 53rd Street, New York, NY 10022.

HarperCollins books may be purchased for educational, business, or sales promotional use. For information, please write: Special Markets Department, HarperCollins Publishers, 10 East 53rd Street, New York, NY 10022.

FIRST EDITION

Designed by Nicola Ferguson

Printed on acid-free paper

Library of Congress Cataloging-in-Publication Data
Mohanraj, Mary Anne.
    Bodies in motion : stories / Mary Anne Mohanraj.—1st ed.
        p.   cm.
    ISBN 0-06-078118-1
    1. Sri Lankan Americans—Fiction. 2. Sri Lanka—Fiction.
    I. Title.
PS3563.O34B63   2005
813'.6—dc22   2004059942

05 06 07 08 09 ❖/RRD 10 9 8 7 6 5 4 3 2 1

For Kevin

Genealogy Charts

THE KANDIAHS

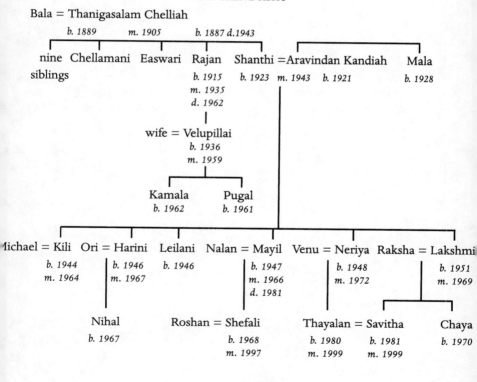

Bala = Thanigasalam Chelliah
b. 1889   *m. 1905*   *b. 1887 d.1943*

nine siblings | Chellamani | Easwari | Rajan | Shanthi = Aravindan Kandiah | Mala

Rajan
b. 1915
m. 1935
d. 1962

Shanthi *b. 1923*   *m. 1943*   Aravindan Kandiah *b. 1921*

Mala *b. 1928*

wife = Velupillai
b. 1936
m. 1959

Kamala
b. 1962

Pugal
b. 1961

Michael = Kili
b. 1944
m. 1964

Ori = Harini
b. 1946
m. 1967

Leilani
b. 1946

Nalan = Mayil
b. 1947
m. 1966
d. 1981

Venu = Neriya
b. 1948
m. 1972

Raksha = Lakshmi
b. 1951
m. 1969

Nihal
b. 1967

Roshan = Shefali
b. 1968
m. 1997

Thayalan = Savitha
b. 1980   *b. 1981*
m. 1999   *m. 1999*

Chaya
b. 1970

THE VALLIPURAMS

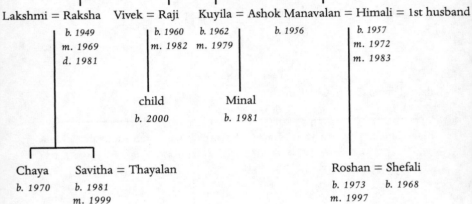

several siblings

Mangai
b. 1931

Sundar Vallipuram = Sushila
b. 1926   b. 1931
m. 1948

"Mary"

Prema = Deepak
b. 1940   b. 1920

Lakshmi = Raksha
b. 1949
m. 1969
d. 1981

Vivek = Raji
b. 1960
m. 1982

Kuyila = Ashok
b. 1962
m. 1979

Manavalan = Himali = 1st husband
b. 1956   b. 1957
                 m. 1972
                 m. 1983

child
b. 2000

Minal
b. 1981

Chaya
b. 1970

Savitha = Thayalan
b. 1981
m. 1999

Roshan = Shefali
b. 1973   b. 1968
m. 1997

Contents

Beginnings

Oceans Bright and Wide

Colombo, 1939

THANI STOOD JUST OUTSIDE THE CONVENT SCHOOL GATES, WAITING
FOR SISTER CATHERINE TO COME AND MEET HIM. BOUGAINVILLEA
spilled over the walls, lush and crimson; he was briefly tempted to
break off a small sprig to present to her. It was her favorite plant, the
brilliantly hued paper-thin leaves hiding their tiny white flowers. But
any flowers he broke off would only wither and die; better to leave
them growing on the vine, surrounded by their own kind, beautiful in
their profusion. Thani watched the young girls instead, demure pairs
walking in their crisp white school uniforms across the wide lawns; he
heard the nuns giving strict instructions to their charges.

An accustomed pleasant thrill of anticipation energized him; after
all these years of friendship, he still looked forward to his walks with
Sister Catherine. Their conversations had started when his daughters
were girls, fatherly duty bringing him to the convent school grounds,
to that large white building, its tall pillars and broad marble floors so
reminiscent of his own Cinnamon Gardens home. When the convent
had put in tennis courts for the girls, and his wife, Bala, had worried
about the propriety of allowing their daughters to play, it was Thani

who had come to talk to the nuns, who had then come home and reassured his wife. Had he been convinced by reason? Or by the bright young face of Sister Catherine, with her sharp green eyes and her red hair forever escaping the confines of her demure garb? Her face had been so fair, like a water lily, too delicate for the touch of the sun. And her mind—quick, rich with the accumulated knowledge of European civilization, the literature and philosophy she taught. When he talked with her, Thani felt like a young coconut tree, growing tall in the bright light of her regard, enriched and enlightened.

There she was, at the top of the white steps, hurrying down, heedless as a girl despite the constrictions of her nun's habit. His heart beat a little faster, and he entered the gates, crossing the broad expanse of grass to meet her. Thani walked slowly; his heavy middle-aged build didn't allow him to move as quickly as she did. He was slow but steady, unreasonably happy. Thani never inquired too closely into his feelings for Sister Catherine. It was enough that for twenty-five years, since the day his first daughter started school, until today, when his last daughter was finally finishing, it had brought him pleasure to come here, to spend an hour or so walking the grounds in Sister Catherine's company, listening to her talk of Chaucer and Milton, Plato and Aristotle.

"Mr. Chelliah! I am so sorry that I've kept you waiting!" She landed beside him, slightly out of breath, hands reaching up to tuck stray wisps of hair back under her wimple. There were a few strands of grey among the red now, but it was still beautiful—so fine and delicate. After all these years, Thani still felt the urge to reach out and touch the strands.

He smiled down at her. "It is never any trouble, Sister. When I received your message that you wanted to see me, I was delighted to come. I hope nothing is wrong."

"No, no." She started to walk, and he fell into step beside her. "It's about Shanthi, but certainly nothing is wrong. Everything is perfectly right, in fact."

"Oh?"

"I wanted to know—what are your plans for her?"

Thani felt mixed apprehension and pride. This had lately been a source of mild contention between him and his wife; Bala was determined to get the girl safely married, as Shanthi's eleven elder sisters and her one brother had been. But Thani wasn't ready to let his youngest daughter go; she was his favorite, the one he could talk to. She was bright, a good companion for his thoughts; he had wondered whether Shanthi might perhaps study for a teacher's certificate. Then she could stay with them a little longer.

"That is not yet decided; my wife and I are not entirely in agreement on this." He flushed, slightly embarrassed, wondering if the nun would think less of him. A man should be able to rule his own house—that was what his friends at the club would say, if they heard him. But whatever men boasted to one another, it was different within a marriage.

Sister Catherine glanced shrewdly at him. "Yes, I thought that might be the case. But if my own words might carry some weight . . ."

"My wife and I have always thought very highly of you, Sister." That was true; the nun had been a frequent visitor to their home, had shared innumerable cups of tea with Bala. They had become friends in their own way, the way of women together, talking of the children. If his wife had been a different woman, Thani might have wondered whether she had carefully chosen to cultivate Sister Catherine, whether she suspected the attraction Thani felt for the pretty nun. But Bala wasn't smart or shrewd enough for such a strategy. That was part of why their marriage was happy and successful; Thani could relax around his wife.

Sister Catherine took a deep breath before saying quickly, "Shanthi must go to Pembroke for a crash course; there are a few girls studying sciences now among the boys at Pembroke. We've taught her what we can in private tutorial, but we have no science courses here. Then she must go on to university; she must continue her physics studies properly. After a year or two there, she can apply to Oxford."

Thani stopped short, shocked, turning to face Sister Catherine. "You're joking, surely, Sister. Pembroke perhaps, although Bala will be worried about her, with all those boys; her reputation might be compromised. And university . . . she's clever, but no girl has ever—"

"That's not true," the nun interrupted. "Shanthi wouldn't be the first to attend, though the few other girls have gone straight into medicine. But Mr. Chelliah—" Sister Catherine put a hand on his arm, and Thani flushed under the bright Colombo late-morning sunshine. "Your daughter is more than clever. She is brilliant. Exceptional. Sixteen, and she has outstripped all the maths and physics we can teach her; she soaks it up like a sponge, her mind leaping ahead of our poor stumbling explanations. She must go on, must go to England. Only there will she get the education she deserves. She will be a beacon at Oxford, proof of what astonishing heights your people are capable of."

Her last words were like a splash of icy water in his face. Thani had been floating in a pleasant haze, flattered by the compliments paid his daughter; Shanthi had gotten her brains from him, after all. He had thought often enough that if he had applied himself more to his studies as a boy, he might have ended up a professor, perhaps even principal of a school. Thani knew that in England Shanthi would get the best education; all the world knew the shining towers of Oxford. But the nun's last words—was his beloved daughter to be a trained monkey, a performing dog? "We are quite aware of our own capabilities, Sister." Thani pulled back from her, surprisingly annoyed. He had never been angry with her before.

"Of course you are." Sister Catherine stared up at him, undaunted, those green eyes earnest and determined. "But don't you want the world to know? Don't you want *us* to know?"

Thani felt disappointed then. She had never allowed her white skin to come between them before. He had almost forgotten she was white—or, rather, forgotten that he was not. "After all this time, Sister, are you still one of them? Or one of us?" His voice was gentler than his words.

SISTER CATHERINE'S VOICE ROSE IN RESPONSE. "CAN'T I BE BOTH? I'm not English, you know." Her voice gentled again. "Ireland has enough reasons to resent England—but are you sorry the British came here? Are you sorry for what they've brought to Ceylon?"

Thani didn't know how to answer. At one point, he would have said, unequivocally, that the British had done great things for his little island. They had brought schools and roads, new systems of law and government, and had brought that great treasure, the English language, the language of Shakespeare. The language that, if a man mastered it, allowed him to rise high in the world. Thani had learned English as his first language, and his family had benefited greatly from the coming of the British, had made fortunes in trade of coffee, tea, cinnamon. They enjoyed high tea with the local white officials and their families; they celebrated the King's birthday with as much pleasure as anyone in England. And yet. He was silent, not knowing how to begin to respond.

The nun said softly into his silence, "Oxford is more beautiful than you can imagine, and full of the brightest minds in the world. Would you deny its benefits to your daughter?" She paused, then asked fiercely, "What will Shanthi's future be, if she stays here? To marry a stranger, to serve him as wife . . . to have a dozen children like her mother?"

There was scorn in the nun's voice, and Thani wanted to recoil, to protest on behalf of his devoted wife. It was honorable to be a good wife, a good mother. But shame held him steady. Hadn't he, occasionally, watching Bala surrounded by their demanding children, watching her tired face, hearing her voice as it turned high and shrill, hadn't he felt exactly the same scorn? Thani shook his head, took a step back. "You have given me much to think about. I will take your words to my wife. Good-bye, Sister." He turned and abruptly made his way from her, across the perfectly manicured lawn.

THANI SENT THE WAITING CAR WITH ITS DRIVER BACK TO THE house; he began walking. He found his heart longing for the clamor of the marketplace, the jumble of voices speaking Tamil and Sinhalese, and yes, English, but not English alone. He had been speaking English for so long, and Sinhalese to the servants—did he even remember how to speak Tamil anymore? Could his children speak it? Thani felt a swift desire to pack them all up, abandon their house and go back to the north, to Jaffna, to his great-grandmother's home, where he could rest his head against her sari-clad knee and hear her soft lilting Tamil again. But his children were grown now, most with homes and children of their own, and his great-grandmother was dead.

The sounds of the market washed over him, the bright colors of the booths, the thin, dark men hawking glass bangles, homespun shirts, sandalwood soap, fresh flowers. The market was dizzying; Thani always shopped at Cargill's, when he shopped for himself at all. British products were of such high quality. He found himself overwhelmed, needing a quieter place to think. Thani wandered from wide paved roads to dirt lanes, bought a fresh coconut and sipped the sweet water under the shade of a palm tree, ventured into the sunshine again.

By late afternoon, he had made his way to the beach market, where the fishermen's wives spread out their husbands' catches. Scraggly women in faded saris, they haggled fiercely with their customers, demanding more rupees, more, more. He paused at one net, where glistening dark fish shone wetly up at him, beckoning. Thani was tempted to buy some—but he didn't know what fish they were, and Vidu, the cook, had undoubtedly already ordered the supplies for supper. Bala would be upset with him if he insulted Vidu; the young Sinhalese man was a genius with spices, and he could produce a mackerel curry so fierce and yet meltingly delicious that every mouthful was a taste of heaven. Bala had never learned to cook herself; she'd had no need. They'd be in real trouble if they lost Vidu, though their son Rajan's new wife had certainly shown a deft hand with last Sunday's hoppers. Her rice pancakes had sides high and a crisp light brown, had centers soft, spongy, and slightly sour.

Perhaps they should have done more to encourage their girls to learn housewifely skills; though, of course, they'd arranged good marriages for them all, to men whose families could easily provide sufficient servants to ensure a comfortable living. None would ever need to cook. They had done well by their daughters, almost entirely. Except for poor Chellamani.

They had arranged a marriage for their eldest daughter, proud of their newfound responsibility. Chellamani had resisted, had said she wasn't sure she liked the boy. Bala and Thani had overridden her, pointed to the many successful arranged marriages of her aunts and uncles, to their own flourishing marriage, had told her that this *like, not-like* business was foolishness. Marriage was not about liking; it was about working together, taking care of each other. They had been so young, so sure of themselves, so strict with their eldest daughter. In the end, Chellamani had bowed her head, had acquiesced—and then.

When she had come home a few months after her marriage for a visit, when Thani had realized that the clumsy makeup smothering her cheek was an attempt to cover a bruise, he had been overcome by a righteous, guilty fury. He had raged that day, shouted dire threats and imprecations, had refused to be calmed until Chella had, sobbing, admitted everything. She had undraped her sari, let them see the welts where her husband had taken a piece of bamboo cane to her back. The child had blamed herself for her husband's brute nature. The boy might have come from one of the finest Tamil families, but apparently that was no guarantee of civilized behavior. Thani had insisted that she move back home immediately. Bala had disagreed.

He remembered her words—his wife had said, "Chella, rasathi, you must go back. You must try to work things out with your husband."

Thani had shouted, astonished. He had asked, "What can a woman possibly work out with a man like that?" Had demanded, "How can Chella put up with this kind of behavior?"

His wife had replied sharply, "You would be surprised what women are able to put up with."

Eventually, Thani had convinced Bala to let their daughter come home. They had barred the door to the man who dared to call himself a husband. He, perhaps ashamed, had soon stopped attempting to see his wife. Chellamani had begun helping Thani with the family accounts, and while she was not as bright as Shanthi, she had always had a good head for numbers and seemed to enjoy the work. It kept her busy. Chella was becoming the prop and comfort of his old age.

Not that Thani was really old. Fifty-two was old in the villages, old for a field-worker, bowed down by work and unrelenting sun. But for a resident of Cinnamon Gardens, one of Colombo's privileged elite, it was nothing. Thani wandered onto an empty patch of beach, away from the fisherwomen's nets. He walked down to the water's edge, his step as steady as if he were a young man. The waves were fierce today, the wind whipping them up to churn, to pound against the shore. He sank down to sit cross-legged on the damp sand, his movements smooth, comfortable despite his bulk.

Thani lived a life of pleasure and ease; he lived, in fact, much as the British colonial administrators did. He had been raised a Christian, though he rarely went to church; his grandfather had converted from Hinduism long ago. Thani had studied with the British children, had worn the same clothes, played the same games of cricket. When he was a boy, he would have thought himself exactly the same as they were.

Sitting here on the sands, gazing north and west, Thani could imagine that he could see England, far across the sunlit waves, could almost imagine himself truly a citizen of His Majesty's empire. But the 1915 troubles, the brutality of the British response—those had made it clear to every Ceylonese aristocrat that an English education, a law degree, and quiet subservience to British rule were no guarantee of true acceptance, of admittance to the ruling class. The vaunted justice of the courts and the philosophies of reason had proven no protection for the brown-skinned.

Thani had been ten years married at the time of the 1915 troubles, with several small children to protect; he remembered the fear he had felt then, the sense of betrayal. The British were better masters of Ceylon, perhaps, than the Dutch or Portuguese had been. But they were still masters. They promised freedom and independence, but those promises had not yet been kept.

He rose slowly and turned away from the water, crossing the beach toward the city, thinking hard. Could he imagine his daughter in Britain? He knew what his friends would say about the idea—they wouldn't allow an unwed daughter to travel to Jaffna by herself, never mind across the oceans. And now seemed a particularly bad time; there was worrying news coming out of Europe, rumblings of troubled times, even war. It seemed unlikely to affect England, but it was possible. Yet Oxford might still be the best place for his Shanthi. If what Sister Catherine had said were true, it might be the only place for her. Should he care what his friends would say? None of them had a daughter as clever as his. Thani felt a swell of pride filling his chest, a glow of satisfaction as he remembered the nun's words. *Exceptional. Brilliant.*

Thani himself had done well under British rule. He was widely read, cultured, prosperous, strong. The patriarch of a growing clan. Thani could easily live into his nineties, as his grandfather had. Or so he had once thought. Lately, his doctor had been saying some worrying things. His heartbeat was a little fast, sometimes irregular, and though Thani felt fine, healthy and strong, the doctor was concerned. Thani hadn't told Bala anything; with no proof of a problem, there was no need to worry his wife. Still, it made a man wonder. Made him think differently about the future, take a wider view. It would be good to have a place in the history books, a place earned not simply by being born in the right place, to the right family. He had always hoped that his son would mark Thani's place in the world, but Rajan seemed content to live a small life with his wife, his first child. Perhaps Thani should be looking to his daughter instead.

Thani paused in the road, lost in contemplation, and was jolted from his thoughts by a bullock cart rumbling past, inches from his nose. The street was lined with vendors shouting, hawking fresh curry buns, steaming hot samosas; it was almost suppertime. His wife would be worrying. Thani hurried toward home.

"YOU'RE A MESS—THERE'S SAND ALL OVER YOUR PANTS. WHAT HAVE you been up to?" Bala's voice was annoyed, but she was smiling. She was sitting at the grand piano, elegant in a green silk sari. Despite thirteen children, his wife was almost as slim as a girl. Thani felt the full weight of the extra kilos that had settled around his belly in the last few years. The doctor hadn't been pleased about those either.

He leaned against the piano, watching her fingers running quiet scales, up and down the keys. She liked to practice for an hour or so before supper, *just to keep her hand in,* she said. Bala had been quite the pianist as a girl; one of the many accomplishments which had made her so very suitable for one of Cinnamon Gardens' most eligible sons. "Just out walking, kunju," Thani said. "Had some thinking to do."

"You and your thinking," she said dismissively yet fondly. "Go and get washed up; we're dressing for dinner tonight. Rajan is joining us; his wife has thrown him out of the house for the evening, and the boy with him. Says they talk so much that she can't hear herself think." Bala played a few loud notes, then quieted again. "What she has to think about, I don't know. Isn't thinking about her husband and son good enough for her?"

Thani smiled. "Ah well—not all wives can be as perfectly patient as you, my rasathi." His princess, he called her, a fair description of the girl she had once been. She was more of a ruling maharani now; they had servants, of course, but it was Bala who arranged everything, who made sure that the servants knew each family member's preferences and desires. She saw to their comfort, their happiness. Bala had worked so hard to find good matches for the children, and Thani knew that she already had her eye on a few suitable boys for Shanthi. Good families, good prospects, good hearts.

Bala blushed at his compliment. "Enough of your foolishness. Go say hello; they're in the library. No need to hurry—Shanthi isn't home from the club yet." Bala was frowning now. "You should never have given her that bicycle; it's become impossible to keep track of her. I'm not going to have an easy time finding a husband willing to put up with her wild ways."

Thani reached down, touched her hand, stilling it on the keys. "She's not really wild, just restless." He hated to hear anything negative about Shanthi, about any of his children. They were gems to him, pearls of great price. He had been blessed.

His wife shrugged helplessly. "I know, I know. She's a good girl. But look at what happened to that poor girl of Ranjee's—caught fooling around with the Sinhalese chauffeur, and now no one will have her. Wild before marriage, wild after—that's what everyone says, and what man wants a wife who will run around? So no husband for her, no children; that girl will die in her parents' house, miserable and alone." Her tone was bitter, grieving. Ranjee's child had brought it on herself, but their Chella faced the same grim future, utterly unwarranted.

Thani's chest felt tight, thick with old sorrow. "I know." He squeezed his wife's hand, released it, took a deep breath. There was nothing they could do now but look to the future of their other children, try not to make the same mistakes again. "But our Shanthi is a good girl. All our children are good—even that lazy boy of ours. I'll go see him now."

Whether she went to Oxford or not, they *would* find a good husband for Shanthi, someone to take care of her, cherish her like the treasure that she was. That was what every parent wanted for their children, to give them every chance at a good life—if possible, a better life than their parents had had.

Thani's own parents had done an excellent job finding a match for him. They hadn't tried to find a girl who was his intellectual equal; Bala wasn't interested in his books, his dabblings into mathematics, physics, philosophy, and literature. It would have been pleasant to have a wife more engaged with the life of the mind—a woman more like Sister Catherine. That's what Thani would have chosen for himself, if his parents had been foolish enough to let him choose. But his parents had known that there were more important properties in a wife than the ability to carry on an interesting conversation. Bala was beautiful, still, and she worked tirelessly to ensure his comfort. He was one of Ceylon's luckiest men.

THANI'S STEP QUICKENED AS HE WALKED DOWN THE CARPETED hall—he could clearly hear his grandson's voice, its brightness seeming to light the hall, to lighten the dark wood. It was a beautiful house, but so empty these days, with most of his children grown and gone. Thani wondered what it would be like to live in a small house on the beach, some place constructed of mud walls, a clay-tiled roof, a dirt floor— and a door always open to the churning sea. He had inherited this vast space from his parents when they retreated to a tea plantation in the high hill country, at Nuwara Eliya, where it was always pleasant and cool. Perhaps it was time to gather the children and visit his parents. It had been too long; it would be good to have all the family in one place again. And then perhaps a trip to Jaffna, visit their ancestral home. Remind them all where they'd come from.

"Father!" Rajan sprang up as Thani entered the library, the small boy rising as well. "It's good to see you again."

"And you as well, son—come, Velu, embrace your old grandfather." The boy came forward shyly for a quick embrace, then pulled back again. He was growing so quickly, only three, but taller than Thani's knees already—he wouldn't be a boy for long. "What have you been showing him?" A book lay open on the floor, thick with text. Not a children's book.

"He wanted a story about kings, so I was trying to tell him about Ceylon's history; I wasn't sure of a few of the details, so I had to look them up." Rajan smiled sheepishly. "Reminded me how much I don't know, actually. Did you know about these irrigation channels? Apparently once they were the most advanced system in the world. Fascinating stuff, quite impressive, considering how backward those people were."

Thani raised an eyebrow. *Those people*, was it? And his son's voice, those intonations—had he never noticed how British his son sounded? "Glad to see you're taking an interest," he said dryly.

"It's Velu, really." The boy was standing quietly by his father; Rajan ruffled his son's hair. "He's completely caught up in this stuff. Can't seem to get enough of our ancient history. It's all kings and elephants right now. I keep telling him that he should be paying attention to English literature, Shakespeare and Dickens and all that. He's a little young for that now, of course, but it's never too early to start. And in a few years, perhaps we'll introduce him to the great philosophers."

"Aristotle and Plato?"

"That's right. That's what will help him get ahead, you know." Rajan frowned in concern. "I say—are you quite all right, Father? You look a bit odd."

Thani forced a reassuring smile, though his head was suddenly pounding. "Just faint with hunger, I suppose, and, oh no"—he pointed out the tall library windows—"there's Shanthi, riding her bicycle across the lawn again. Your mother will be annoyed. I must go wash up and dress. I'll see you in the dining room." Thani patted Velu's head and turned to head out the door.

"Look, Shanthi's taken a bit of a fall on her bicycle." Thani turned quickly, following his son's gaze out the library windows to where his daughter sprawled on the grass in a tumble of limbs. The girl appeared all right—and though he couldn't hear her, she certainly looked as if she were cursing her bicycle. Kicking it too, despite her prone position.

Rajan continued cheerfully, "Think her sari's gotten caught on the chain again; that'll take her a bit to put right. So you have plenty of time to wash up."

AFTER DINNER, WHILE THEY LINGERED OVER CARAMEL PUDDING AND coffee, it was Bala who brought up the subject of Shanthi's future. "So, mahal, I've had word of a few exciting prospects."

Thani glanced at Chellamani, but his eldest daughter seemed calm, unbothered by this reminder of her own unfortunate state. She was serving a little extra pudding to Velu, her slender hands steady on the porcelain dish, its accompanying silver spoon. Chella would have been a good mother, Thani was sure of that. It was too late to think of such things now.

"Oh-ho, is it time for little Sammie to be married off?" Rajan asked cheerfully.

"No one's being married off here," Bala said, frowning. "You make it sound like we're putting her up on an auction block. We're not barbarians. We've just found a few nice, handsome boys for Shanthi to meet, in appropriate circumstances. She might like them. What do you think, Shanthi? Are you ready?"

There was an uncomfortable pause, with Shanthi quiet and blushing, her eyes cast down. It was impossible to tell what the girl was thinking. Into that pause, Thani found himself speaking.

"Actually, Sister Catherine had a suggestion for Shanthi."

"Oh?" Bala said, a bit sharply. "I wouldn't think she would have had much . . . opportunity, to meet suitable young men."

"Not that kind of suggestion." Thani wasn't sure why he was bringing this up now; he had meant to discuss this quietly with his wife, in private. Something was pushing him to say the words now, out loud, for everyone to hear. "She thinks Shanthi should go to Pembroke, then university—and then, if they'll take her, to Oxford."

The table erupted into a storm of voices, arguments, protests. Velu was asking his father if *he* could go to Oxford; Rajan was congratulating Shanthi heartily, with just the slightest tone of smothered envy. Chellamani was asking questions, wanting more details, while Bala was simply refusing, flat out, saying that it was an impossible idea, what was that ridiculous woman thinking? Thani ignored them all, his eyes locked on his youngest daughter. When Shanthi looked up, her face was shining with a mix of fear and excitement. Thani hadn't known before he said the words, hadn't known what the girl would want. Now he knew.

It shouldn't have made any difference, but it did.

"SHE'D BE ALONE," BALA SAID, AS HE CLOSED THE BEDROOM DOOR behind him, shutting them into their own private world. Nothing had been resolved over dinner; the arguing had continued while the food grew cold, until Thani had shouted for silence, told them all to be quiet and eat. They had obeyed him, eventually.

"There's no guarantee they'd take her," Thani said. He would be sending his daughter, his little flower, to a cold country, to a land where people would look on her as an exotic stranger at best, a half-civilized barbarian at worst. They wouldn't want to believe that she could be as smart, or smarter, than their sons. That she could do the work. They would want to send her back.

"Of course they'll take her," his wife said sharply. "Don't be foolish."

Thani knew, of course, had always known that while all his children were clever enough, like himself, Shanthi was special. She learned everything fast, too fast, remembered everything that was told her, could repeat it back flawlessly. Thani had taught her a little math when she was just a child, and he remembered how quickly she'd learned it. It had been a game between them, he posing simple problems, and her solving them. He'd come to tell her bedtime stories from the *Ra-*

mayana, and she'd want to do math problems instead. A pretty girl, a sweet girl—but above all, a smart girl. *Brilliant.* Shining, like the sea, sparkling in the sunlight. Could he dim that brightness, draw down the clouds? Had he the right? However anxious he felt at the idea of putting his child into British hands—could Thani deny her every opportunity to shine?

And if he himself wanted to bask in her reflected glory—wasn't that a father's privilege?

He reached for his wife, pulled Bala close, into the circle of his arms. After all these years, he still took comfort from the shape of her body pressed against his. More now, perhaps, than ever. "It's years away. She may not want to go by then. She may want to marry instead."

"She'll want to go." Bala added softly, "I would, if I were her."

Thani was startled to hear that; he couldn't imagine Bala on the grounds of Oxford, striding across the quadrangle in a black scholar's robe. His daughter, yes, perhaps, but his wife? It was a ridiculous idea—so why did it disturb him so? He put it aside and came back to the real issues.

"What worries me," Thani said, "is the idea of her among all those white boys. What if one of them tries to take advantage of her? What if she is seduced by one of them?"

Bala shook her head, dismissing that concern. "Not worth worrying about. She would just as soon fall in love with Vidu."

Thani chuckled at the idea—his daughter and the cook? Impossible.

His wife continued, "Shanthi understands that like is only happy with like. The whites can never think of us as equals; they've ruled us for too long. A brown-white match would never work." Bala pulled back then, looking steadily up at him. She said softly, "Only a fool would even entertain the possibility."

Thani realized then that his wife knew—knew the thoughts he'd had about Sister Catherine, the years of idle fantasies.

He had been so sure that he had been utterly discreet—after all, nothing had ever happened. He had done *nothing*. But the way his wife gazed at him told him she knew, that she had always known. He felt a sudden sharp fear that Bala would say it out loud, would be angry, feel betrayed—might she even leave him? The thought was terrifying; Thani had grown entirely dependent on her care. If she left him, he would be like a tree in a monsoon storm, torn up by the roots.

He could see the possibility in her eyes—Bala *could* walk away from him. He had never known that about his wife.

She leaned back against him then, her cheek pressed against his thumping heart. The moment of danger passed.

When his pulse had calmed, he said, "Maybe you're right." Bala's head nodded against his chest.

Thani was no longer a tree alone; they were two trees, twined together. Together, they would withstand such storms—that was what a marriage was, after all. Protection against life's storms. The kind of marriage his parents had given him, sheltering, safe. The kind of marriage he would like to give his youngest daughter. If that were only what she needed, what she wanted. If he *knew* what was the right thing to do.

"I need to talk to her," he said. He expected his wife to protest, to say that it wasn't Shanthi's decision to make. They were her parents, it was their responsibility to decide what was best for their child. But Bala only nodded, said, "Go."

HIS DAUGHTER'S DOOR STOOD OPEN; SHE WAS SITTING CROSS-LEGGED on her bed, as if waiting for him. Had she known he would come? *He* hadn't even known. Shanthi looked worried.

"What are you thinking, mahal?" he asked her. Thani expected her to answer something about the distance, the foreignness, the fear of being surrounded by whites, by young men—the difficulty of being a stranger in a strange land.

"What if I'm not good enough?" Shanthi asked quietly.

He sat down beside his daughter on the bed, drew her head to rest on his sturdy shoulder. Thani stroked her hair, trying to think what to say. He wanted to reassure her, to tell her that she was brilliant, would be able to accomplish whatever she wanted.

Instead he said, "You may not be. You may go, and try, and fail." He felt the girl shiver against him, and he wanted nothing more in that moment than to pull her close, keep her here, near him, protected, safe. Wasn't that a father's job? Instead, he forced himself to ask, "The question is, do you want to try anyway?"

Shanthi nodded, quick, like a bird. Said, "Oh, yes." No hesitation. He had known she would, hadn't he? Thani hadn't needed to come here to know her response. But perhaps he had needed to hear it, to be able to stifle his own fears.

He stroked her hair one last time, feeling it so soft, so young, beneath his thick fingers. Then he stood to leave, saying as he did, "I'll talk to your mother." Shanthi nodded and pulled her knees up, wrapping her arms around her legs and resting her head against them. Trusting her father to take care of everything, already lost in thought again.

WHEN THEY WERE BOTH IN BED, THE LIGHTS OUT, THE COVERS PULLED UP tight, enclosing them, Bala turned to her husband. "It's so far," Bala said softly.

That was the heart of the problem after all. Not worries about white boys seducing his daughter, or even concerns about how the British would treat the poor brown colonial; Shanthi was strong enough for either of those. Thani simply didn't want to let his daughter go. To let her go so far, all alone. Shanthi was excited, eager for the opportunity. She would be changed, inevitably, when she returned.

Thani squeezed his wife, trying to reassure her, to reassure himself. "Uncle knows people in London, studying law. She would have family nearby. We would write letters."

"But how would we know that she was safe?" Those words almost a wail, his wife's hands pressed hard against his chest.

"We wouldn't know," he said heavily, his heart sore. It was so very far. There would be difficulties for Shanthi there—insults, slights, dangers, and hardships. "But can you tell her no?"

Bala was silent for a long time. Then she shook her head, as he had known she would. She was thinking of the same thing he was, he knew. You grew to know things like that about your wife, in a marriage. Thinking of their poor Chellamani.

Since the day she had returned to them, neither Thani nor his wife had been willing to take the chance of forcing another child down the wrong path. Did it make them bad parents, that in the end, after giving out advice, passing out as much wisdom as they had, arranging introductions, they had allowed the rest of their children to choose their own way? Many of their friends thought so, Thani knew. His own parents thought it hopelessly indulgent. Dangerous, to let children make such important decisions, decisions that could bring them such heartache. Thani's own father had told him that he had taken a coward's path, an abrogation of parental responsibility.

Perhaps. But it was the path they had chosen to take. They no longer lived in the village, safe in a thousand years of tradition. Their island was no longer isolated, if it ever really had been. The colonizers had come to Ceylon, and would someday go. The world was changing, and they were changing with it.

"It will only be for a few years," Thani said. "She'll get the degree, she'll come home to us." There were no guarantees, but he said it anyway, said it as if he knew.

There was a long silence. Then Bala asked, in a whisper, "After years in that country, with them, what will she be? Will we know her, when she returns?"

"We are her parents," Thani said. "We will always know her."

THE NEXT MORNING HE WOKE LATE, STUMBLED FROM BED FEELING exhausted, sluggish. Thani found his way to the washroom, splashed water on his face. Delicious scents perfumed the air—was it breakfast time already? Had he missed it?

Thani made his way to the kitchen, still in his pyjamas. There he found Shanthi, her mother, and Vidu, the cook, all bent intently over a simmering pot.

"What's going on here?" Thani asked, bewildered. He couldn't remember the last time he'd found his wife in the kitchen.

Bala turned, smiling. "Shanthi woke me this morning. You were fast asleep, snoring like a sick cow." His wife was teasing him, still punishing him perhaps for his thoughts about the white nun. It was a gentle enough punishment, and deserved. "The girl said she wanted to learn how to cook."

Shanthi grinned up at her father. "If I do go all the way to England, I need to have something decent to eat."

Bala added, "I had to confess that I can hardly cook anything—so we're both going to learn, together. Vidu has kindly agreed to teach us." She reached out then, in a spontaneous gesture of affection, and pulled her daughter close. Shanthi looked startled, but then leaned her head against her mother's shoulder.

Thani smiled slowly. His wife had never truly understood their youngest daughter, had never felt close to her. Shanthi was too bright, too quick, for Bala to be comfortable. Perhaps that would change now. This wasn't a consequence that Sister Catherine had been anticipating, but Thani would take such blessings where he found them. He knew himself to be a lucky man.

He felt an urge to shake up his wife a little; she was growing too complacent. "Well, move over. I might as well learn, too."

"You?!" Bala was startled, about to protest—but then she surprised him, smiling. "Why not? Might as well learn something useful, instead of just sitting around with those musty books all the time. Come— we'll make room." She and Shanthi took a few steps closer to the wall.

"Vidu was just showing us how to fry curry leaves in oil. *"Tell Mr. Chelliah what you're doing, Vidu,"* she said in Sinhalese.

"I'm just frying the curry leaves, sir, with mustard and cumin seed."

"He says that's how he starts all our curries. I never knew that, but it does smell like home, doesn't it?"

"It does." It was Thani's turn to pull his daughter close, to lean into the pot, their heads wreathed in scent.

He closed his eyes and breathed in deep, willing himself to record this moment, to fix this memory and hold it close, a talisman against the time when his daughter would be gone, far across the churning seas.

Seven Cups of Water

Jaffna, 1948

MY BROTHER'S WEDDING DAY. THE FEASTING LASTED LONG PAST
DARK, AND I WENT TO BED EXHAUSTED. I PEELED OFF MY SWEAT-
soaked sari, rinsing my body with cool well water before changing
into the soft cotton sari I wore to sleep. The old women had con-
sulted the horoscopes of my brother and his young bride, had pronounced that this day, in this month, would be the luckiest, in fact the
only day that would not bring down a thousand curses on the young
couple—never mind that it was also one of the hottest days of the
year. There was no flesh left on the old women's bones, nothing that
could drip sweat; I was sure they enjoyed making the young ones
miserable.

I thought that for once, I would be able to sleep. I'd been allowed a
little arrack whiskey to celebrate Sundar's wedding, had danced with
the other unmarried girls. My sisters' friends giggled and preened as
they danced, flashing dark eyes and slim brown bellies at the young
men who lounged by the door, drinking. I just danced; I had no interest in catching a man. Not that any would have spared a glance for me,
too-short, too-plump Mangai with her coarse hair and flat chest. I

danced for myself, not for them. Danced until my feet were aching, until my arms and legs were lead weights.

I danced until Sundar and his lovely Sushila were escorted to his bedroom, until the last piece of rich wedding cake was eaten, and the last guest had gone. Only then did I bathe and change, only then did I lie down on my bamboo mat, a few feet from my peacefully sleeping sisters. And still I could not sleep.

It might have been the heat. Our house is near the ocean, and usually cool breezes fill the small rooms, but that night it was so hot that it was hard to breathe. I kept thinking it would get cooler, but instead it got hotter and hotter. Sweat dripped in uncomfortable trickles from my neck to my throat, from my breasts to the hollow between them, pooling in my navel. My mouth was dry as dead leaves, and I finally rose to get some water.

The house was silent. I left my sisters sleeping, passed my parents' room, and my brother's. I passed the main room, where dying flowers and bits of colored foil testified to the day's happy event, and finally entered my mother's vast kitchen. We weren't rich, but we did have one of the largest houses in the village. We needed it; I was the youngest of eight, and cooking enough food for all of us took many hands and pots. The moonlight streamed in the window, illuminating the rickety table where my mother worked, the baskets of onions and garlic and ginger and chilies, the pitcher of water that was always kept filled. It was one of my mother's rules—if you drank from the pitcher, you refilled it from the well. With five daughters and three sons, she needed many rules to keep peace in the house. Not that we always obeyed them.

I stepped over to the pitcher, took a tin cup from the shelf, and poured myself a cupful. Then I saw her. Sushila huddled in a far corner of the kitchen, her back pressed flat against the baked mud walls, her crimson wedding sari pulled tight around her, so tight that the heavy silk seemed to cut into her fair skin. Folds of gold-embroidered fabric were wrapped around her fists, and those in turn were pressed tight against her open mouth. She looked as if she were trying not to scream, but she didn't move, or make a single sound.

I stepped toward her. "Sushila?" I knelt at her feet. Her knees were pulled up tight against her chest, and I rested a hand on one. "Is something wrong?" It was a foolish question, and after a moment I understood that I didn't deserve an answer. The cup was still in my other hand; at last I stretched it out to her. "Would you like a cup of water?"

She nodded, and slowly lowered her fists. I raised the cup to her lips and tilted it so that she could drink. Sushila took a deep gulp, draining half the cup. Her whole body shivered then, though the water couldn't have been cooler than lukewarm, after sitting all night. She shivered again, and again, her arms now hanging loose at her sides, her eyes wide.

I didn't want to ask my next question. "Did Sundar—did he hurt you?" The words almost choked in my throat. I knew that there were men like that in the world. But Sundar had always been the gentlest of us all. He had even converted to Buddhism almost two years ago, had turned vegetarian and mourned every time he accidentally stepped on an insect. He had never teased me like the others had; he'd protected me from the worst of our oldest sister's rages. I didn't want to believe my favorite brother had hurt his wife—but there she was, shaking before me.

Sushila shook her head. No. After a moment, the word came up and out of her throat—"No." I was almost as glad to hear the sound of the word as the sense of it; there was a crippled child who lived in the alley nearby who could not speak at all. I raised the cup again, and she drained it in another gulp. I put it down, not sure what to do next.

She was still shaking. I leaned forward, pulled her into my arms. When she was completely enclosed in my arms, the white of my sari covering the red of hers, she turned her head, so that her mouth was against my ear. Her breath was hot against my neck as she whispered, "I'm bleeding . . ." Before I could speak, she reached up and took my right arm, her fingers sliding down to my hand, pulling it down between us, under the sari to the space between her thighs. Her legs were wet, and when I brought my hand up, the tips of my fingers were stained red. When Sushila saw the blood, she started to cry.

I wrapped my arms around her and held her tightly, letting her cry against me. My second sister had shared every detail of her wedding night with us; she seemed to enjoy our shock and fascination. I knew that Sushila was the oldest daughter in her family, that her mother had died years ago of a fever. But didn't she have any aunts? I stroked her hair, so soft and fine, and told her quietly, "It's all right . . . shh . . ." Her shaking eased, slowly, though the tears still fell hot against my neck, sliding down my chest and mixing with my sweat, an indistinguishable mix of salty waters. I held her, and rubbed her smooth back, and whispered the words, over and over, until she understood.

THE NEXT MORNING, OVER THE FIRST MEAL OF THE DAY, I ASKED HER if she had slept well. Everyone laughed, and Sundar's face reddened. He had inherited my mother's pale skin, and every emotion showed through. Sushila smiled demurely and assured me that she had. I was glad for her, but I hadn't slept at all. I had drunk cup after cup of water after she'd left, then refilled the pitcher from the well. A breeze had finally picked up, and the ocean's salt air filled the rooms, cooling my body stretched out on its mat, but still, I couldn't sleep.

While cooking the midday meal, while eating, throughout the day, I watched Sushila, though I didn't speak to her again. She was slender and fair, a perfect foil to tall Sundar, and she moved as if she were dancing. She was clever too, telling small jokes that made everyone laugh. If I could only look like her, talk like her . . . but I might as well wish for Lord Krishna to come down and carry me off.

That night I dozed for a few hours, but in the deepest hours I woke, sweaty and damp. I needed water. I got up and walked down the hall.

She was standing near the kitchen window, drenched in moonlight.

"I hoped you'd be awake," she said, turning as I came in.

My tongue stumbled, but I managed to say, "I just woke."

"Thank you, for last night." Her face flushed, but her voice was firm and clear. There was no sign of the trembling girl I'd held in my arms; Sushila held herself straight and poised. "You must think I'm very foolish."

"I don't think you're foolish." The moonlight shaded the planes of her face, the delicate curves; it was almost like looking at a statue. I could have stood there, watching her, for hours. "Shouldn't you be in bed...with your husband?" My brother.

"I was thirsty. I often get thirsty at night." She was wearing white tonight, a thin gauze sari that barely covered her limbs. Sushila's small arms and legs made her look almost like a child, but she was seventeen, a few months older than me. "I came for some water, but I couldn't find a cup."

The cups were in plain sight. I reached up, pulling down the same one I'd used the night before. It had a small notch in one side; you had to drink carefully or you might scratch yourself. It was different from all the others, and my favorite. I lifted the pitcher and found that it was almost empty. Someone hadn't refilled it. I poured what water was left into the cup and held it out to her. As she stepped forward to take it from me, she stumbled, and her outstretched hand knocked against mine, spilling the water over both our hands, splashing onto the dirt floor.

"Sorry!" She seemed frightened, though it was only water.

"It's all right—but that was all the water." I could draw more from the well, of course.

Sushila sighed. I could see her breasts move under the thin fabric of her blouse. "I'm really very thirsty." She lifted her dripping hand to her mouth then and started to lick the water from it. Her tongue was small and licked very delicately, with determination. She licked away every drop, slowly, as I watched.

"Still thirsty?" I asked. Sushila hesitated and then nodded. I took a small step forward, bringing up my wet hand, up to her opening mouth. She reached out a hand and gripped my wrist, surprisingly tight. She took the cup out of my hand and set it on the table. Then she brought my hand to her mouth and started to lick.

I shivered.

When she finished, having licked first the back of my hand, then the palm, and then taken each finger into her mouth, Sushila let go of my wrist. My arm dropped limply to my side. Her eyes were wide and still, her head cocked to its side like a little startled bird. She bit her lip, then said, "I have to go back. Sundar might miss me."

I nodded, wordless. She turned away and stepped quickly and quietly down the hall. I heard her closing the door to their bedroom behind her. I picked up the pitcher and went out to the well.

THE THIRD NIGHT, I DIDN'T EVEN TRY TO SLEEP. I HAD NAPPED A little during the day, and my mother had called me a lazybones. Sushila was only staying three more days, and then she was getting on a train, leaving the north, going down the coast to Trincomalee, where Sundar had secured a good job with one of our uncles. The tickets were bought, plans had been made. This night, and then three more—that was all.

That night, I picked shoeflowers from the garden, lush and crimson, picked them with feverish haste until my arms were full. I arranged them in circles on my mother's table, and in the center of the circle, I placed the filled tin cup. I was bent over them, straightening a crooked flower, when I heard her step behind me. Her arms slid around my waist and Sushila rested her face against my back. She whispered, "It's dry in that room. My mouth and skin are dry; the air is like breathing chalk. The heat is outside and inside, burning. It hurts to breathe."

I said nothing, feeling her slim arms around my too-solid bare waist, the heat of her cheek pressed against the bare flesh above my blouse. I felt dizzy with lack of sleep, exhausted and yet intensely awake. None of this seemed real.

"Mangai," she whispered, "I'm thirsty."

I picked up the cup, raised it to my lips. I filled my mouth with water, soaking the dry roof, my parched tongue. I turned to face her, still enclosed in the circle of her arms. I leaned forward, placed my lips on hers, and gave her water. She sucked the water deep down her throat, swallowed, and I felt the motion in my lips. I took more water from the cup and fed her water from my lips, making each mouthful smaller and smaller, each transfer taking longer and longer, until the cup was not just empty, but dry.

This was impossible, so impossible that it wasn't even forbidden. I couldn't imagine what would happen if my father found us.

Sushila released me and returned to her husband.

Three more nights.

THE FOURTH NIGHT, SHE TOOK THE CUP AWAY FROM ME. SUSHILA pulled down my sari, so that the sheer fabric fell to my waist, leaving my upper body dressed only in my blouse. I felt naked. She smiled and, scooping up half a cup of water in her palm, drenched my left breast.

She put her mouth to the fabric, sucking the moisture from it, the water mixed with my own sweat. I raised my hand to my mouth again, teeth closing down on flesh. Sushila started with the underside of my small breast, then circled up and around, spirals circling closer and closer until finally her mouth closed on the center and I bit down hard on the web of skin between thumb and forefinger, breaking the skin, drawing bitter blood. When she released my sore breast and lifted her mouth away, she smiled to see my bleeding hand. Her eyes dared me to continue. I could stop this at any time, could smother the fire and walk away. If I did, she would return to her husband; her body would lie under his, and he would bend to taste her breast.

I nodded acquiescence. She poured the rest of the cup's water onto my right breast, and lowered her head again.

FIFTH NIGHT; ONE MORE TO GO. WHEN SUSHILA CAME INTO THE
kitchen, I opened my mouth to speak, but she laid a soft finger against
my lips.

"You seem thirsty," she said. She filled the tin cup, filled it to the
brim, and then handed it carefully to me.

"I am thirsty," I said. I was dizzy, weak. I couldn't remember what
it felt like to sleep, to close my eyes and rest. During the day, I had
moved around the house in a daze. I forced myself not to talk to
Sushila, not to look at her, so that no one would suspect—but I carried
the sweet curves of her face with me, fixed in my mind's eye.

In the heat of the day, I burned. I'd been thinking all day and all
night of how to make Sushila burn as well. I needed to match her, to
push the game forward. I needed her to understand that this was not a
game. We couldn't stop here, or even slow down.

I put my hand on her shoulder and pushed down gently; she
obediently sank to sit cross-legged on the floor. Sushila could wait
forever, unmoved. I needed to move her. The words pulsed through
me—*one more night, one more night*. I didn't have time to be patient. I
pushed her down again; her eyes widened, but Sushila obediently lay
down, stretching her legs out straight, with arms at her sides, her sari
stark and white in the moonlight, against the dark dirt floor.

I touched her eyelids, and she closed them. I stood and picked up
my mother's chopping knife, cold and heavy in my hand. I had always
been clumsy; I had dropped it many times, and had cut myself as I
chopped. But tonight I would be careful.

I pulled over a basket and, lifting out a handful of chilies, began to
chop as quietly as I could. The wind whistled through the palm trees,
and down the hall my father snored loudly, but still . . . I chopped the
chilies finely, minced them the way my mother could never get me to
do when it was only for cooking. I minced them until they were oil and
ground bits, almost paste. Then I scooped them into a tin bowl, my
fingers covered in hot oil and slowly starting to burn.

I knelt beside Sushila and placed the bowl and cup by her still body.

I pulled loose the sari fabric, pulled it down so that her upper body was only covered by her blouse, as mine had been the night before. Then I started to unhook her blouse.

I expected her to protest, but she said nothing, didn't move. I don't know what I would have done if she had tried to stop me; stopped, I suppose. But she didn't, and so I unhooked each clasp. I peeled back the fabric, baring her breasts. They were ripe, dark mangoes bursting with juice. I was so thirsty. If we were interrupted now, there could be no innocent excuse . . . and yet it wasn't enough. *One more night.* I smeared the chili paste in a weaving line, starting with her navel, curving up over her belly, looping and swirling until I reached her breasts, then circling in as she had done, to the centers.

Chilies don't burn at once, on the skin. They take time. To Sushila it would have felt like some slightly gritty chutney. Perhaps she thought I planned to lick it off—but there was a whole cup of water to use up, and first I wanted her burning. When I finished drawing my patterns, I put down the bowl. I sat back on my heels and waited.

She felt it first on her belly, the slight, growing burn. Sushila shifted a little, uncomfortably. I watched. Her eyes started to open, and I placed a hand, the clean one, over them. She kept her arms at her sides, but her body began to twist, to raise up from the floor, to arch. It was useless. Her belly was heated, her breasts. They were getting hotter. Soon it would be unbearable.

"Please . . ." The word broke from her lips. I took the tin cup. I started with her navel, started rinsing the chili paste away, caressing the skin with wet fingers, relieving the pain. But there wasn't much water in the cup. I could only dilute the essence, soften the intensity, and by the time I reached her breasts, the water was more than half gone. There just wasn't enough water left to do her nipples, their darkness crowned by fiery red paste. I let Sushila open her eyes then, raised the cup and showed her its emptiness.

There were tears in her eyes, but her arms stayed perfectly still at her sides. I smiled down at her.

"Do you want to go back to your husband now?"

"I'm burning, Mangai. I'm burning up."

My heart thumped. I lay down beside her, moved my head to her breast and took the fire into my mouth. I have never been able to eat spicy food. I swirled the chili paste on my tongue; I savored the burning flavor of it, mixed with sweat. My tongue was being stabbed by millions of tiny pins. I wanted to suffer for her.

I suckled at her right breast, feeling her body shifting against mine, hearing her whimpers. I was afraid we would be heard. Her hand came up to tangle in my hair, to keep me there. Her leg slid between mine, and I moved to her left breast, suckling again, rocking our bodies together as I did. Her breath left her in a tiny sigh, and at the sound, my chest exploded.

I went to bed that night knowing that traces of oil lingered on her body, that she lay beside Sundar still burning for me.

THE NEXT NIGHT, I WAS READY WITH MY ARGUMENTS.

I took her hands in mine, caressing her soft skin under my rough fingers. When she smiled, I said, "Come away with me."

"What?" Sushila tried to pull away, but I held tight. Her eyes were wide and frightened, and I squeezed her fingers, trying to reassure her.

"Come away. Take the tickets; we can trade them for another town and leave together. We can go to the capital, far away. I can find work."

Her mouth twisted in a way I had never seen before. Ugly. "Work? What can we do?" Her voice was carefully low, scornful. "Should we end up washing someone's filthy clothes? Lose caste, lose family, lose the future?" She pulled away then, sharply.

I wrapped my arms tightly around my body, trying to slow my thumping heart.

"*You* are my future." I wanted to shout the words. "It doesn't matter what we do; nothing matters but that we leave, together."

"I can't leave him—you have nothing and I have nothing. All I own are my wedding saris, the gold jewelry your family gave me; would you have me sell that so that we can buy rice and lentils?"

"Yes, if we must. How can we be separated? It's not right!" I reached for her hand, but she pulled away. Sushila walked to the window, stared out into the night. Her voice grew even softer, so I could barely hear her.

"It's not right to leave, Mangai. The jewelry, even my saris, belong to him. I belong to him. Would you have me abandon your brother, leave him alone and shamed, without wife or the hope of children?" She paused, then said, "I have to go with Sundar."

What had happened to my Sushila, who had burned for me last night? She sounded so cold.

"It doesn't matter what's right or wrong. What's wrong is the idea of you leaving me . . ." I didn't know if I was making any sense; I was desperate to say something that might keep her. But she wasn't listening.

Sushila turned back to face me. "I'm sorry." She sounded like the statue I had once thought her, as if she were built of stone.

"But I love you!" My heart was breaking. It had broken, and she was crushing the pieces under her heel. "Don't you love me?"

Her voice gentled a little. "I care for you, Mangai. But if they found us, they'd drag us back in shame. They might do worse. My friend— her husband died, and his family said she'd poisoned him with bad cooking. They burned her alive."

I sucked in my breath, shocked. "My family wouldn't—" She cut me off.

"No, you're right. They wouldn't. But Mangai—my place is with Sundar. There's no place for us out there. Just here in the kitchen, without words. Just you, me, and the cup full of water." Her voice had turned soft, persuasive, but I would not be persuaded.

"The cup! Is that what matters to you? The cup is *nothing*, Sushila. The cup is just a game, it's *your* game. You just want to play your game and then go off, safe in the arms of your husband, leaving me here." Leaving me alone.

"Safe? You think I'm safe with Sundar?" Passion in her voice, finally—but not the kind I'd wanted.

"My brother would never hurt you." I was sure of that.

She closed her eyes, squeezed them tight, opened them again.

"Oh no. He's sweet, and gentle, and kind. He will try to be a good husband to me, and I will try to be a good wife to him. We will have children, if the gods are kind." There was the pain I felt, there in her voice. But it wasn't for me. "And after ten or twenty or thirty years of that, I will have all the juices sucked out of me; I will be dry as dust. I will die of my thirst and blow away on the wind. That's the way it is, the way it always is. You're the lucky one, Mangai."

"Lucky?" I didn't understand her, didn't know her. Who was this woman with flat eyes, speaking of dust?

"You're sixteen, almost as old as me, old enough to be married, but you're still free. They're not even talking of arranging your marriage yet. Take what pleasure you can of it. That's all we can do, Mangai. Take a little pleasure when we can."

Sushila fell silent and I did too, still thinking that there must be some other argument, some persuasion I could offer. But I thought for too long.

"Come," she said softly. "Take up the cup." It waited full on the table. She was trying to save what she could; it was our last night, the very last. I grabbed the cup, held it in my shaking hands.

Then I turned it over, spilling every drop of water to the floor.

I didn't know what she'd do, if she'd rage and shout, if she'd drag me to the ground. But Sushila just turned and walked away.

I SLEPT LIKE THE DEAD THAT NIGHT. I DIDN'T WANT TO FACE THE morning, hoped that she would just slip away without my having to see her again. My mother shook me awake.

"What, are you sick too? Get up, Mangai—I need your help. Sushila's sick and they can't leave today. I need you to take care of her."

I dressed quickly, rushed to Sundar's room to find him standing over his wife, his cheeks pulled in. Sushila's eyes were closed, and she looked pale.

"Mangai, she's nauseated. She's been vomiting all morning. Stay with her? I need to go change our tickets."

I nodded and sat down in the chair beside her; he patted me on the head and then left the room. Once he'd gone, her eyes opened, and she motioned for me to bend closer. She whispered in my ear, "I made myself throw up. I'm giving you one more chance." When I pulled back, Sushila was smiling, and I was too. Perhaps I looked too happy, because all too soon she was saying, "Sundar and I will leave tomorrow."

"But—"

"No, Mangai. It's too dangerous."

I knew she was right. Each night we'd gone further, taken more risks. If we kept this up, we would be caught. I finally nodded agreement.

I stayed with her through the day; we didn't touch.

It was an eternity until nightfall.

When I arrived in the kitchen, she was waiting. Something was different. The tin cup sat on the table, and the pitcher, but something else as well—a stone. My mother's sharpening stone that she used for her knives.

"Help me," she said. Sushila picked up the cup and ran the stone along the jagged edge. I thought at first that she was dulling it, making it safer—but after a few strokes, I realized she was making it sharper. Sushila handed it to me, and I stroked it to greater sharpness. We passed the two items back and forth, the cup and stone, sharpening the edge to match that of a blade. Finally, she put down the stone and called the cup done. Three-quarters of the rim was still that of a cup, safe and dull. But one quarter had a sheen of sharpness to it, seemed more than just a cup.

"Pull up your sari," she said. I obeyed, pulling it up past my ankle, my calf, my knee, until almost all of my thigh was visible. "Stop." I stopped obediently and watched her do the same with her sari. Her legs were so smooth and fragile; for a moment, I felt like a hairy cow. But the moment passed; we were past that now.

"Cut me." She pointed to her thigh, and, suddenly understanding, I took the cup in my hand. I reached out, pressed it against her soft flesh, bit my lip, and sliced down. A short, sharp cut, barely half the length of my palm. She exhaled once, sharply, but made no other sound. She took the cup from my hand and, with a swift motion, made an identical cut in my thigh. The beads of blood welled bright, shining in the moonlight, and for a moment I was so dizzy I thought I would faint. But then I steadied, and when she leaned forward and pressed the cuts together, blending our blood, I held firm. She kissed me then, and the world spun around us.

"Pour the water." I poured the water into the cup with my left hand, spilling some onto the table. It didn't matter. I poured until the cup was full. She took it then, and carefully sluiced some onto our joined legs, pulling away as she did. The bright blood ran down, mixing with the water, diluting.

"Don't pour it all!"

"I haven't. See?" She showed me the water left in the cup, barely a mouthful.

"Good." But we had a problem. "If we let the fabric go, the saris will be stained. People will notice."

Sushila said solemnly, "We'd better remove them, then."

It was so risky; it was the last time.

We carefully removed our clothes, holding them away from the now trickling blood. We piled the fabric on the table and then, carefully, eased to the floor. My hand found her breast, and her arms wrapped around me. We lingered over our pleasure until the sky began to lighten, and then we shared the last mouthful of water. By the time the household wakened I was back in my room, one hand pressed to the ache in my thigh, trying to remember everything.

WHEN SHE LEFT, SHE LEANED TO MY EAR IN FULL SIGHT OF EVERY-
one and whispered, "It's for the best, Mangai. You'll be married
soon—try to be happy."

I didn't say anything. I knew that I would never marry, and that I
would never love anyone as I had loved her.

THE SCAR FADED INTO NOTHING WITHIN A YEAR.

Sister Mary

Colombo, 1949

SHE COMES IN THE EARLY DAYS OF THE DRY SEASON, WITH THE BABE
IN HER ARMS, CLOTHED IN WIDOW'S WHITE. THE THIN CHIFFON SARI
that wraps around her tall, slender bones is clearly of good quality, but
is sadly torn and dark with dust, dark like her smooth skin. She is too
thin—the nuns all agree on that. When two nuns find her wandering
mute in the road near Holy Family convent, the bones stand out sharp
under the skin of her face, her back, her ribs. The woman might have
been beautiful if she hadn't been so thin, and so very dark.

The baby is fair, and almost as thin as the mother. When they find
her, the smaller nun, Sister Anne, starts to put a supporting hand on
the woman's arm, since she seems dazed, close to fainting. But the
woman screams and hunches down in the dirt road, her entire body
huddled around the child; the nun pulls back. The taller nun, Sister
Teresa, speaks sharply; though she is younger, she was of high caste
before coming to the convent and misses no opportunity to remind
the other nuns. But when she reaches out, the woman screams again
and almost falls backward as she scuttles away. Sister Anne bites back
a smile.

Sister Anne speaks softly, gently to the woman. Despite the baby in her arms, she seems no more than a girl—perhaps eighteen or so in years, her face tear-streaked and open. Sister Anne's words are low and rhythmic, more a croon than speech. Without touching the woman, she coaxes her to rise to her feet again, to start walking down the road. The sun is high in the sky when they meet her; it is almost down to the top of the nearby coconut palm before they manage to lead her inside the convent gates.

Sister Anne takes her to the Mother Superior, and leaves her in the Mother's small, dark office. The woman is closeted with the Mother for a long time; when they come out, the Mother instructs that the woman be given a small northern cell, and an opportunity to bathe, and some food. The Mother goes back into her office and shuts the door, leaving the woman in the care of the nuns. The northern rooms are coveted in the dry season for their coolness, and the nuns think it unfair that one be given to a stranger.

The woman cannot immediately make friends, for she is mute. She has a tongue, but does not seem to know how to use it. Had she talked to the Mother Superior? No one knows, but rumors quickly fly among the nuns. Sister Anne is the most generous among them; she staunchly claims that the poor woman must have been widowed and left without family in some terrible accident.

She had been beautiful, a girl of good family who had married and borne a child. Perhaps it had even been a love match. She had a good life, cooking and caring for her husband and baby. Barely a year into her marriage, her husband had been hit by a bus, or lost in a train crash, or drowned in a river, or, most likely, taken by disease, and the poor woman was left alone and bereft, driven mad.

The capital is large and crowded enough that tragedies occur daily and are swallowed in the rush of life. Anne is sure that once the grief passes, the woman will begin to speak. Others, led by Teresa, look at the baby and the woman and tell a different tale.

A darkie, unmarried, falls in love with a fair man. She offers herself to him, and he takes advantage. She becomes pregnant; her family finds out. They press for marriage, but he is of higher caste; his family laughs. The girl is disgraced, ruined, thrown out. She works, shamefully—in a shadowed room, men do not care that she is dark. She gets large and has difficulty finding such work. She grows thin; she gives birth. She is driven mad by the shame. She takes to wandering the roads, slowly starving herself to death as penance, an atonement for her sins.

Teresa is certain of this version and tells it often, until many of the others are convinced. There are other stories told, of course, but none so well liked. The convent is divided between the two tales, and one of the nuns names the woman Mary. So they call her, each in her own mind deciding whether they are speaking to one more like the Holy Virgin Mother, or more like Magdalene the whore.

IN A NORTHERN VILLAGE, A WOMAN IS WASHING DISHES, FACING THE sink.

"You weren't to leave them alone!" A man stands behind her, tall, straight-shouldered. He is fair-skinned, handsome as an actor. She does not turn to him; all he can see is her back. It is an attractive back—the skin at her waist and above the scoop of her cotton sari blouse is fair, unblemished.

"It was only for a few minutes, while I washed my face. I was tired, Sundar." She scrubs a dinner plate; she washes a cup. Water splashes up onto the front of her bright green blouse. He takes her shoulder with his right hand; he pulls her around.

"Tired? Why?" His voice is sharp. "You do nothing, Sushila. She washed him, fed him, played with him. You had her do it all."

She holds a half-washed glass in her hands. "I know how to manage her. I always have."

"She's a half-wit. We should never—"

Sushila looks up at him, eyebrows raised. "Husband dead, baby dead. A woman alone—where could she go? What life did my sister have?" She looks down again. "And I needed her."

He turns and paces away a few steps, turns back. "How could you leave them alone?" His voice is low, anguished.

"I just—had to wash my face. Just for a few minutes." She looks down at her plump hands, wrapped around the wet glass. They are covered in gold rings. "Sundar—what happens now?"

"The police keep looking. We keep looking. We'll find her." He sits down, as far from Sushila as he can. "How far could she have gone?" he asks softly.

She says nothing in response, only turns back to the sink. But she does not start washing again. The glass lies cradled in her hand, delicate, fragile.

THE BABY CHUCKLES HAPPILY, NO MATTER WHO IS HOLDING HIM. He is not quite so thin as he was; once the woman has been fed, she begins to produce good milk again. He is getting better, and with each day, he seems more beautiful. He is the most beautiful baby the nuns have seen—though they don't see so many, other than the scrawny, sickly babies of the parish destitute. They do not name him—he is *the baby*. Within a few days, he is their baby.

He is as happy with Anne as with Mary, and, more surprisingly, as happy with Teresa as with Anne. The youngest novice is so enamored of the child that she begins to whisper that perhaps he is more than a baby, that he is the Christ child come again. But the others laugh at her, and when she persists, Sister Anne sets her to chapel-cleaning.

As Mary's health improves, she begins working. She is competent in the kitchen, but seems happiest in the garden. The dry season is ending; it is time to turn the soil, to weed, to plant the seeds and seedlings. She wears the baby in a sling and works peacefully. When she tires, there is always a nun happy to take the child. After a few weeks of this, she seems much better.

THEY WERE SITTING IN HER GARDEN WHEN IT HAPPENED, SUSHILA IN a bright sari, pink like the bougainvillea arching overhead. Her sister, dressed in widow's white, held the baby, humming to it wordlessly. Her sister had not spoken since the sickness carried away her husband, her own baby. But she had been a good wet-nurse for the baby, had taken such care with it. Even now, she held a hand above its face, shading it from the sun. Before she came to join them, Sushila never took such care.

Sushila watches them, her heart beating faster. She has had an idea. The words are fluttering in her head, aching to get out. She has been beating them back for days, for weeks. But she is about to lose that battle. In a few minutes, she will start talking, softly, quietly, almost as if she is speaking to herself. She will say that there are places for a woman to go. Not here, perhaps, but far away, in the capital city, where Sushila had gone with her mother, her sisters, to buy her wedding jewels and sari. There are places that will take a woman in, will care for her.

She will mention one such place, Holy Family convent, where they had once visited, had had a nice cup of thick, sweet milk tea with the Mother Superior. Sushila will say that a child would be happy in a place like that, sheltered, safe. She will say, even softer, that a child should have a mother who loves him. Then she will rise, will go into the house, leaving them alone there in the garden. She will leave them alone for a long time. Her sister is silent, not stupid.

THE BABY IS SICK. THE CONVENT IS IN CHAOS. THE FLOOR HAS NOT been swept. The rice is burned. Sister Catherine's mother once mentioned feeding a sick baby drops of ginger juice, and two nuns run to the kitchen to chop and mince and squeeze. The doctor has come once, twice, three times.

The child is pale; he will not drink milk. He sucks for a minute—maybe two—then turns away fretful, crying. The pitiful wail echoes through the long white halls. Mary does not leave him for a moment. She paces the room, she does not sleep. She coaxes him to eat, offering her breast again and again. She hums and murmurs—nonsense sounds, nothing that makes any sense at all. As his face grows hotter, she grows colder. Her hands and feet turn cold as mountain snow, and as the days pass and the baby becomes more ill, she stays on her feet through sheer determination.

The Mother Superior has even come out of her office, once, to look in on Mary, the child, the huddle of nuns with their panicked whispers and scurrying feet. She shakes her head, then turns and goes back in, closing the door behind her.

SUSHILA IS FINISHING HER BATH. SHE TAKES THE TIN DIPPER, POURS the water over her head, down her long black hair and lush body. It has softened in the last year, becoming uncomfortably heavy. Her belly is marked now, her thighs rub together when she walks. Her breasts are finally getting smaller again, but they still hang from her chest. Sushila cannot bear to touch her alien flesh.

Her hands move smoothly, mechanically—dipping the water, pouring it down. It is cold; she shudders. She finishes and steps out of the small room. She dries herself, eyes closed. She wraps a blue silk sari around herself and steps lightly across the corridor, into the bedroom. Sundar is sleeping. His clothes are scattered here and there, wherever he has flung them. She picks his shirt up, quietly, and folds it awkwardly. She looks around the room, uncertain, and then places it on a chair. She picks it up again, and puts it on top of the chest. Then back on the chair.

Sushila sits down on the packed dirt floor, arms wrapped around her knees, and watches her husband sleep. His face is smooth, unlined. He is still as handsome as the day she was married to him. She hadn't objected when her parents had first brought her to his parents' house. She had looked up at him once, then cast her eyes down and remained silent. He seemed as good as any other that day, and her mother had said, leaving, that they would have beautiful children. A streak of silver has appeared in his dark hair over the last few weeks, and he sleeps curled in on himself, huddled like an animal in distress. His hands are buried under the sheet, but she knows that they will be tight fists against his body, fingers digging into the palms. She has felt them that way for many nights.

He has not been a bad husband to her. Perhaps she should have taken the road to the convent herself, vowed silence and disappeared into a black robe, a cowl hiding her wealth of silky hair. It had not occurred to her then, that solution. It was not much of a solution.

When the sun's early light enters the room, Sushila rises, her limbs stiff. She walks into the kitchen, sits down at the table with pen and paper. She has a letter to write.

THE CHILD'S FEVER BREAKS, AND MARY FINALLY SLEEPS A FULL night through again. The doctor gives all the credit to their devoted nursing, and the nuns are pleased with themselves. The baby cuddles content against Mary's breast; Mary's smile stretches across her face even in sleep. Her teeth shine, white and beautiful against her dark face. The youngest nun looks in on her and thinks that this is how Christ himself must have looked, as he rested, after battling the devil's temptation for forty days and nights in the barren desert. But she knows to keep that particular blasphemous thought to herself, and walks away singing a Gloria softly, under her breath.

THE MOTHER RECEIVES THE YOUNG COUPLE GRACIOUSLY; AS THE door closes behind them, the whispers start among the nuns. How handsome they are! See how fair their skin! Does the baby have his eyes? Is he a husband? A brother?

Mary sleeps soundly through the morning, through the hours that the couple spends closeted with the Mother. When the three finally emerge, they walk down the long white hall to her room, together. At the door, they see Mary and the baby, sleeping. Sushila steps forward and touches Mary gently on the shoulder. She wakes at once and at the sight of her sister begins to moan. The moan rises, louder and louder, into a panicked, broken wail. The nuns clustered in the hall move to defend, but the Mother stops them with an outstretched iron arm.

Sundar steps in, looks at his wife. Looks at Mary. Then he reaches forward and takes the baby from her limp arms. He turns away, cradling the child, tears bright in his eyes. He turns and walks out. Sushila brushes a few strands of hair from Mary's forehead, then turns as well, following her husband, leaving her sister behind, to the nuns' gentle care. She does not weep, but in the next few weeks, she is never more than a few steps away from her husband, her son.

The wails eventually lessen to low moans, almost inaudible. A day comes when Mary goes back to working in the garden. She does not smile, and she never does speak. The nuns continue to speculate, to conjecture, but though they discuss this for the rest of her life, invent a thousand different stories, they will never know the truth of it. They will never even come close.

A dark girl, married off. Love, unexpected, and a child. A terrible disease, deaths. A sister, beautiful and fair, married off. A baby, a wet-nurse. A gift, a theft. Flight from a garden. A desperate search; a weeping man. The lost, found. Two women, lost.

The Kandiahs

The Princess in the Forest

Chicago, 1955

It is always summer in the forest. The sun shines down through the tall trees, the leaves of spreading banyan and coconut palm. Monkeys race from limb to limb, hanging precariously by single arm or leg; parakeets swoop and glide, silhouetted for dark moments against the brightness of sky.

The princess walks for hours, her face smooth as an undisturbed pool of water, her eyes laughing, light as butterflies. Newly married, full of adoration for her husband, her prince. Rama hunts in the forest; he pursues the slender hart, lays traps for cunning rabbits. But always he comes to his Sita before the sun is down, comes to their modest hut, their gentle home in exile. He smiles to see her, lays the game aside and takes her in his arms, draws her down to the forest floor, the soft grasses, and she loves him then, as the gopis loved blue Krishna, she loves him with everything she has, everything she is.

"SHANTHI—YOU'LL BE LATE!" HER HUSBAND SCOLDS FROM THE kitchen doorway, their youngest daughter tucked under one arm, a book nestled in the other. Three days a week he watches the children, the days he doesn't teach, so that they can spend that time with a parent instead of with the hired black nanny. Shanthi doesn't know how he can read and mind the girls at the same time; she can't even think when she's with them. She can't understand now what had possessed her to keep having children, one after another, until there were six small heads to be tucked into bed. It was only after giving birth to Lakshmi that she had finally come to her senses.

Shanthi had told Aravindan that she would have no more children, that as soon as Lakshmi was weaned, she wanted to find a job. She had been ready with her arguments—had expected that she would have to win her husband over, talk him around. None of the other professors' wives worked. But she was different; she was smart, special. Shanthi had left Ceylon at nineteen, had attended graduate school at Oxford, one of very few women admitted. She possessed a doctorate in physics from Oxford—even though it was now a decade out of date, surely *someone* would hire her to teach. Shanthi had been unaccountably angry when Aravindan hadn't given her a chance to use her readied arguments, had only placidly agreed to her proposal.

Lately, even his gentlest words have driven her into a fury.

"I'm going, I'm going. I can't find my gloves. Where's my coat? What did you do with it?" She's frenzied, stomping from one room to the next, looking behind overstuffed leather chairs, under sofa cushions.

"Your coat's in the closet; I hung it up. The gloves are in the left pocket." Lakshmi has fallen asleep against Aravindan's shoulder, soothed by the solidity of his thick body. She is four now, too old to be carried around on her father's arm, but she has been a strange, slow child from the beginning, and Aravindan doesn't seem to mind the extra attention she needs.

Shanthi should be grateful for his care for the children, for her, but a wave of resentment sweeps through her instead, at the criticism implied. It isn't fair, but she can't help it. Should she be grateful that the important University of Chicago professor allows his wife to work, takes time out of his busy day so that she can teach at the high school for money they don't need? Other wives would be grateful; her own mother would tell her to thank Mother Mary for such a saint of a husband, and would then scold her for not spending more time at home, taking good care of such a kind, brilliant man.

"You'll have to reheat the rice and curries from yesterday; I need to meet with a parent after school; I'll be home late." Instead of feeling grateful, Shanthi takes a small, petty pleasure in making Aravindan eat old food, a pleasure somehow more intense because she knows he would not have noticed if she hadn't pointed it out. And without a kiss, or another word, she pulls on the coat, storms down the hallway and out the door, not bothering to button the buttons or pull on her gloves, taking satisfaction in the winter wind that will undoubtedly give her a cold before nightfall. Let Aravindan work a little harder the next few days. It will be good for him.

In the evenings, Rama cleans and dresses the game; Sita slices wild onions, cooks savory curries and coconut roti over a small fire. They each have their appointed tasks and perform them together, companionably, in perfect harmony. The prince's brother arrives, just before the meal is ready. Lakshman is a lazy thing; he rarely brings anything to add to the pot. What does he do in the forest, all day long? There is nowhere to go, no one to see.

They have been in the forest for days, weeks, years. They have been in exile so long that the princess has forgotten what it is to see a familiar face, a face other than that of her husband or his brother. Sita has only monkeys for company, who screech and gibber in the day, in the night, endless in their complaints. With wide faces and brazen eyes, they follow her as she moves barefoot through her days, her crimson wedding sari (all she owns in this exile) like a slender flame in the forest. The monkeys do not worry her; she is a princess, after all, and her husband is a prince. She has nothing to fear from monkeys.

But his brother watches too, with eyes wide and shameless. Rama is oblivious, will think no evil of his brother. But Sita knows; she feels it. His heated gaze strips the silk from her skin, leaving her naked and trembling.

SHANTHI CANNOT PAY ANY ATTENTION TO THE WHITE MAN, THE concerned father who sits across from her desk. There was a time when Shanthi would have worried about a student of hers who was doing so poorly, would have taken extra trouble, extra time to tutor the child. In her first year of teaching, she'd been so grateful to be out of the house, away from the endless rounds of washing diapers and cooking dishes (two sets—one spicy for her husband, one mild for the children), that she'd thrown all her frustrated mental energy into her students. But the endless weeks, one after another, teaching the same things to the same slow minds—it was just as bad as diapers. What they called algebra, geometry—it was only arithmetic, really. It wasn't anything that stretched her mind, made her feel like she was actually doing something interesting, worthwhile, important. Only the novelty had made it seem an improvement over diapers and dishes.

As the man drones on about his errant daughter, Shanthi slips into her familiar daydream, the epic story her own father had told her, at night, as she fell asleep. He had filled her head with stories of brave Rama, his beloved wife Sita, loyal Lakshman. As a child, Shanthi had believed every word, had absorbed them as she slowly fell asleep. Her father had sat under the mosquito netting with her, smoothed sweat-damp hair from Shanthi's forehead in the heat of the Colombo summer. He'd even fanned her with a handy piece of paper so that she could fall asleep, the paper invariably scribbled over with math. It was from her father that Shanthi had learned to love math and physics, the clean sense of their underlying structures. He had taught his youngest daughter as a game, an amusement, at first. But she had been quick to learn, eager for the challenge; he had become caught up in her excitement, ignoring her mother's protestations, until the day when Shanthi stepped on the boat for England. Only then did she see the stricken realization in his eyes, that everything he had taught her had only served to send her away from him. She had wanted to tell him that fathers always lost their daughters in the end, but she hadn't had the words.

He had gotten sick in the midst of the war, while she was away at school. Mail, already slow, had been disrupted by the war; letters took months longer than normal to traverse the long distances. He had died before her letter back had arrived; she had heedlessly offered to come home, though there was no guarantee that she could even find someone to carry her back across the dark waters. Aravindan had already proposed by then, and Shanthi had accepted, though she had not yet had the courage to write to her father, to tell him that she had met a man, had fallen in love, that she wasn't coming home, not yet. And then it was too late. Would her father have wanted her to marry Aravindan, to move with him to his new job in America? Would he have worried about her, as this father worries about his own daughter?

The poor student's plight is not enough to focus Shanthi's attention—now she considers the body of the white man sitting across from her, at a student's desk. His long legs fit awkwardly under the low desktop, and Shanthi wonders what he would look like if he could stretch out properly. On a low sofa, perhaps, or a broad bed. He stares fixedly at her, and she wonders what he sees. A brown woman who should better know her place? Or does he see an exotic beauty, a princess from the storybooks? After six children, she is no longer slender, but her breasts are full, her broad hips might seem appealing. Shanthi is a respectable woman, a professor's wife, a Catholic. She would never accede to any invitation. But she does wonder what it would be like to be looked at, to be desired again by hot and feverish eyes—that, she imagines, would be satisfying. That would be some compensation.

Someone has stolen the princess! It is a demon, a monster, who stole her away, who flew Sita up over the mountains, across the sea, to the barbaric island of Lanka. The prince was away, hunting; the prince was not paying proper attention. And no one knows what Lakshman was doing; he has served his purpose, his part in the story is done. But now Rama gathers a great army, and it is the monkey king who leads them, through the dark forests, over the churning sea.

The princess waits in a tall tower, resisting the demon's advances. Sita wants to be a good wife; if the demon comes too close, she threatens to throw herself off the edge, down onto the sharp rocks. She has never been in a tower so high, and secretly, she wants to jump, to feel the wind rushing again as it did when the demon snatched her. His glossy obsidian claws came down around her, caging her in, sweeping her through the air, her crimson sari trailing like a banner behind them. Nothing in her life has been as exciting as that flight. But Sita does her duty, she clings to the crumbling stone of the ancient tower, she teeters over the edge but does not, in fact, fall.

SHANTHI KNOWS SHE SHOULD GO STRAIGHT HOME. THE GIRLS WILL be fed by now, but they will still be raucous, full of energy. Leilani will be running up and down the stairs, Harini and Kili will undoubtedly be fighting, over dolls, or clothes, or makeup they aren't yet allowed to wear. Mayil will be drawing in her sketchbook; Shanthi thanks God every day for giving her one quiet child, and tries not to worry that all the girl seems to want to draw are human skeletons. Neriya won't have eaten enough, and Aravindan will be coaxing her to eat a little more, and Lakshmi—Lakshmi will be sitting on the floor, sucking her thumb. Shanthi knows exactly what it will be like, and so she turns east instead of west, heading along the Midway to the lake, heedless of the cold that bites her nose, her cheeks.

She kicks her way along snowy sidewalks until the hem of her sari is drenched. Aravindan is always trying to convince her to wear Western clothes, insisting that she will be more comfortable; he has never understood that it is only the clothing from home that makes her feel comfortable. When Shanthi wears her saris, she can close her eyes and block out the brutal cold; she can imagine herself back in Colombo, in her father's study perhaps, sitting beside him under the lazy ceiling fan, working out the answer to a problem he's set her—or in the market with her mother, listening to the cries of the fruit and vegetable sellers, fingering the rows of cheap glass bangles. She would throw a few coins to an armless beggar and feel rich, and blessed, and lucky. Once, Aravindan had refused to buy her new saris, and so Shanthi had worn the same green sari every day for a month, to faculty dinners and receptions, until he was so ashamed that he gave in.

She crosses the bridge over Lake Shore Drive, her fingers icy against the metal handrail. She walks out onto the broken stones, the massive rocks leaning into the lake. Her feet are still nimble, and for a moment she remembers the dancer she was as a little girl. If she had never studied physics, never gone to England, whom would she have married? Would she have become the perfect wife, the Sita of the story? Shanthi stands there a long time, watching the waves crash hard against the unyielding stone, feeling the wind whip against her, before turning back for the long walk home.

It has become apparent that the demon Ravana is only going through the motions. Sita does not know why he stole her away at all; he appears to have lost all interest. If he really wanted her, he could have taken her by now, before she ever made it to the tower's edge. If she jumped, he could snatch her out of the falling air. What could she do to resist him?

"SHANTHI, COME TO BED. COME TO BED, RASATHI."

Rasathi. Aravindan is full of soft touches and honeyed words these days, the guilt lacing through him. She can tell. You don't marry a man against your mother's wishes, you don't give up your work to have his children, you don't spend a decade sleeping by his side without knowing when something has changed. Shanthi doesn't know who the woman was, but she knew when it started, and when it ended. Months of carrying on, and Shanthi never said a word, to anyone. If she had written to her mother in Colombo, she knows what would have come back—written in a pale hand on fragile onionskin paper, instructions to be patient, be understanding, and perhaps to take a little more trouble with her appearance. Instead Shanthi cooked with abandoned fury, dissolving entire sticks of butter into the uppuma, tossing the rice with toasted almond oil, heaping her plate high with spicy potatoes. Ate bite after bite until her stomach felt swollen, painful, and the sweat rolled down her face. When the affair ended, she almost relented, almost gave in. Almost.

"Soon. When the news is finished, I'll come." Let him toss and turn in the bed, hungry for relief that will not come from her. A brief, warm pleasure kindles in her stomach at the thought. Perhaps this is why she hates Aravindan most of all—because he has turned her mean and spiteful, bitter and old. When they met, Shanthi placed her hand in his, let herself be drawn down, down to the sweet green grass. She listened to his words of love and thought she had found her prince, her Rama. Later, she felt herself betrayed; she comforted herself with bitterness, thought herself trapped with an uncaring demon, a Ravana. But she finds it harder these days to disappear into either fairy tale, either fantasy.

When Shanthi is feeling particularly fair, she doesn't hate Aravindan at all. Sometimes, she only hates herself.

At the end of the story, Sita is rescued, the demon is killed, the monkey king dances in triumph. But the people demand that she die, for she is only a woman, and undoubtedly she has betrayed her husband by now. She could not live so long in a barbarian land and not open her thighs for the demon. They know that all women are faithless, in the end.

She is lost, alone, and when Sita turns to her prince, he does not stand by her, he does not hold her up, exhausted as she is by all of these difficulties, more than any princess should bear. Rama claims to love her, to believe her— yet he gestures to the screaming crowds and says sadly that he cannot defy them. He is not an evil man, but he is, in the final analysis, weak.

What should happen now? Should Sita walk away from her prince?

EVENTUALLY, SHANTHI CANNOT KEEP HER EYES OPEN ANY LONGER; she checks on the sleeping girls, then goes to her bedroom, to her marriage bed. Aravindan is long asleep, turned toward her half of the bed. She stands there, watching him sleep—then climbs under the covers and lies down with her back to him. Shanthi closes her eyes, feels the heat of Aravindan's body beside her, slowly warming the chilled sheets. She wishes she knew how to open to him again, wonders if he could warm her. Or, if it is too late for them, wonders if there might be another path for her.

But what would she do, without her husband, her children? Whatever else she might have been is long gone; the paths are barred by walls of thorns.

It is late, and Shanthi knows how this story ends.

Sita volunteers to undergo the trial by fire, to have her virtue tested; what else can she do to keep Rama by her side? She is nothing without her husband, so what can she do, alone in a strange forest, with the sun going down?

Sita walks into the flames, her body consumed, her spirit rising up, up, up. The princess flees home, to her sisters' bedrooms, her mother's arms. But they do not know her, they shriek in horror at this ghost, this pale monster. Her father might have known her, but he is long since dead. So she returns, weeping salt tears in the night, her spirit crossing the bitter sea once more. Sita returns to her burning body, walks out of the fire, cooling so quickly as she goes, until

*she is solid again, composed of ice and snow. She never knew ice until her ex-
ile began. Sita walks out of the fire, her body transparent and brittle, but the
prince does not notice. Perhaps he chooses not to notice. He takes her in his
arms to the crowd's acclaim, he lays her down in the forest grass.*

This is supposed to be a happy ending.

Other Cities

Chicago, 1962

TWENTY YEARS AGO, IN THE LIBRARY AT OXFORD; THE DECEMBER
SUN SHAFTING DOWN THROUGH TALL WINDOWS, ILLUMINATING THE
long wood tables with the gift of peace. Silence. It had never been
silent in Jaffna, in his parents' house, with his mother and sister always
talking talking. Talking and never doing, and all Aravindan wanted
was to *do*, to get up and go, somewhere, anywhere. Somewhere where
he could be more than his parents' son, his sister's brother. And so he
worked, worked all the time because that was the only way to get
away. He liked it too, the math. Liked it well enough, though perhaps
never quite as well as he was supposed to. But well enough to get him
out. Passing exams with high marks, getting a scholarship to graduate
study at Oxford. His parents had sent him off with their best wishes
and many tears. His heart had been beating faster than he could count,
and once he was on the boat, standing up against the rail, he pressed
his hand to his chest, hard. His mouth alternately dry with fear and
wet with excitement.

He had abandoned the sterile math library that Christmas break to
take refuge in the Bodleian, in its faded stone walls and high arched

ceilings, in its comfortable wood chairs, worn down by decades of students. He studied in the deserted library until his brain ached, the symbols spinning in his head, until he had to rest, had to put his head down against the fine-grained wood. Aravindan heard her then, crying in the next aisle. Crying softly; if the library hadn't been absolutely silent, he would never have heard a thing. He knew then that she wasn't a white girl; white girls were noisy and cheerful—he'd never seen one cry, but there was no quietness in them, even for tears. This girl cried just like his sister, Mala, had, at the docks, so close to silent that only he, only her brother, could have heard her over their mother's wailing. Aravindan hadn't said a word to his sister then—what could he say? He was abandoning her, though she had begged him not to go. Mala was fourteen; she understood nothing. She didn't know what it was to feel that urge to fly, that craving in his throat, the sick shifting in his stomach, like a bird fluttering there, that said he could not stand it here, not a day, not a moment more. And then be forced to stay, day after day after day.

Because he had left his sister behind, left her without a word or a touch, he got up from his books, went to this weeping girl—and yes, he knew who she was. Shanthi, a year behind him and in physics instead of math, from Colombo rather than Jaffna, but what was a small stretch of ground between two lost travelers in a cold land? Their cities were neighbors, and though he was not sorry for his flight, he knew what it was to long for the sun, for the sour tang of his mother's rusum on his tongue, for the songs of his sister in the evening with chirping crickets for company. Aravindan came to Shanthi in the library and sat down in the next chair; he reached out to her head buried in her arms upon her books and stroked her hair, long and black, sweetly redolent of sandalwood and coconut oil. Like Mala's hair, like his mother's hair, but softer, a waterfall of silk, a river down to a dark sea. She looked up at him once, then put her head down again. He stroked her hair as she cried, until the last of the sun had disappeared from the long windows, the wide wood tables. His hand was shaking.

He first kissed her under the tall trees, the spreading oaks and ash; he walked with her in early spring gardens full of daffodils and pale irises. These plants his parents had never seen; they wouldn't, couldn't carry tales back across the wide wide ocean, to the banyan trees, the coconut palms, the bougainvillea climbing brilliantly pink over his mother's kitchen window.

They did not speak the same language. Both Tamil, yes, but her Tamil was not the same as his. Their ancestors had crossed the ocean in small boats, crossing to the island, three hundred years before the birth of Christ, but his family had stayed in the north, immersed in Tamil language and culture, while her family had moved south to the capital, spoken Sinhalese to the servants in the evenings, and Tamil rarely. They murmured their love words in English instead, in the language of knowledge, hope, the future. Not even an errant breeze could carry these words back to their parents. Aravindan kissed Shanthi's *neck*, her *breast*, her *navel*. His fingers cupped her silk-clad *thigh*. That word, *thigh*—like *sigh*, like the sounds she made as his fingers slid under her shirt, dipped inside her skirt. She never removed her clothes, so neither did he, though he ached for the length of her body to be pressed against his, without such artificial barriers.

They married in Oxford in the sweet summer, amid the climbing roses and over her mother's distant wails. The church choir couldn't drown out the voice in his head, the voice that said he had gone too far. Wealthy high-caste girl and only middling-high-caste boy. Though the father was dead, so what could her mother do to prevent them? If her parents had been wise, they would never have let Shanthi go so far away. Shanthi's mother cried for three weeks straight, according to her eldest sister's letters, written in steady hand on translucent blue paper.

England was caught up in the war, but they built a space for themselves, isolated and alone together. Quiet despite the screech of air-raid sirens; bright, despite the blackout curtains. They studied, they made love—Shanthi became pregnant, and in June they had a daughter. A year later the peace was signed, and their interlude was ended.

Aravindan graduated, and there was a job, in America, so far away. He left his wife and daughter in the rain at Oxford that September—Shanthi agreed it was wise. She only had a year left, and they'd hired a woman to help her—soon Shanthi would finish, and then she and the baby could join him. He took the long boat trip, started research in Boston, working with bright minds, pushing harder and harder, and how he longed for his wife, for her curries almost as tasty as his mother's, though always somewhat strange, ginger instead of garlic, fenugreek along with the fennel. He longed for the way she moved through the halls, swaying like a dancer, for the length of her body (only in the dark, but that was enough), pressed against the length of his. His head hurt at night; he lay on the rough wood floor in the dark, a wet cloth on his forehead, trying to think of math, thinking, instead, of her. Shanthi, sweet and creamy cool, like a mango lassi, chilled with ice. He was lying on the floor when the letter came that November. She was pregnant again.

Aravindan wanted to go to her then. To feel her belly swelling with his son. To rub coconut oil onto its sore stretching. To hold her in the mornings when the shudders racked through her. But the ocean was wide, the journey long, and she said that she could manage. It was a crucial time, a most important time, with his work getting harder, harder, harder. And more exciting too, he must admit. At times it seemed that perhaps he might love this after all, the quest to find out what and why and how. To unravel creation, to find a piece of the grand puzzle, to understand the underlying structure. He sent her letters, long letters full of English words. Words like *love* and *heart* and *dearest*. Words like *patient* and *work* and *soon*. Shanthi sent him pressed petals of roses from her small English garden, sketches of his first child, Kili, his daughter.

Two children were born, twin girls. Harini, Leilani. Aravindan went to her in Oxford, just after the birth, and held his new daughters in his arms. He smiled at his wife, but she didn't smile back. Shanthi wept, and he did not know why; he held her, in the small room in the small house that she shared with two other women; he promised to fix whatever was wrong, but she could not tell him what it was. Darkness had come over her, and Aravindan did not know how to lift it. He told her that he had been offered a better position in Philadelphia. It was a great chance, an opportunity, an adventure. He asked her if she thought he should take it. Or should they stay in Boston, where she had been promised a job? Shanthi lay in his arms, her face pressed against his shoulder; she did not answer. She finished her degree a few weeks later, not well.

They got a girl from Ceylon to cook and clean; they had another child in Philadelphia, a girl, Mayil. They moved to New York, then Chicago. Aravindan continued to work, but the patterns that had seemed so clear began to fracture. Some days they all came together in a shining shape, a moment of perfection—and then they fell apart again, into confusion and dissonance. Shanthi started a new garden in Chicago, grew curry plants alongside the roses. He watched his daughters grow like weeds. Four daughters, five, six.

The fifth daughter almost killed his wife; the child came out sideways, tearing through Shanthi's delicate skin like paper, like a careless gardener pruning petals along with dead matter. Aravindan asked her to stop, not to try again, but she wanted to continue. Shanthi insisted, and he wondered if she wanted to give him a son. It would have been important, in Ceylon. Here, it seemed to matter less. After every child, her hair grew coarse, her eyes darker, her body thicker. Her voice grew harsh when she spoke to him, harsh and dry and thick with regrets. After their sixth daughter, Lakshmi, Shanthi started teaching high school, taught children algebra and geometry, forgot her physics.

Sometimes Aravindan closed his eyes and imagined himself back in the library at Oxford, hearing the weeping in the next aisle. Would he get up; would he stroke that silky hair? His throat closed up; the bird in his stomach fluttered fragile wings.

When his daughters were nine, seven, seven, six, five, and two, he kissed another woman. Carol Sawyer, a graduate student, the only woman in the math department, unless one counted the secretaries. A plain face, but long blonde hair like satin that curved over her knit sweater, brushed the waist of her skirt. Three years they'd worked together, and if he had wondered what it would be like to run his hands over her large pale breasts, to hide his face between her white thighs, to see her lying naked in the sunlight on the floor of his office, naked to his eyes the way his wife refused to be—if he'd wondered these things, at least he hadn't acted. Aravindan kept his hands to himself, on his desk, at his side, clasped behind his back. He left the door open, always. He looked at Carol's eyes, never her full lips, her slope of bared neck, the curve of arm, and long, thin fingers on graceful hands. When she wrote on the board, his eyes focused on the chalk, white marks crossing the green surface. She was brilliant, this girl. She might be better than he was, better than he'd ever been.

He found her crying that day, in his office. The door was closed when Aravindan came to it, though not locked. His hand on the knob, he heard her crying, just the way he had known that white women must cry, full-throated sobs. He knew her hair would be disheveled, her eyes puffy and red, that Carol would be gasping for breath. Ugly, surely, no temptation. So he opened the door, went in, closed it behind him. *Miss Sawyer?* And yes, she was ugly, with tears leaking from her eyes, and fluids dripping from her nose, rising to her feet, still sobbing, saying *sorry sorry sorry professor*. Her father had died, suddenly. She had known for days, had kept working steadily, but while she had sat in his office, waiting for their meeting, the knowledge had risen up and overwhelmed her, dragging her out to drown in a sea of untouched grief. Aravindan took her in his arms, a brotherly, fatherly embrace. He held her as he had not held Mala, as he had held Shanthi, though he could not comfort his wife. He held this girl, and she was comforted. She raised up her head to his, after a time, and kissed his thin lips, his pointed chin. She whispered his name, *Aravindan*. He felt the bird fluttering inside his bound ribs, the sudden lift and dip of it. How many years had it been, since his wife had said his name with love, with desire? He kissed Carol's rich lips, the tip of her tongue darting into the gap between his upper front teeth, startling him so that he almost, almost pulled away.

It ended a few months later, unexpectedly. They had not quite locked the door; they had gotten careless. Anyone could have come in—a secretary, a colleague, a student. It might have been a scandal; it might have been hushed up. But instead, it was his daughter, Leilani, eight years old, who stumbled in the office door. A cut on her head, blood dripping down her face in a thin line. She had been running again, heedless, the way she always would, impatient with any fatherly cautions to *slow down, be careful.* His eyes recorded her image; long after she fled down the hall he could pull the picture up, run it like a movie in his mind. The shocked wide eyes, the thin line of red. They were only kissing, only pressing Aravindan's dark lips against Carol's pink ones. The child might not have understood—but she had run away, instead of seeking comfort in his arms. She had always been his favorite.

So many years ago, and still he could not talk to her. When he looked at Leilani's face, at ten, twelve, fourteen—the recorded image intervened, the taste of Carol on his lips. A rock sat in his stomach, heavy and unmoving. His throat so tight that not a word escaped it.

And now—a job in California, another chance. He'd been asking around, quietly, and this possibility had emerged. A small step down in prestige, but a new department, with fresh new faces, new energy. Aravindan was growing stale, he could feel it. So little new work in the past few years. He had become instead a good teacher—one of the best. Carol was only one of a string of bright young students coming through his office, the only one he'd kissed, but not the only one he'd taught, and helped, and cared for. One of them was bound to be more than just brilliant. One of them would change the shape of the world, would unlock its deepest secrets. Or it might, just possibly, be him— Aravindan could take this job, drag his family up from their roots, leave his wife's garden behind and take them to a new city, a new world. A new life.

Only just last year, the curry plants had finally gotten sturdy enough that Shanthi felt safe cutting and pruning them, using their leaves to delicately flavor crab curries, uppuma, his favorite fried garlic-ginger chicken. Her roses had climbed up and over the kitchen window; they had bloomed all summer in rich crimson profusion. Roses the exact same shade as his wife's wedding sari, just as startling against the white-painted wood as she had been, standing in the tall, cold English church, smiling up at him, her face as bright as Jaffna sunshine.

Acts of Faith

Chicago, 1963

NALAN REMEMBERS WHEN HE FIRST HEARD HER NAME, AS HER PAR-
TICULAR NAME—SINGLY, COMPELLING ATTENTION, RATHER THAN AS
one of a set of children, of sisters. A start-of-semester party in Eckhart,
professors and their wives, their children, swirling through the tea
room and the halls, the cold building filled with unaccustomed laughter. He was the only English professor in the room—he'd only come
by to see if Aravindan Kandiah had heard any news from Ceylon
over the summer. The man's mother could usually be relied on to
write pages-long letters, full of news; Nalan's own mother had passed
away a few years ago. His quest for news had led him straight into
chaos, a frenzy of noise that almost turned him right around, sent him
scurrying back to the haven of his tiny office on the top floor of Gates-
Blake.

"Hello, Nalan! Good to see you!" The man was shaking his hand
too hard—a habit, he'd always thought, of nervous, overambitious
men. "You know my daughter, Harini? Starting here this year. She'll be
taking your class soon—be good to her!" Kandiah was pushing forward a shy girl, head tilted forward, hair falling to shield her face.

"Of course, of course." Nalan couldn't actually tell any of the man's six daughters apart, but he was glad they were in the room nonetheless; he enjoyed their slender sari-clad bodies, reminding him of his own sunny college days, fifteen years past in Colombo. Fifteen long, cold years, here in Chicago. Sometimes he couldn't remember why he'd ever come. Shakespeare was probably to blame. Nalan smiled gently at the girl, who might be pretty under that veil of hair—it was impossible to tell. "I remember when you barely came up to my knee; it's hard to believe you're starting college already."

That was the right tone, cheerful and avuncular. Not a role he'd had much practice with, but he could remember it from his youth—the uncles who had patted his head, surreptitiously passed him sweets he hadn't needed and, later, prophylactics he had needed even less. Nalan had been a chubby boy, terrified of girls, grateful for the refuge he'd found in English books. He'd grown into a plump, intellectual man. If he'd stayed in Ceylon, he'd undoubtedly have been married off regardless of his fears. Perhaps that would have been better, though he'd gotten used to his solitary existence, the company of great minds, long since dust. If occasionally Nalan wished for some experience of those emotions he'd read of, the passions of a Romeo, or even the jealous rages of an Othello, for the most part he was reconciled to a quiet life and grateful for the peace of it.

"She's not the only one," her father said, beaming. "Leilani starts this year, and Mayil too! Come here, little prodigy!" Reaching down the long table piled high with cookies and teacups, calling one more girl out of the group surrounding his rather round wife. One of the girls headed toward them, her hair pulled neatly back into a long braid, her eyes bright. Her sari-wrapped hips swayed gently as she walked, and Nalan felt a sudden unwelcome throb in his pants—this wasn't the time, the place, or the girl. Besides, she couldn't possibly be old enough to go to college ...

"She can't be more than fifteen," he protested, feeling particularly old and creaky in response.

"Mayil is sixteen, and smart as a whip! Tell Nalan Uncle your SAT scores, Mayil." The other girl had disappeared into the crowd, leaving Mayil now alone with the two men, uncomfortably close. Nalan fought the urge to take an uneasy, obvious step backward. She didn't say a word, just looked at him, with unusual poise.

"She's shy—but we'll soon cure her of that, won't we?" Kandiah clapped his colleague on the arm, hard enough to bruise. "Seven-eighty English and a perfect eight hundred math! Shanthi didn't think it was a good idea to let her skip grades in grammar school, but the girl was the one who wanted it, and it hasn't hurt her, has it? Mayil's always known her own mind, this one—and what a mind it is!"

"That's certainly very impressive," Nalan agreed, though he wasn't sure it was a good idea to let children skip ahead. In his experience, they tended to either get conceited or socially inept, or, in the worst cases, both. He wondered which category this girl fell into—conceited was his bet. Mayil was overly restrained for a child; she seemed arrogant, in a way that Nalan found irritating. She wasn't pretty enough to justify her coldness; a plain girl who should have been more accommodating.

"I can't cook," she offered up, without any hint of apology—or explanation, for that matter. Nalan couldn't see why the girl thought it might matter to him whether she could cook or not.

Her father laughed. "No man will care, my rasathi, not with such a brilliant wife. Not that I'll let you go to just any man—the one who takes you away will have to be quite a catch himself. My clever daughters deserve the best—don't you agree, Nalan?" He pulled Mayil close, squeezed her shoulders affectionately. She turned and smiled up at her father, a smile of such unexpected sweetness that Nalan had to catch his breath.

Nalan, who had learned to be quite a good cook in twenty years of lonely bachelorhood, could only nod and silently agree.

The clock slowly ticked its way from two to three, from three to four. The man sat in the chair, very still, waiting with his hands in his lap. Outwardly he seemed the picture of calm, but if you walked up to him, if you laid your fingers on his upturned wrist, you would feel a pulse leaping wildly.

HE DIDN'T SEE MAYIL AGAIN FOR TWO YEARS, THOUGH HE RAN INTO her father fairly often, and one of her sisters did take his Renaissance Drama class, what he privately thought of as "Marlowe, et cetera," that spring. Harini was competent enough, but no more so than any of his other students, and he wasn't surprised when she confided in office hours that she planned to become an engineer. Nalan was sure she'd be a good one, inheriting her father's science skills. When he did finally see Mayil again, it was in the fall of 1965. He walked into his Survey of English Drama class and there she was, in the front row.

After class, she came up to the front, after the other students had left.

"So, did you like it?" he asked, strangely anxious, desiring her approval.

"Very much," Mayil said, smiling.

"I'm afraid my class wasn't so much to your sister's taste. I thought you might feel similarly." Mayil could easily still drop the course—so many students did in the first few weeks. In fact, he wished some of them would; the class was fuller than he liked. But he'd rather she stayed.

"I'm not a science person—I'm more interested in learning about people." Was it his imagination, or did she give that last word a lingering, sensual stress? Nalan knew that few of his students made it through college with virginity intact; he wondered what exactly this girl had learned about people so far. Mayil went on to say, "I'm going to be a historian, and history is all about what particular people did. That's all it is, really."

"You can't know for sure what you'll be doing—you must be,

what, starting your third year now?" Mayil had been sixteen when they'd met—she'd be eighteen now. A rather beddable eighteen, with wide hips encased in a flowing grass-green skirt, curves of breasts quite visible under a peasant-style white shirt. In a Shakespearean play, she'd be ready to be tumbled, in a field of daffydowndillies, under the warm summer sun. Or so he imagined. "You'll have just finished your core requirements . . . you're only now starting on your specialty."

Mayil smiled. "You have a good memory, Professor," she said, her head tilted up inquisitively.

"Please, call me Nalan." That sounded much too intimate, inappropriate, and he hurried to explain, "I don't like formality with my students—I find it interferes with the learning process. I'm supposed to be teaching them to think for themselves, and they have such sheeplike tendencies already . . ." He'd rambled on too long, now she'd think he was insulting her. Nalan didn't know what it was about this girl that made him stumble so, made him feel twenty again. Her self-possession, perhaps.

"Nalan," she said. "You're quite right that I would normally have two more years—but I've been quite sure what I wanted to study for some time, and I've been able to double up some classes. I'll be graduating in the spring, and I was actually hoping you might be able to help me? I'd like some advice on which grad schools I should apply to, if I want to do interdepartmental work in Renaissance history and literature."

"I'd be pleased to advise you, of course." So that was why she had come to talk to him, a perfectly innocent, sensible reason—Nalan felt relieved, and disappointed.

Mayil smiled. That smile once again took her rather plain face and lent it undeniable charm. The girl wasn't beautiful, but when she smiled, he couldn't seem to stop looking at her. She said, "If you're free this period, let me buy you a cup of coffee at the Reynolds Club, please."

There was nothing objectionable in that—they'd be in full view of many students, some professors. But it would be more appropriate to meet in his office, with the door open. He hesitated a long moment, and then leaped.

"That sounds very nice." Nalan's heart beat faster, as he gathered up his papers and followed her out the door.

"Sir?"

"Is there any word?"

"No, not yet. We just need you to fill out this form . . ."

"Of course."

EVERYTHING WENT VERY QUICKLY AFTER THAT—EVERYTHING EXCEPT THE physical consummation he woke up from dreaming about, with sheets embarrassingly wet. Mayil never said anything, but somehow she let him know that sex wasn't actually an option—and it was for the best, of course. She was his student, he was her teacher, and even after the course finished, and the grades were handed out (hers one of only two As), she was still a student, still barely eighteen, and he was almost forty. Nalan was somewhat relieved.

While he wouldn't have wanted to admit it, as a liberal professor of English literature, a literature that sometimes seemed to be entirely about sex, it would have disturbed him if Mayil had wanted to make love. If an eighteen-year-old girl were willing to have sex with a man twice her age, it would imply, wouldn't it, that this wasn't an activity entirely new to her? Nalan was already jealous enough of the slender, pale boys in class who sat near her, who leaned too close to borrow a pen or paper—he couldn't believe that she might actually prefer him, pudgy and dark as he was. Othello's emotions were becoming entirely too real. And, of course, it would be humiliating if she found him less experienced than herself. Better by far to learn together— eventually. Someday. Mayil didn't want to have sex, but she did make it utterly clear that she wanted to spend time with him, wanted to talk to him, listen to him. Perhaps, morally speaking, Nalan should have dismissed it all as a schoolgirl crush, gently steered her away. He did try once.

They were walking on the Fifty-seventh Street beach, late at night. It was February, the middle of winter term, and the wind was still brutally cold. The beach was deserted—even the street people had found better shelter that night.

"Your father will not be pleased with this." Nalan wasn't even sure what "this" was, but whatever it was, her father would not be happy, that was certain.

Mayil paced alongside him, her body painfully near, her eyes gazing out into the darkness of the water, the few far lights. "We'll have to wait until I graduate. If Northwestern takes me for grad school with a fellowship, Appa won't be able to say a word."

Nalan asked, "Wait for . . . ?" His heart was thumping, most distracting.

"If you don't ask me to marry you the day I graduate, I shall be very disappointed." Mayil still wasn't looking at him, but her hand slid into his, interlacing their fingers. It was one of the few times she'd touched him, and the fragility of her slender hand made his throat feel tight. He felt a simultaneous desire to protect her and to shake her—didn't she know how ridiculous this was? How people would laugh? There were so many cruel things they could say. Nalan felt a sharp pang at the thought of putting her through that kind of gauntlet.

He was quiet for a long time, walking slowly down the beach, her hand in his. Then, "Maybe someone your own age . . . ," he offered.

"Don't be stupid," she said sharply, squeezing his hand and digging in her nails. "I've known since the day I met you."

She was so sure of herself, so certain. Mayil never seemed to have any doubts, about anything, and somehow, she made it all happen, despite inexperience, despite youth. She made it happen by sheer intelligence and force of will. "All right, then." He put himself into her hands.

He remembered how she'd looked yesterday, boiling water for spaghetti at the stove, hands resting on her hips, leaning back. She couldn't stand curry when she was pregnant—the onions were too much for her. So she made spaghetti while his sauce simmered; she never had learned to cook. Soon it would be ready, and then she'd shake crushed red pepper into the lush red sauce, shake over and over, angrily waiting for the day when all of this would be over and she could eat properly again. He was waiting for that day too, when he could make her the most delicate of chicken kormas, with toasted almonds scattered across the top. Until then, he ate crushed pepper with her, his tongue burning, and waited.

NALAN CAME TO HER FATHER'S HOUSE THE EVENING AFTER THE morning when he'd gotten down on one knee, in his office, and asked Mayil to marry him. She'd gone ahead to prepare the way, his ring heavy on her finger. He was calm on the outside, but his stomach was doing acrobatics; he had to pause before ringing their doorbell, swallowing hard to keep from vomiting in the profusion of rosebushes. When he finally pushed the buzzer, no one answered at first. He pushed it again, and again, wondering if he'd simply been banned from the house. Finally the door flung open, and there was her father, his face flushed deep red, his fist clenched.

"You!"

"Yes, sir." The man was only a few years older than him, but Nalan suddenly felt like a schoolboy.

Kandiah stared at him, steam not quite visible from his nostrils, his chest heaving. When he spoke, the words weren't the ones Nalan had expected. "At least you aren't a whitey. And you've had the courtesy to tell me beforehand, instead of just running off. Apparently, these days, a father should be grateful for such small blessings. Daughters! The woman gave me six daughters!" And then he turned, stomping down the hallway, leaving Mayil to come to the door, beckon Nalan inside.

"I'm afraid we've been upstaged," she whispered, smiling as she closed the door. It was set with stained glass, deep reds and purples that caught the sun and sent it refracting across the hallway, their bodies. "Kili's gone and married a white boy."

"You're joking!" Nalan was astonished. Not that he knew Kili at all, but still—he couldn't think of a single Tamil woman he knew who had married outside her caste, either here or at home.

Mayil nodded firmly. "And to make it even better, she did it two years ago! She kept it a secret until she'd graduated. Didn't want Appa to stop paying the bills, I suppose. His name's Michael. He's inside."

Kili was the eldest, premed if Nalan remembered correctly.

"What about med school?" He was rather appalled at the girl's nerve. Were all of the sisters so determined, so bold?

"Appa says he isn't going to pay a penny. Kili says she'll take out loans—and maybe she will, but I think Appa will back down. He's all roar and fuss, but it never lasts. You'll see." Mayil reached out a hand to him, smiling. His diamond glinted in the stained light, suddenly crimson, a bloody ruby.

Nalan felt like a character inside a play, a story full of sudden reverses, shifts of fortune, revelations of identity mistaken, loved ones deceived. He wanted to turn, to run, but he had made his decision, months ago. He had cast his lot with her, to walk by her side. So he took her hand, followed her down the hall, to the kitchen where her family waited.

"Just a few questions, if you don't mind. Your wife was how far along?"

"Eight months."

"And is this her first pregnancy?"

"No."

THEY HADN'T PLANNED ON GETTING PREGNANT SO QUICKLY. MAYIL had only been in grad school a year; they'd celebrated the successful completion of that first year with an endless night of sex. It should have been safe—she was conscientious about keeping track of the days, knowing which ones were safe, which risky, which downright dangerous. If it had been up to him, he would have taken further precautions, but Mayil had surprised him with a firm devoutness in this regard. The Church said it wasn't acceptable, and so. Nalan wasn't religious himself, and hadn't really realized how religious she was, but there was little he could deny her.

The pregnancy had gone well enough, and she'd managed to work straight through fall semester without trouble. By December, Mayil was positively lumbering, irritated with him, with her body—all of her old grace disappeared. And yet, when she smiled, Nalan still couldn't take his eyes off her.

He came home with roses that day, bought on impulse at the grocery store, a rich profusion of crimson petals, an exuberant two dozen. Because they reminded him of her, the curve of the petals like the curve of her breasts, her swollen thighs. Because he couldn't remember what his life had been for, before she came into it. Nalan put his key in the door, almost dropped a bag of groceries, and shifted to catch it. He heard a woman weeping—he put down the groceries, the roses, put his ear to the door.

"What is it, what's wrong?" His wife's voice, gentle and soft. Nalan let out a breath in relief and put his hand on the key, ready to turn it. Then he heard her sister's response:

"I lost the baby." Kili's voice harsh, rough with many tears.

He sat down on the steps, heavily, fear rising up to smother him. The two women had become pregnant within a few weeks of each other; Kili was due only a few months from now, a month after Mayil. It was disastrous, to lose a baby so late. Nalan bent forward, pressed his forehead against his knees, taking deep breaths. He had been waiting for such a disaster—waiting, it sometimes seemed, since the day they met.

It was foolish to worry, he knew. Most pregnancies went smoothly, by far. There were doctors, and hospitals and procedures—and women had been giving birth in barns, in open fields, for millennia. He told himself this, again and again. But the curse of being a good student of antique literature, and therefore, by necessity, of antique history, was that Nalan couldn't comfort himself with the thought of how many women had survived. He knew just how often medicine and biology failed. He lifted his head, pressed it to the door again. The voices seemed more muffled, but still distinguishable.

"Shh . . . shh . . . oh, don't cry, kunju. Don't cry. There'll be others." He could imagine Mayil, leaning across the dining table, stroking her sister's hand.

"No, no . . . there won't be any others." The crying stopped; Kili sounded certain, sure.

"Don't be foolish—Amma miscarried too, and look at us. Six children!" Mayil's own voice, usually so solid and certain, was shaken, cracking. Nalan pressed his palms flat against the door, his chest aching. He relied on his wife's surety.

Kili paused, then said, "This isn't the first time. I was pregnant my second year, not long after we married."

"You never said anything."

He could almost hear the shrug in the pause this time, and now her sister's voice was very dry and cold, almost clinical. "I wasn't ready to tell Appa; I got rid of it. Apparently, I damaged myself. I knew it was a risk, trying to get pregnant again. I knew the risks . . ." And the coldness failed her, the tears rising again.

"You're sure?" Mayil asked.

"I'm sure. It would be . . . unwise. To try again." And that desolation Nalan couldn't bear. He stood up abruptly, left the groceries and roses by the door, and started walking, blindly. Mayil would find them; she'd understand. Nalan could do nothing now but walk, and wait. And if a small, ancient part of him hoped that it was the mixing of the races that had gone awry, the miscegenation that had led to calamity, then his conscious mind was properly appalled, and stifled the thought before it could surface.

"And that pregnancy . . ."
  "It was fine. We had a daughter, Shefali. She's thirteen now."
  "No other children?"
  "No, none."

MAYIL HAD WANTED OTHER CHILDREN, AND HE DID FIND IT HARD TO resist her when he looked at their daughter. Tiny, delicate, perfect. After her birth, Nalan had cooked for them both, cooked richly, until, over the years, both he and Mayil acquired a comfortable weight on their bellies. The soft flesh reassured him. But he couldn't seem to feed his daughter enough—however much she ate, she stayed small, slender. It didn't seem to hurt her, though—Shefali was full of energy, a dancing sprite of a child, an active young teen. She had, with her aunt Leilani's encouragement, joined the track team, had gone to state championships. Shefali talked loudly, laughed prodigiously, and would, with no provocation, sometimes burst into song. Nalan's own movements felt more solid, more slow, with each passing year, and he found himself bewildered that somehow he had engendered this flighty Puck, this delightful Ariel.

Stranger still were Shefali's other interests—the child could not have cared less for her father's books, her mother's history; she dismissed it all as unreal, boring. Instead, she begged for a computer all through her last year of grammar school; he'd finally gotten her one, an Apple II Plus, for her birthday. She'd spent the next three months engrossed in it, programming, of all things. Who'd ever heard of a girl-child wanting to spend all her free hours programming? It was absurd. It was just as well, though—neither he nor her mother had had much time to spare for her.

They were sufficiently busy with a second unexpected pregnancy, one that had somehow managed to slide by every barrier placed in its way. Nalan had overruled his wife's Catholic objections after Shefali's long and difficult birth, and she had, surprisingly, given way. Nalan still didn't know how the second pregnancy had happened—God's will, was all Mayil would say. And if there was more of the hand of his wife in it than of God, well, Nalan didn't want to know. As the pregnancy progressed, he continued to cook, more and more dishes, to tempt her stomach. Again, he ate too much crushed red pepper, endless tomato sauces. He ate them in place of religious belief, as his own private prayer and pledge, a silent bargain with the universe, to keep her safe.

"When did you first suspect that something was wrong?"

HE HAD WOKEN IN THE DARK TO WET SHEETS—THAT WAS WHAT HE had first noticed. A dampness around his hips and groin. He'd put his hand down to feel the sticky wet; his first thought was that he had somehow returned to the embarrassing days of nocturnal emissions— his second, that Mayil's water had broken. Early, but not impossibly so. He'd said her name as he reached for the light, twisting to find the switch—and then it had come on, and he had seen his fingers, stained a ridiculous, shining red. Turned in the bed, yanked back the covers to see blood, covering her thighs, pooling under her hips. And her face clammy, her ears deaf to his entreaties. He felt for the pulse with red fingers, felt and found it, then, his mind abruptly cold, logical, sending him up to get a towel, to press it between her thighs. And then the phone, the three digits quickly dialed, the address recited. The phone again, to call a sister to come stay with the child. And then he was wrapping a clean blanket around his wife, lifting her up—he didn't know if it was wise, but he couldn't just wait. Couldn't just sit still. Somehow he lifted her up, and she was heavy but not impossibly so. He carried her down the dark hall; the child was still sleeping, undisturbed. Carried his wife to the front door, to the end of the walk, talking to her all the while, saying her name, whispering nonsense words. Anything she might respond to. The names of Shakespeare plays. Historical dates. Then the siren came, red and screaming, and they were taking her out of his arms, they were loading her into the back, and he went, leaving the child alone in the empty house. A sister was coming, and he, he had to go.

They had let him clean up at the hospital, had packaged up his clothes and given him patient pyjamas, a robe. Eventually, her parents had come, her sisters. Leilani, sensible, solid Leilani, had brought clothes for him, and he had changed again. She had told Kili to stay with Shefali, been wise enough to spare her this; Leilani knew about the miscarriages, knew all their secrets. He would not have expected a poet to be the most sensible one of the set, before he'd gotten to know them. But it was true. He was, distantly, grateful for her. And furious with her too, with all of them, every single sister—this one with Mayil's eyes, that one with her hair, her slender hands. He could have strangled them all, and gladly, to simply turn the clock back six hours, knowing what he knew now. It might have been enough.

The clock ticked from four to five. At five-fifteen, the nurse called him into a small room. The doctor came in, in his white coat, unspattered. Nalan wondered if the man had changed before coming to see him. If that was hospital policy in this sort of situation. Because he knew—he knew when he saw the man's face. Exhausted. And already abstracted, thinking ahead to the next patient, the one he might be able to save.

"I'm sorry to tell you..."

"I know. I've always known."

And he is walking away, leaving the doctor standing there, the family in the waiting room, he is walking away, her small, slender hand in his, so fragile, so easily lost.

Marry in Haste

Chicago, 1964

CEYLON IS EVERYWHERE IN THE TINY HYDE PARK APARTMENT—IN
KILI'S BRASS CANDLESTICKS ON THEIR TINY BLACK-AND-WHITE TV, IN
the demon masks and batiks of sari-clad dancers hanging on the wall.
Michael's great-grandparents were immigrants, but their blood was already mongrel, a mix of English and Scottish. His counterpoint lies in
the scattered papers on the pine table, in the sink of dirty dishes, the
clothes piled on the bedroom floor. Michael works at home most
nights, as does she. Kili rustles pages, committing to memory an endless stream of medical terminology. His pen scritches across long
sheets of yellow lined paper. Med student and physics student, they
work in companionable silence. He often fills pages of the yellow paper without a single word, living in a world of jumbled letters and
symbols. When Kili pauses in her work to peer over his shoulder, her
long hair brushing in a black curtain against his cheek, she will not understand a word he has written. But it is only fair—her own languages
are equally impenetrable.

"Why didn't you marry someone from Ceylon?" Michael asks one
night as they lie in bed; he is at his most talkative at these times. They

have only been married a few weeks and it is perhaps not the best time for such a question—but he has been wanting to ask it, or something like it, for years. Only now, with her naked, vulnerable beside him, has he found the courage. She twists in his arms, looks up at him, smiles. "I fell in love with you." It is a true answer; he lets it stand for the night. But it is not the only truth.

KILI DIDN'T FALL IN LOVE RIGHT AWAY; HE HAD TO PURSUE HER. Michael had been sitting on the grass under a tree in Hutchinson Commons, unfolding a peanut butter sandwich from its paper wrapper. He was intent on the task at hand, and it was laughter that first drew his attention, the sound of several girls laughing together. He'd looked up to see them coming out of Ryerson, mostly voluptuous undergrad blondes, not so different from Kate, the girl he'd been with for the last two years, the girl who had dumped him a few weeks previous. At the periphery of the group was a small, slender brown-skinned girl, conspicuous because she was the only one not laughing. She was smiling, though, with a sweet indulgence evident in her expression—she was not actually amused by the joke, he understood, but she was glad that her friends were happy. Her hair was pulled up into a neat coil at the nape of her neck, unlike the short bobbed styles of her friends; the skirt of her dark dress was long, and her arms were covered to the wrist. Among the brightly patterned sleeveless shifts of her friends, she stood out, a dark rose in a field of daisies.

He took to having his lunch there, at that time, regularly, until he had determined exactly when she came out of her class. It gave him time to gather his courage. He had only dated white girls up until now. But even though Michael knew his parents wouldn't understand it, he couldn't think of any good reason not to ask her out—not a real reason. Weren't they all the same, under the skin? Eventually he walked over and asked her name, and she admitted it was Kili. Then he asked if she'd like to have lunch with him sometime, and she looked up at

Michael, flustered, and stammered a *No, sorry,* while her friends gig-gled and his face flushed red. As he walked away, he heard one of the blondes whispering, *Can you believe that? Are you okay?* As if his words to her had been an insult, an assault.

Perhaps he should have given up, but what would have discour-aged him with a girl like Kate somehow enflamed him coming from Kili. Her eyes were large and dark; on her thin face, they seemed inde-cisive, persuadable. Michael courted Kili—picked stolen flowers from Botany Pond and brought them to where she sat, surrounded by the intimidating bevy of girlfriends who laughed and teased and, eventu-ally, encouraged him. He paid her extravagant compliments, even went to the library and memorized lines of poetry to recite to her. Michael compared Kili to a summer's day and surprised a laugh out of her; her face opened up then, a lotus unfolding. Or so he imagined— he had never seen a lotus.

Eventually, he charmed her; Kili allowed him to sit by her side, still surrounded, guarded by her friends. She tried a bite of his peanut butter sandwich. Kili didn't like it. But she agreed to meet him again, and again. Her father didn't allow her to date at all, and certainly not to date white boys, so when they met alone, they met secretly. The first time Michael kissed her, in a dark stairwell in Eckhart, she froze for a moment. Then Kili's lips moved, soft under his; her hands slid up to rest against his chest. He could feel his heart, pounding, under her fingertips.

KILI SITS, HUNCHED, ON A CORNER OF THEIR NARROW BED, LEGS pulled up under her long, dark skirt, the phone handle pressed tight against her ear. Michael sits cross-legged behind her, his hands gently massaging her shoulders through the fabric of her thin white blouse. The voice on the line is loud enough that he can hear every word.

"Rasathi, I called your room last night at eleven-thirty! Where were you?" Her father has a strong British accent, but he is otherwise not hard to understand.

"Appa," she says softly, "I work late at the library sometimes. I've told you that."

Kili does, sometimes. So that is true. But last night—last night they were otherwise occupied when the phone rang, and she chose to ignore it. Michael, of course, never answers the phone. It is part of their agreement.

Her father is talking louder now, faster, and Kili hunches in on herself, shrugs her shoulders away from his hands, impatiently. Michael lets his hands drop, fighting back a sudden impotent fury, an urge to snatch the phone from her hand, to tell everything. Michael has seen her father, a pudgy math professor who strides quickly across the Chicago campus; he has even sat in on one of his lectures, and cannot believe that the man is as old-fashioned, as unreasonable, as his daughter insists. But Kili has begged Michael not to say anything, has made him promise to wait. She folds in on herself when they discuss it, fades and withers, like a flower deprived of water. Michael will promise anything then to make her smile.

Michael entertains brief fantasies sometimes, listening to her father's British inflections; he wishes they lived in Ceylon a few decades earlier, when the British were still in charge. Then, he could have loved Kili as he wanted to, could have seen Kili as often as he wished, without her father daring to interfere. He pictures Kili in a thin sari, perhaps drawing water from a well, and himself striding into the courtyard, a white man rich with power, authority. Pictures the older man forced to sit silent, while Michael takes his daughter boldly in his arms, kisses her for all the world to see. Kili would have never allowed it.

He gets up, walks over to the counter of their kitchenette, where six onions sit waiting for dinner. Kili is a good cook, and he has been an eager student; after two years, he can make a curry almost as well as she can. Michael starts to chop onions, thin, the way she likes them. As the conversation continues, her voice growing more frantic, pleading, he chops harder, faster, turning the pile of chopped onions into mush.

Before long, the onions are nothing more than a heap of white fiber and eye-stinging water, useless.

He turns then, to find her watching him with the phone pressed hard against her ear, her eyes wide, her face unusually pale. Guilt makes him put down the knife, walk over and brush the sweaty hair back from her forehead, bend down and drop a kiss there, reassuring. Michael wishes, though, that her father might hear it, the almost-sound of pink lips on dark flesh. And he wonders whether the onion juices on his fingers have left a residue on her skin, whether the fumes will make her cry.

"MARRY IN HASTE, REPENT AT LEISURE." THAT'S WHAT HIS OWN father had said when Michael had called with the news that he had married a brown-skinned girl. His father had been polite to Kili's face—Michael even thought he might approve of her slender frame, her swift medical mind. Michael's own mother, who was rather enormously fat and spent her days weeping over romance novels, had been a sad disappointment, his father had once drunkenly confessed. Michael hadn't told his father the reason for the hasty civil marriage, bereft of church or family—but it couldn't be too hard to guess.

He and Kili had walked out to the Point that morning that April, had sat on the damp grass under a tree, watching the waters of the lake wash in and out. Michael hadn't suspected anything—not until she took his hand, something she never did in public. Kili had pressed his hand so hard that pink imprints had risen to the surface of the white skin, had whispered her suspicions even though there was no one else in sight, as though the very wind and waves might betray her, might carry the words to her family. She had been so terrified that Michael had risen to one knee and proposed. It was the only thing to do.

Kili had said yes, had even smiled before kissing him, but she refused to tell her family—as she had refused to tell them they were dating, for the past two years. Michael had guiltily agreed, agreed to everything she wanted. It seemed easy enough to agree—soon enough Kili would be showing, would have to tell her parents, whether she wanted to or not. They had filled out the necessary paperwork and gotten married without ceremony a few days after his college graduation. Housing was harder, but after being turned down, once with veiled insults, by two apartment managers for places near the lake, they had managed to find a manager on Woodlawn who cared more about their money than about the color of their respective, different, skins. They settled there into an appearance of wedded bliss—but the baby, the threat and promise of it, had disappeared not long after that.

He was afraid to ask what had happened to it, afraid he knew what his wife had done. She had been so scared.

THE ONIONS ARE DECLARED A LOSS AND HE PICKS UP PIZZA INSTEAD. They can afford to buy pizza often; they are only paying the rent for a small studio, so that her parents believe she is living there, and paying for it, by herself. He picks up pizza often, since Kili is unwilling to go out to eat with him, unless they gather a crowd of friends to join them. Her father teaches on this campus, after all; her younger sisters are in school here. There are ten thousand students in Hyde Park, but according to Kili, spies are everywhere. None of their friends know that they've married—they have been so secret, so careful, that most didn't even know that they were dating. Michael isn't sure how his friends will react, but he wants to find out. She promises that they can tell them, soon. Kili has been saying soon, in her soft voice, since that first stolen kiss.

She has lit candles for their dinner; as they sit on the floor, cross-legged, sharing thick stuffed spinach slices, Michael finds himself entranced by the play of light across her face. Kili is not beautiful, according to her own report. She is too thin, too dark; her nose is sharp, and she has no breasts to speak of. But her skin is perfectly smooth, and nothing is as soft as the insides of her thighs. She eats pizza with both hands, smothers the slices in extra chili sauce before stuffing them into her small mouth. When Michael abandons his own pizza to taste a bite of hers, the chili burns his lips, his tongue, the inside of his cheeks. It hurts, but he cannot seem to stop. He presses forward, presses his burning lips to her mouth, bites down, gently, then less gently. Kili leans backward, and he presses forward, until she is trapped against the hardwood floor, her slight body entirely hidden beneath him. The pizza lies forgotten beside them.

IN THE WEEKS AFTER THAT FIRST KISS, MICHAEL PRESSED KILI FOR details about her family, her parents' country, her culture. She steadfastly avoided any such discussion; talking of her family would only lead to grief, she claimed, and as for her country—she was born in England, raised entirely in America. She was as American as he was.

Michael took refuge in the library; he raided the card catalog for anything relating to Ceylon but only unearthed the driest of historical texts. He widened his search to include India, reasoning that it was surely close enough. First he found the *National Geographics,* with their photos of sari-clad women bathing under waterfalls; then he found the library's many editions of the Kama Sutra, which more than satisfied his desires. Michael took them down to the subbasement, to the levels where once, when there had only been a football field instead of a library, physicists had split the atom. There, amid deserted, dimly lit stacks, his excitement would sometimes overwhelm him; it was only by retreating to a sudden focus on equations that he avoided embarrassing accidents.

Michael studied his favorite edition in the weeks when they were progressing from kisses to caresses, from above Kili's blouse to underneath her bra. His limited experiences with Kate were overshadowed by his eager studies. By the time he had the virginal Kili entirely undressed, the contrast of his white hands sharp and exciting against her dark brown skin, he had read through the book at least three times.

Kili was unfamiliar with the poses, but proved willing, even eager, to be taught, though she raised an eyebrow at him when he referred to it as the lore of her country. Generally, she didn't openly contradict him; she was willing to let him take the lead in making most decisions, in friendly arguments with their friends. It was only when he actually made a mistake, claimed something incorrect, that Kili would speak up and correct him—but she was surprisingly firm on those occasions. Michael found those rare challenges to his authority disconcerting—and that, in turn, left him feeling guilty.

KATE HAD BEEN A SCREAMER. SHE THREW PLATES AT HIM, AND THEN threw her promise ring, screeched sharp accusations before turning and storming from the room, slamming the door behind her. Michael was bewildered at the time, and only later theorized that Kate had been concealing her own infidelities in that last brutal scene. Even before that, the relationship was punctuated by frequent fights, passionate arguments; only her equivalent passion when pleased kept them together at all.

When Michael makes love to his wife, she is almost silent. He encourages Kili to make more noise—it is not as if the rather deaf downstairs neighbor will report them to her parents. But she remains obstinately quiet, and it is only by paying the closest attention that he can chart her response to his touch. At first Michael doesn't mind. Her body does respond; Kili moves eagerly against him, whether below or in front or above. It was enough, for a long time. Lately, though, he has wanted more from his wife. Michael finds himself digging his fingers into her skin, biting at the flesh of her breasts, her stomach. Love bites, he could call them, but is it love that shoves her thighs apart, roughly, that grasps her wrists and pulls them high above her head? Her eyes are dark in the candlelight, and they gaze at him without reproach—and when he bites a nipple hard, Kili arches, twisting underneath him, whimpering slightly. Michael cannot tell whether she enjoys this, or whether she wants to get away. All he knows is that she will not protest—that for as long as he wants to maul her frail body, she will allow it, will arch to meet his every move; there will be no surrender in her face, her body, until finally he must concede defeat, shuddering to a finish, exhausted.

Michael hates knowing that when they finish, Kili will rise, will shower, will wash away all trace of him. His wife's body will be smooth, dark, and, despite his efforts, entirely unmarked. Perhaps this is the punishment for his guilty pleasure in her subservience, that despite all his efforts, all his fantasies, she remains inaccessible, inviolate. Or perhaps she wants this violence, wants more than he can give her. Michael wonders if Kili wants him to hurt her, if that is what excites her in the end. Michael is afraid to ask why she really married him. He will take what Kili allows him. He will try to convince himself that it is enough.

Pieces of the Heart

Chicago, 1966

I SAT IN HARPER LIBRARY, IN A SHAFT OF SUNLIGHT FROM ONE OF THE TALL, SLENDER WINDOWS IN THE HIGH HALL, WRITING IN MY notebook. A few hours before my final physiology exam, but the dutiful delineations of the chambers of the heart had slid into lines that swooped and scanned along the page.

"Poetry. You're writing poetry again?" Sue's eyes were fixed on my page, reading the writing upside down. Her eyes were clear blue, like Lake Michigan on a sunny June day. We could have studied at the lake that day instead of in the library; she'd wanted to. But then I would have gotten nothing done. "This is a sign, Leilani—God's sneaking into your mind and telling us that we need to take a break."

"God doesn't work that way, Sue." She'd been my roommate for two years now, and while she appeared a good Catholic on the surface—she even went to Mass with me on Sundays, which made my parents happy—Sue had an oddly irreverent streak in her. It made me uncomfortable, but it was exciting too. That's what it was always like, being around Sue.

"How do you know how God works? Are *you* omniscient and omnipotent?" She grinned across the table at me.

I didn't have an answer to that and just shook my head, smiling.

"There's something I've been wanting to show you. Meaning to for weeks and weeks, actually. C'mon." She stood up, extending a hand toward me. I stood too, but my hand remained on the page, the pen cupped lightly in my fingers. The words were dancing across the paper.

WHEN I WAS A LITTLE GIRL, MAYBE THREE YEARS OLD, APPA TAUGHT me to read. He got me interested by reading to me; he'd read almost anything, but mostly I liked fairy tales. Adventure stories, where the prince would have three impossible tasks that he'd somehow manage to fulfill, if he were only strong enough, smart enough, fast enough. And then he'd win the crown, the gold, the princess's undying love. Appa loved stories—mostly he read them to me, but every once in a while, he'd make them up. Those were the best ones—he'd steal bits out of the *Ramayana,* and while he told the story I would lie in his arms and close my eyes and become noble Prince Rama, who went into the dark forest with his beloved wife, Sita, and his loyal brother, Lakshman.

I have five sisters, but I was Appa's favorite—I knew it, though I wasn't supposed to talk about it. He told me so, though he didn't tell me why. Maybe it was because I liked to read. He said that if he didn't have six naughty little girls to feed and clothe and shelter, he might have just stayed at home and read books all day. He got to read at work sometimes too, but that was math, what he taught at the college, what he researched. There wasn't so much time, with six daughters, for curling up in a comfortable chair and reading stories. Maybe he loved me best because I loved the stories too.

Or maybe it was because I loved the adventure stories best. He and Amma had had an adventure themselves—they'd left Ceylon (the land of the demon Ravana in the stories) to travel all the way to England as math and physics students. They had met at Oxford, met and fallen in love, and had then gone on to America, to become teachers here, to leave everyone else behind. They had been young, and brave, and had been rewarded for their bravery. Appa loved America, and almost everything American. This was a good country, Appa said. Full of decent, hardworking people. And even if white Americans were a little distrustful of foreigners, that was to be expected. The other professors respected Appa, and that was what mattered.

I wanted to have adventures too, to travel to foreign countries, to take on impossible tasks. When I told him this, he never laughed at me. He just held me close, so close that I could feel his heart beating against my shoulder, and then started another story.

"I HAVE TO PASS THIS CLASS. MY PARENTS . . ." MY EYES SLID TO THE heart diagram, and then, treacherously, to the half-finished sonnet. I had my first two stanzas, but it was time for the turn, which was always tricky.

Sue's eyebrows drew together; her forehead crinkled. "You'll pass, you know you will—and if you only get a C, your parents will handle it. You've got plenty of time to pull your grades up; you can still get into med school if you really want to. It's not like you ever do anything but study anyway . . . no drinking, no drugs . . . no sex."

"Sue!" She talked this way in our room all the time, but in the middle of a library . . . My father could walk by at any minute. He probably wouldn't, but he could. It had been wonderful growing up with a professor for a father and a teacher for a mother when I was younger—most of my friends' mothers didn't even work. I was so proud of them both. It hadn't been so bad, going to the grammar school my mother taught at. But now that I was going to the same college my father taught at, it was not fun. It was not fun at all.

"Okay, okay." She shrugged. "You could stand to have a good time, you know. Once in a while."

Sue used to be a frat girl. She didn't join a sorority—hardly anyone did at the U of C—but she did chase frat boys. She usually caught them too. This year had been different; these days, Sue's idea of a good time was to go to a sit-in, a protest against the war. Maybe because those often turned into something else; after one of those, she generally didn't come back to our room at night. She'd invited me to come along, but I could always hear my mother's voice in my head.

Plenty of time for that sort of thing after you're done with your education. Not that my mother really meant *that* sort of thing, not without the priest's blessing.

"I'm sorry ..." I was sorry, I really was.

Sue sighed. "I know, I know. You're a nice Tamil girl." When she said that, she sounded just like my mother. She'd really been a very patient roommate. Sue had quickly stopped trying to persuade me to have a drink with her; she never said a word as I knelt and said my rosary each night; she had taught me how to cook pot roast, and I had introduced her to chicken curry. The first time she tried it, Sue valiantly stuck it out through the whole meal without a single sip from her glass of water, though her face had gotten pinker and pinker until I had to squeeze my stomach muscles tight to keep from laughing.

She reached out her hand to me again. "Just this one time—trust me. You'll love this! Please?" Her face was fey and sparkling, with her mass of blonde hair tightly curled around her curving cheeks and wicked grin.

I sighed and put my hand in hers, letting her draw me out of the room, down the hall, and into a dark stairwell.

WHEN I WAS TEN, I KISSED A BOY.

It was dark in the stairwell. All the other kids were out on the playground; we ate quickly, then ran outside to play four-square and jump rope. I usually ended up running with the boys, playing soccer in the far end of the blacktop. I ran fast, faster than all the girls and most of the boys. That was why they let me play. I was even faster than some of the sixth-graders who would sometimes come and play with us. It wasn't real soccer—we didn't have goals. But it was fast and fun, trying to get the ball and keep it, dribbling it hard with your feet down the blacktop, sometimes falling and scraping your knees badly, so the nurse had to paint them with iodine. Amma always got mad when that happened, but I didn't care.

That day I wasn't on the blacktop. I was in the stairwell, with Jesús Gonzalez. He had touched my arm at lunch, leaning over the table. He was tall—more than six feet, even though he was only twelve. He wasn't too bright, either; he'd been held back twice, which was why he was in my grade. But he was nice, so when he asked me if he could talk to me after lunch, I said okay. My friends hung around at the table, but I sipped my milk so slowly that eventually they got bored and went out to play. He came back to the table then, and I threw out my trash and followed him up the stairs.

We were kissing in the stairwell, a long, dark length of concrete steps and walls. I was standing on the step above him, almost as tall as he was with the help of the step, and my lips were pressed against his, my hands were wrapped tight into the fabric of his leather jacket. I don't remember what it felt like, kissing Jesús. We kissed for a long time, five minutes, or maybe ten. Just pressing our lips together. Then I remembered something I'd read about, and opened my mouth and stuck my tongue out. Jesús lost his balance and started falling backward down the stairs. I pulled harder at his jacket and tried to lean back, but I started falling too—I heard the awful sound of the jacket tearing. Then he grabbed the rail and straightened up, banging into me, knocking me backward again so I ended up letting go of his jacket and sitting down on the concrete step, banging my elbows hard behind me.

"Aw, God. My jacket! My mom's gonna kill me! She's gonna kill me!"

He looked like he was going to cry. I felt like crying too, but instead I told him to give me the coat. I'd sew it up. I'd fix it. He started to say no—then slid out of it and handed it to me, ran off to the far end of the blacktop. He must have been cold; it was October, which can be cold in Chicago. He could have stayed in the stairwell.

I took the jacket home that afternoon. I had sewn buttons back onto my skirts before—I was always popping them, running and wrestling with the boys. But the jacket hadn't ripped along a seam; the actual leather had ripped. I did the best I could, choosing dark brown thread that matched the color of the leather, sewing the tiniest stitches. It took more than an hour, but when I was done, it still looked awful. The tears were near the armpits, though—maybe no one would notice. I didn't know what else to do.

I gave Jesús his jacket back the next day, in the morning, while we waited for the bell. He was shivering in a sweater; he'd told his folks that he'd forgotten his jacket at school. He said thanks, quickly, and then he went off to join the boys again. I didn't know what to do; usually we played a little soccer before school started. I just hung out by the stairwell. Eventually, the bell rang and we all went in.

That night, Appa and Amma came up to the room I shared with two of my sisters. Jesús's mother had called; she had immediately noticed the tear, and he had told her everything. Amma started shouting at me, but Appa didn't say anything. He wouldn't look at me. I wanted him to look at me, even if he was shouting while he did. But he wouldn't. He said he'd pay Mrs. Gonzalez for the cost of a replacement jacket. A hundred dollars we couldn't afford easily. Amma always worried about money. When she started shouting again, he said, "Let her be, Shanthi."

Amma said, "Kissing boys—she's going to ruin herself!"

He said, "She's just a child. She didn't know what she was doing."

"You're too soft on her—you're always too soft on this one ..."

"Please, Shanthi, kunju ..."

Amma looked like she wanted to yell some more, but she wouldn't argue with him in front of me. She always waited until she thought we were all asleep before she started shouting. Amma shut her mouth tight, lips pressed flat and thin. He took her arm and led her down-stairs, leaving me alone.

I didn't speak to Jesús again; it was easy, because he avoided me af-ter that. And I stopped playing soccer with the boys. I spent my recess breaks doing homework, and my grades went up.

Appa avoided me too.

THE AIR INSIDE THE STAIRWELL WAS CHILL, EVEN IN JUNE. TO MY surprise, Sue led me up instead of down. We climbed up a flight. At the top of the stairs, there was a door. She pushed it open, and there was sky beyond it.

"They never seem to lock this. I think they've forgotten it's here." She grinned again as she pulled me out onto the roof. The tiles were slanted, and we balanced precariously, looking down across campus. The business school and the divinity school before us, the social sci-ence and humanities buildings to either side. "C'mere...," she called. She had let go of my hand and walked across the tiles, heading over the peak, toward the view south across the grassy strips of the Midway. She seemed to have no trouble at all walking; my right hand still clung tightly to the doorknob. "Don't worry, it won't lock if you let it go..."

"We're going to get in trouble, Sue."

She turned and came back across the tiles, looking annoyed. "Please, Leilani. Can't you just enjoy something for once in your life?"

"But it must be against the rules to be on the roof." If my father finished the exam he was giving and decided to come and take a little nap in the library; he often took naps in Harper...

"We're not hurting anything! I come up here all the time. No one ever notices—nobody ever looks up. Leilani, please. For ten minutes, just relax, okay?"

I felt trapped—I hadn't even come fully out onto the roof. One foot was still on the inside landing, one hand tight to the door. I glanced down at the grass far below; my stomach was churning, and I felt dizzy. I didn't know why I hadn't already fallen. Sue must have seen that on my face, because suddenly she was beside me, her body blocking my view of the grass, her hands firm around mine.

"Hey. Hey . . . I'm sorry. I'm so stupid. Sit down. Just slide down . . . yeah, that's right. Put your head between your knees. Take a deep breath. Just breathe."

WHEN YOU RUN, REALLY RUN, YOU HAVE TO BREATHE PROPERLY. Little quick breaths will make you light-headed; huge, gasping breaths won't do you much good. You need to breathe normally, just as if you were walking, or standing still. If you can't breathe normally, you need to slow down.

I started really running at fourteen. My breasts were small, and I had long legs. No one was surprised, though my sisters teased me and said I'd never get a date if I acted like a boy. Amma wasn't sure it was a good thing for a girl to do, but Appa said to let me be. That's what he always said about me, and Amma was enough of a traditionalist that, at least in public, his word ruled the house. So I got to do what I wanted, and what I wanted to do at fourteen was keep running.

I ran at school. At home. I'd get up in the early morning, even before Amma rose to iron our uniforms and make our hot, sweet milk. I walked out the door when the sky was cold and dark and dry, the air so clear that even an hour later, it was amazing that you could still breathe. I started running when the tip of my sneaker touched the bottom of the last step—with a push from those toes, going as fast as I could.

I never ran far. Down the street, to the small patch of woods that still existed back then, through the woods between the trees, ignoring scratches on my arms that would later have Amma squawking and casting reproachful looks at Appa over his toast and fish curry. Through the woods to the lake. I'd stop there, sit down on the shore. Sometimes, if it was early enough, if I had time, I'd take off my sneakers and socks, slip dirty brown feet into even dirtier water. Watch the sun rise. Wipe off my feet on the grass, put the socks and sneakers back on. Turn around. Start running. There wasn't much time.

Less than two miles to the lake and back. I was always back before any of my five sisters had woken.

At home, I removed my shoes, threw the socks in the laundry basket, washed my body and my hair. I'd cut it short when I started running. It was too much trouble brushing it afterward, and I never had the patience to braid it the way Amma wanted me to. Amma took her hairbrush to me that day and got in a few good smacks before Appa intervened. "Please, Shanthi, please let her be." And she did.

I ran all through high school. At home. At school. I was the best sprinter on the team, and when I won my first trophy, Amma was there at the ceremony, in her blue and silver sari, with her hair up and her glasses in her purse. She was almost blind without them, but she hated wearing them in public. She wouldn't even wear them to teach; she memorized her math lectures and hardly used the blackboard at all. When I came down after receiving the trophy, she looked right past me.

The summer after my senior year of high school, my breasts suddenly grew two sizes. I couldn't run the way I had, pounding through the woods, hardly noticing the ups and downs. Even with my oldest, tightest bra, they jiggled and distracted. They had gone from barely plums to grapefruit. The family doctor didn't know why, though he seemed to think it was wonderful. Maybe it was all that hot milk.

I took up tennis instead, when I started college at Chicago. Amma had new complaints; my arms were getting unfeminine, too muscular. I ignored her. Tennis was good at first, slamming the ball across the court, the competitive charge. But the audience at games was distracting, and even my opponent was more than I wanted; it wasn't the same as running alone. Tennis didn't give me the same rush of blood through my body, from my toes to the top of my head. Eventually, I stopped bothering to cut my hair; I let it grow long, like my sisters, and braided it.

In the fall of my second year, I dropped tennis. I was too busy studying to practice daily, to make every scheduled meeting, every event at home and away. Amma was happy.

I WAS SHAKING. MY EYES WERE PRESSED TIGHTLY CLOSED, MY HEAD was tucked between my knees, and Sue's head was pressed against mine. Her hands were wrapped around mine, and I could feel her breath on my calves; I was wearing a knee-length skirt, though my father didn't really approve. My mother had convinced him to allow all of us to wear them, since they were still longer than the miniskirts all the white girls were wearing. She said we had to adapt—but not too much. We had to remember where we came from.

It was difficult remembering anything with Sue's breath warm and quick against my shivering skin.

I took deep breaths, trying to slow my thumping heart. Left ventricle, right ventricle, aorta, pulmonary artery . . . Names, words were calming. That's what I knew, all I knew. I had forgotten the language of my body. All I did those days was read and write and study the words. Right atrium, left atrium, inferior vena cava . . . The dizziness faded; I lifted my head—and promptly became dizzy again.

Sue's softly rounded face was just an inch or two away from mine, and the words had fled. All I could think about was how warm and solid her lips looked, how the curve of them contrasted so sharply with the empty air behind her, the sharp angles of tilted roof and vertical wall and hard horizontal ground three stories below. I couldn't breathe, and I could feel my eyes widening, my throat swallowing convulsively. She looked frightened, with blue eyes gone dark and stormy—and then she leaned forward and pressed her lips against mine.

WHEN WE WERE LITTLE, MY SISTERS AND I RAN FREELY AROUND campus in the hours after school and before dinner, making friends with the students and teachers. We watched each other, and everyone kept an eye on us, so my parents didn't worry. They were busy with their teaching schedules. Appa was a mathematician, in Eckhart Hall on the main quadrangle; Amma was a few streets away at the Lab School. We weren't supposed to bother them while they were working.

I hadn't meant to bother him. I was eight, and I liked to run. That day, I was running from the Reynolds Club fountain to the tennis courts, just running back and forth, seeing how fast I could go. There was a tricky bit, crossing the open archway between Eckhart and Ryerson Halls. Three steps up, four steps across, three steps down. I could skip steps, but I didn't actually go faster then. So I usually hit them all, thump thump thump. My head down, and my arms at my sides, pumping to help me run faster. I must have run it a hundred times that day before I tripped and fell.

I cut my forehead on the stone. It didn't hurt much. But it was bleeding, blood running down my face, onto my favorite blue dress. Appa's office was right there—just inside Eckhart, up two flights of stairs, three doors down. I pressed my hand over the cut, trying to stop the bleeding. I ran inside, up the stairs, down the hall. And when I got to his door, I pushed it open, without knocking.

He was kissing a woman. A blonde woman, with long, straight hair that fell down her back. It looked just like Amma's hair—but the wrong color. And she was much younger than Amma. I turned around and ran away, leaving the door open behind me.

I didn't tell anyone.

I COULD HAVE PULLED AWAY AND PULLED MYSELF INTO THE STAIRwell and run down the stairs and away. But instead I slid forward, just an inch, but an inch further out onto the roof. I slid forward and pressed my lips back against hers, tentatively opened my mouth and I was breathing her breath, swallowing her air, and I could breathe again. I was still dizzy but her lips were so warm and solid and her mouth was wet and her hands tightened on mine as if she would pin me to the roof, pin me down so that I couldn't possibly fall off. I was grateful for their pressure, because my body felt light, my bones felt hollow, as if I could fly away on them.

Her hands slid up my arms. They slid up to my shoulders and wrapped around, pressing against my spine, pulling my body against hers. She was crouching now, her knees pressed against the outside of mine, and I could feel the heat of them, the damp sweat cooling in the breeze that blew across the roof. They slid against my own sweaty skin; and I didn't dare to look down. I knew that her skirt must have slid up and up. Sue kept kissing me. That was what we were doing. She was kissing me, and I was kissing her back. I was kissing Sue on the roof of the college library, the college where my father was currently giving an exam; we were kissing on the roof where anyone who looked up could see us.

Her mouth moved hard against mine, her tongue licking out in tiny licks against my tongue, my teeth, the inside of my lips. Then she started sliding her mouth down, down my chin, and I tilted my head back. Sue was licking my neck, sucking on the hollow of my throat, and I was sure there was a name for that part but I couldn't remember what it was. The blood was still thumping through my heart, the aorta filling and pulsing and pumping it along. Her hands were still tight against my spine, grounding me against her solid body, keeping my skin attached though my bones wanted to fly. And my hands were off the ground and on her bare legs. My hands were sliding up and down her damp thighs and she moaned in her throat, and at the sound of it a burn started between my thighs, a quick convulsion shook through me.

Sue pulled away; she started to open her mouth to speak.

IN THE FALL OF MY THIRD YEAR, I WOULD SWITCH MAJORS TO English lit. I would write poetry and win a few awards. I wouldn't tell my parents what I'd done until Christmas, when the grades would arrive, with my straight As in the wrong field. Amma would say that I had never been a very good science student, and that science had only given her heartache anyway. Appa would not say anything.

I would graduate in June. Three of my sisters would have married, and Harini would be pregnant. I would have already turned down half a dozen arranged proposals; though I was not beautiful, I was not ugly either. Some of the proposals would have been from Ceylon; I would tell my parents I didn't want to marry a boy who just wanted a green card. Some would be from local boys whom I had known my whole life; I would tell my parents that it would have felt like marrying my brother, if I had had a brother. I would hold them off until gradua-tion with such excuses. My mother and I would fight about it, often. Once, she would get so angry that she would throw a pot of boiling crab curry at my head. She would miss, but the splashing liquid would burn us both.

On graduation day, with my degree safe in my hand, I would tell my parents that I had a job as a secretary at the university, and that I was going to move out, to share a house with other girls. I would tell them that I was hoping to be a poet. I would not tell them how many lovers (mostly female, a few male) I had had. I would tell them that I might never marry.

They would say nothing. Amma would turn and walk away. Appa would hesitate and then follow her. I would not talk to them, or they to me, for some years.

I would be maid of honor at Sue's wedding. I would dance for her.

I REACHED OUT AND PULLED SUE TO ME AGAIN. I CUPPED MY HANDS around her thighs and pulled her legs against mine, between mine. I arched up and placed my mouth on hers and kissed her hard. Her tongue slipped into my mouth, her teeth bit my bottom lip, and sound climbed up from my spine to my throat to my tongue to hers.

Sue captured my moan with her lips and tongue hard against my throat, and then she was pushing me back, tilting me back against the tiles, laying my body down and kneeling above me. Her hands were on my arms now, still holding me, still grounding me, and then her teeth were on my shirt, pulling buttons open with such skill that I knew she had done this before, many times, and then my shirt was open, my bra pulled down and my left breast was in her mouth, my heart was under her lips and tongue and my skin was naked to the air and I was lost and found and nothing would ever be the same again.

The shudders shook through me, as her lips tightened on my breast and her fingers dug into my arms; my thighs clenched and my heart opened.

I was not running. I was not falling.

Was this the adventure I'd been searching for?

I was holding very still, and flying.

Lakshmi's Diary

Chicago, 1969

JULY 2, 1969—MY WEDDING DAY.

Today I'm getting married. Raksha is a handsome man—smooth skin, nice cheekbones. He's cheerful, generous, and owns his own business, a sari shop. Easwari Aunty has done well by me, though I thought she was going to have a heart attack when I wrote to her and asked her to find me a husband. She protested—of course my parents, both teachers, would object to my getting married instead of going to college, but I can be just as stubborn as any of my five sisters when I need to be. And she knew it. Aunty also knew there wasn't much else for me. The dark horse of the family, the one who didn't get into U of C, or Northwestern, or even UIC—who didn't get into college at all. Dark-skinned too, which made Aunty's job harder. But she agreed that I had better get married.

I'm going to have babies. That's one thing my sisters have done little of. Only three of them married so far, and only two babies in the lot. I will have hundreds of babies.

Maybe not hundreds. But seven or eight or nine or more—my grandmother had thirteen living children, and that was in Ceylon, without the benefit of modern medicine! I will have many children, and a beautiful home, and I will cook perfect meals for my Raksha—at least I can cook. I will sing Tamil songs to him when he comes home tired from work; that's something Leilani can't do. She croaks like a frog. And none of them can dance. I will take good care of my husband, and I will be happy.

LATER—ALMOST MIDNIGHT.

Easwari Aunty said it would hurt a little, but then it would get better.

Raksha was different tonight. Maybe it was all the wine and champagne at the wedding. The men were drinking hard liquor too. He wasn't himself. He didn't give me time to think. Maybe there's something wrong with me. If this is what it takes to make many children—maybe I'll wait a while.

It must get better.

He sleeps like a log, snoring loudly, sprawling over the hotel bed. I want my own bed, with its crazy quilt in scraps of silk and sari fabric, cornflower blue, lavender, and rose. Silver threads through it, and an occasional hint of gold. I want it to be that winter again, and me sixteen, sitting in front of the fireplace and leaning against Appa's knee, sewing together the pieces of my quilt.

AUGUST 10, 1969—PREGNANT.

It didn't happen the way I'd planned. The morning after the wedding, Raksha did it again in the morning. It hurt more. He tried to touch me again that night, but I wouldn't let him. I told him I'd scream if he touched me, and since we were back in my old room, in my old bed, with my parents and sisters just down the hall, someone would come. They'd all come running. He left me alone for a while and said he was sorry he'd hurt me. I believed him; I just needed a little time.

But now I'm going to have a baby. Already.

He can't touch me now—it might hurt the baby.

I'm going to learn how to knit. I've already crocheted a blanket for her, white and soft and warm. I'll make her socks and sweaters and pink hats. I'll start making her clothes too—I have the patterns picked out, the fabrics neatly folded in my drawer, in sunny yellow and grass-green.

I'm going to be a perfect mother. They'll see.

DECEMBER 25, 1969—CHRISTMAS.

I'm a married woman now, and pregnant—they should treat me with more respect. They won't even let me have a glass of wine at Christmas dinner. Kili, who thinks she's such a big doctor now, says it might hurt the baby. I've never heard of any such thing, but when I poured myself a glass, she just reached out and took it out of my hand, while everyone laughed.

Raksha gets to drink whatever he wants—and he's not drinking wine. All the men drink whiskey or vodka, and Appa tells stories of when he was a boy in Ceylon, sneaking sips of arrack. Raksha hangs on my father's every word, laughs when he does, and when Kili took my glass, he just laughed with the rest of my family, my father, my sisters. He wouldn't let me have a sip of his whiskey either. Sometimes I hate them all.

FEBRUARY 18, 1970—HE HIT ME.

I married a drunk. Leilani was right. I'm an idiot.

He had a bad day at the store. I don't know what happened, and it doesn't matter. He went drinking with his friends afterward; he does that every night. He came home, and I could smell the whiskey on him. I'm sure Amma and Appa could smell it too. I'm the embarrassment of my family—the stupid girl who didn't go to college, got married too young, got pregnant, and, finally, picked a drunk to spend her life with.

Raksha wants to move out of my parents' house. I want that too, but not now. Not yet. If we stay here, Amma will be close, in case anything goes wrong with the baby. And I'll need help afterward. We've been arguing for weeks, but tonight he got angry. I got angry too and threw a cushion at him. He grabbed it in the air, twisted it in his hand, tore the fabric. He knew I made that cushion. He knew I'd sewn it to match the quilt, with a little more silver, shining. I came at him, screaming, my hands raised, and maybe I would have scratched him, clawed his face—I wanted to. But he grabbed my hands in one of his, and then slapped my face, hard, with his other hand. Shouting nonsense I couldn't understand. I just stood there, my hands still caught in his. It didn't hurt. And then the anger melted from his face, and he started crying. He let go of my hands.

I turned and left then—went into the bathroom and locked the door. He stopped crying after a while, and then I heard the front door slam. He'd gone out to drink more. That was fine; he could sleep on a park bench, or in the driveway. I didn't care. I went to the front door and bolted it shut.

It didn't hurt. Not when he hit me, though it aches now. That was the strangest part.

FEBRUARY 19, 1970—CONTRACTIONS.

He came back. He broke the lock on the kitchen door and came in and woke me up and shook me, shouting. He hit me again, and this time he knocked me down. Amma and Appa came and Appa threw him out—I didn't know Appa was strong enough. But now I'm having contractions, and it's so early. We're going to the hospital in a few minutes. Amma is packing a bag for me, and Leilani is coming to drive us. There is a huge black bruise on my cheek—everyone will know.

Please, let the baby be all right.

Let me do something right.

FEBRUARY 21, 1970—CHAYA.

They argued with me. Everyone said, "What a bad-luck name! You can't name her that!" But she is small and dark and born under her mother's shadow of misery and pain, and so I'm going to name her

Chaya, which means shadow, and they can't stop me. Raksha isn't here, and the nurse is listening to me.

One small shadow to follow me. Thirty-seven hours of labor. I won't have another child. It would kill me. And I won't let him touch me again.

MARCH I, 1970—RAKSHA MOVED OUT.

Everything of his is gone. He tried to argue. He was waiting for us, sitting on the steps outside the kitchen door. His face crumpled when he saw Chaya's tiny hands and feet. He has fallen in love with his little daughter, says he wants to be with her, wants to take care of her.

He can take care of her by sending money. I'll take care of Chaya.

JUNE 6, 1970—MY BIRTHDAY. HE SENDS ROSES.

Does he think I'm stupid?

Amma loves them; Appa never brings her flowers. She insisted on displaying them in the hall, three dozen, long-stemmed, deepest red. Will rose scent hide the whiskey reek?

Appa says Raksha has joined some group for alcoholics, that he attends weekly meetings. So what? Let him keep sending money, for now, and when Chaya's a little older, I'll go back to school. I'll graduate, and get a good job—we'll move out, and I'll take care of my daughter by myself.

NOVEMBER II, 1970—CHAYA'S FIRST WORD.

I haven't recorded every first—not the first time she really looked at me, or the first time she smiled, or the first time she got sick, when I thought my heart would pound its way out of my chest.

My little shadow is with me always, carried in a small shoulder sling I made myself, soft well-washed cottons in red and amber and gold. I started helping Amma in the garden this summer, learning the weeds and the flowers. Chaya rode with me, and I told her the names—the late autumn roses, the chrysanthemums, the crimson snapdragons. I thought maybe she would say a flower name for her first word; we spent so much time in the garden together.

She said *Appa*. I'm sure she's heard me call my father that a thousand times.

But still. I'm sorry Raksha didn't hear it.

FEBRUARY 21, 1971—CHAYA'S FIRST BIRTHDAY.

Raksha came to the party. They didn't warn me. They must have all contrived together—he arrived with Kili and her husband, and the rest of my sisters came sweeping in after. He looked small, and so alone. It reminded me of how alone he really is. No family. His father cut Raksha off, years ago, for no good reason; he was only a teenager at the time. Forbade him to call his mother, his little sisters. All he has is me, and Chaya. And the store, of course—he started that store all by himself, with money borrowed from friends and the bank, and built it into a thriving business. He has a right to be proud of the store. I should have written to his parents when Chaya was born. They should have met their granddaughter.

He hasn't taken a drink in eighteen weeks. He told me that in the kitchen, in the one moment when we were alone. I said *So?* and then I lit the last candle and took Chaya's birthday cake in, singing in perfect key. He followed quietly.

He looks thin. He hasn't been eating right.

Chaya is scared of her father. She started crying when Raksha bent over her to kiss her forehead and wish her happy birthday. He left a few minutes later.

SEPTEMBER 9, 1972—RAKSHA MOVES BACK IN.

He is sleeping on a cot in the basement, not in our bedroom. But he's been visiting since Chaya's first birthday—just a few times a month. He always called first. Chaya knows who he is now. It's been good, having his help with her.

Appa retired last June, or semiretired. He's a professor emeritus now, only teaches an occasional class. He wanted to keep teaching full-time, but Amma made him stop. He was getting so tired. They're not young, either of them.

I've taken over about half the garden work, though I plant herbs and vegetables instead of Amma's flowers. I do all the digging and heavy work. They can't really keep up with an energetic toddler, especially not one as strong and fast and willful as Chaya. You'd never guess that she was born early.

Appa says a child needs both her parents.

Raksha hasn't had a drink in almost two years. The store is doing well; he's thinking of opening a second store. I think it'll be good for Chaya to have him here. So far, he's been on his best behavior.

DECEMBER 25, 1972—CHRISTMAS.

Everyone was here for Christmas. All my sisters and all their husbands (four of them married now, everyone but Leilani). Four small cousins for Chaya to play with. Amma and Appa presiding over it all and Raksha quiet in a corner. He's been so good the last few months. He takes Chaya to work with him sometimes, so I can have a day to myself. He changes diapers in the back of the shop and carries her on his hip while he works. How many husbands would do that? He says it's pure self-interest, that he sells more saris when she's with him, but I can see the tenderness in his hands, in his eyes. He gave up the drinking for her, so he could be with her. That's fine. That's enough for me.

We felt like a family today.

JANUARY 1, 1973—WE HAD SEX AGAIN.

It wasn't the champagne—it was just time. The family's been working on me. Amma pointed out that Raksha had a cough and said it must be cold down in the basement. Kili managed to get in a few comments about how she took better care of her husband. Hah! That poor man goes around with his ribs sticking out from hunger, that's how good care she takes of him. Never mind the fine clothes she buys with her doctor money. If he has to eat cold sandwiches for dinner, no wonder he doesn't eat. At least Raksha eats properly. He's tall now, and strong. He's more handsome now than he was when I married him.

It's Leilani's fault, really. She's not married, but she isn't a virgin either—I think Amma knows that, but she won't ever talk about it. Leilani has been telling me about sex; she made it sound good. So when Raksha came to my door last night to say good night before going down to the basement, I took his hand. I pulled him inside and shut the door. I wasn't sure what to do then. He just stood there, looking sad and hopeful at the same time, until I tilted my head up and closed my eyes, like the girls in the movies. I'm pretty enough, even if I'm not as beautiful as my sisters, and my breasts are bigger after having Chaya. He kissed me so carefully, like a butterfly kissing a flower. I kissed back.

Leilani was right. It wasn't bad the first time; he was gentle. Slow. In the morning, it was nice. And the way he looked at me—as if he'd been starving, and I'd laid out a feast.

I'm going to make sure we use something every time; Leilani showed me that too. But from now on, I think I'll let my husband sleep in my bedroom.

Maybe I'll even make him a shirt.

MARCH 5, 1975—OUR OWN HOUSE!

More than two years since I last wrote here. Raksha still hasn't had a drink, as far as I know. The second store is doing well, and we can afford a house—not a big one, but ours, with enough space in the backyard for a real garden. It's only ten minutes drive away from Amma and Appa. And I've done it up nicely—I just made new drapes for the living room, floor-length, in a pale spring green. Soon the rains will stop, and we'll have real spring here at last. I've made curtains for all the rooms and chosen wallpaper to match. Leilani says I have an eye for beauty. She's a poet, so she should know.

Chaya starts school in September. I'm thinking of going back to college then. I don't want my daughter to think her mother is ignorant.

SEPTEMBER 19, 1975—CHAYA'S FIRST DAY OF SCHOOL.

The house is so empty. It's harvest time in my garden, but soon there won't be anything to do there. I've decided—I'm going to take some classes, and if I do all right in them, I'm going to college. I don't know what I'll study—but I don't think it matters, as long as I pick something and stick with it. I learned that from my marriage—sometimes, you just have to keep working at something, even when you don't understand exactly why. Eventually, things work out.

JUNE 20, 1980—GRADUATION DAY.

College graduate—that's me. A degree in art history, which I enjoyed, even though I'm not sure it will do me any good. Classes seemed easier than they did in high school, eleven years ago.

Chaya is ten now, and she looked beautiful in her white dress, sitting proudly in the audience. She may be dark like her mother, but she's still lovely. Everyone says so. She's doing so well in school—the highest scores in the class!—and at her piano lessons too. Her teacher says she has real talent. And she's so affectionate. I'm proud of my little girl.

Maybe I should have another child. Maybe I should have several, the way I planned. I'm not so old yet—not even thirty.

Raksha looked handsome too, holding his daughter's little hand, beaming as he watched me walk down the aisle. He never understood why I wanted this degree, but he paid for the classes, for the babysitting when I needed the time to study. He looked happier today than he did at our wedding. I am growing fond of my husband, after all these years. We may not have the perfect understanding, the great love affair, that Kili claims to have with her husband, but we have a beautiful daughter together. We are gentle with each other. That's more than many marriages can claim.

SEPTEMBER 18, 1980—PREGNANT AGAIN.

I hope this birth is easier.

I'm knitting again. When I was pregnant with Chaya, all my socks and sweaters came out malformed. I didn't have any patience back then; when I made a mistake, I'd just keep going. It's going better this time around. I fix the mistakes before continuing, even if it means pulling out half the rows I've already done.

OCTOBER 10, 1980.

It is nothing. Nothing. I'm not even sure why I'm writing this. Nothing has happened.

I woke up in the middle of the night. Raksha wasn't in bed. I went to Chaya's room. He was standing by her bed, watching her.

This is nothing. Every parent does this—every parent wakes in the middle of the night and goes to check on their child. Is she healthy, is she sleeping soundly, is she breathing well? Raksha has a weak heart, and we've always worried that Chaya might develop problems too. He loves her so much—of course he goes to check on her at night, sometimes. And if he stands and watches her for a while, so what?

The expression on his face . . . it's nothing.

I called him softly, and he turned and smiled. No guilty start, nothing. "Just checking," he said. "I'll be there in a minute." And I nodded, and smiled, and went back to bed. He was there beside me a few minutes later.

What's wrong with me? Pregnant-woman fancies, that's all.

NOVEMBER 28, 1980. HE'S DRINKING AGAIN.

I'm sure of it. And I don't know how long he's been doing it, because there are so few signs. He doesn't come home reeking of whiskey—he doesn't go out drinking with his friends from work. I haven't found any bottles around the house; maybe he picks them up in the morning and drinks them at lunchtime. I don't know. But I've been watching him closely the last few weeks. Something is different.

He's louder, noisier. More energetic when he plays with Chaya—he throws her up in the air as if she's still a little girl. And when he sits her on his lap and reads to her, they're action and adventure stories, full of rocket ships and robots. She loves them—right now she's planning to be an astronaut when she grows up. And she adores her father, who can do no wrong. Chaya gets angry at me; she screams and shouts when she doesn't want to clean her room, but let Appa come home and say the word, and that room is clean before you can turn around. It's good for a little girl to love her father, and for him to love her. But the way he gets engrossed in playing with her . . . He often doesn't notice when I call them to dinner. He gets annoyed if I call again. "Leave us alone, Lakshmi—we're busy!" he'll shout, and Chaya will giggle. Conspirators together.

I've seen nothing wrong.

It's the drinking again. I'll watch him for a while. I'll make sure. And then I'll make him get help. I'm not going to just panic and kick him out—I'm not the frightened little girl I was when we married. I will fight for this man, for my marriage, for our family. We'll get through this.

FEBRUARY 20, 1981—TALKED TO THE LAWYER.
Leilani took me. I haven't told anyone else. I'm going to ask for a divorce.

No one in my family has ever been divorced. I always wanted to be first at something.

I caught him last night. Not drinking, though I'm sure he's been doing that too. Maybe that's why—who knows? Maybe it would be too easy to blame it on the drinking. Maybe he's just a man who loves his daughter too much.

I woke up again in the middle of the night. Raksha wasn't there. I found him in Chaya's room. He wasn't touching her—she was fast asleep. But she had kicked off the sheet the way she always does, so that her bare legs stuck out, and his eyes were fixed on her, on my daughter. His daughter. My stomach began to churn. I couldn't breathe.

Something was wrong with my baby, my little girl. Something was wrong with him.

He didn't see me at all.

I wanted to rush in, to push him away from her, to scream. Instead, I went back to our room, walking as quickly and silently as I could. I climbed into bed and called his name, just loudly enough for him to hear me, as if I had just woken from sleep, and a moment later he came back.

"Bad dreams?"

Yes, bad dreams. The worst. He climbed into bed and held me, and I tried not to pull away, counting my breaths, forcing them to be calm, even. If I told him what I'd seen, would he hit me again? How hard? Or would he just start to cry?

I lay in his arms all night, wide awake. This morning, after Raksha left for work, I called Amma and told her the pregnancy was making me tired. I asked her if she'd mind taking Chaya for a while. Then I called Leilani and told her everything.

We'll keep it quiet—Leilani thinks that's best. But I am not going to leave my daughter in the same house with that man for even one more day.

MARCH 3, 1981—CHAYA'S PIANO RECITAL.

We bought the tickets weeks ago; everyone expected Raksha to be there. Leilani won't say anything, but the others think I should let him come. Kili thinks I just had a bad dream that night; I'm sure the others think that too, though none of the others actually say it. I know what I saw. I know what it would become.

Chaya will be surrounded by other people throughout the recital. She hasn't seen her father in days, not since we moved back to Amma's and Appa's house, and she's started asking questions I don't know how to answer. I tuck her into bed, wrap the blue silk patchwork quilt around her small body, kiss her forehead and tell her I'll explain it all soon. Then I curl up on a mattress on the floor beside her, trying to think what I can possibly say.

I don't think Raksha will fight the divorce; he sounds like a whipped dog on the phone. He's drinking all the time, I think—he cries every time he calls. I make him calm down before I let him talk to Chaya. He sounds so small.

He can come to the recital; he deserves the chance to say good-bye to her in person. He can pretend to be a good father for one more day.

JULY 20, 2000—CHAYA LEAVES FOR HER NEW JOB IN CALIFORNIA.

I thought about burning this journal, so Chaya would never find it and suspect. But I saved it instead, buried it in the back of my closet, in a hamper full of scraps and rags. I was saving it for this day, it seems.

Chaya is leaving to start her new position; I don't know how often I'll see her after this. Christmas and New Year and perhaps a birthday or two. Maybe she should know what really happened that day, the day her father died. She should read these words and know the truth. I almost told her when she got involved with that white boy—I didn't trust him. But she got free of him quickly enough. I didn't need to say the words. But they're here. If anyone has a right to judge me, she does.

On that day in early March, Raksha at first seemed sober. But when we got to the recital hall, he slipped away. When he joined us in our seats, I could smell it on him. Chaya waited in the wings for her turn to go up. I said nothing. He drank more at intermission. Leilani sat on my other side; when Chaya went up, she took my hand. Chaya played beautifully that day. I never told her that. She was full of smiles as she curtseyed and the audience applauded.

Raksha hugged her when she came down. He hugged her and hugged her and when we left to go to the car, he swung her up on his shoulders. I should have stopped him then—but we were surrounded by people. I didn't want to embarrass him in front of our friends and family and Chaya's piano teacher. I don't know why I cared.

When we got back to the car, Leilani offered to drive; Raksha refused. It was still winter in Chicago—we'd just been through a bad ice storm, and the roads were slippery. I tried to convince him to give her the keys, but he wouldn't listen. He started to get angry; his voice got louder, and Leilani tried to take the keys from his hand. He shoved her away, hard, so that she fell on the ground. Chaya looked scared; she opened her mouth to yell, and Raksha pushed her inside the car, into the front passenger's seat, shoving down the lock and slamming the door shut.

I couldn't let him drive off with Chaya. He was running around the front, climbing into the driver's seat. Chaya was crying loudly now, and I couldn't breathe. I was on the wrong side of the car to reach him, to stop him. I opened the back door and climbed in. It took a few minutes—my stomach was so huge—but it seemed like it took forever. He had already turned on the engine. Before I closed the door, the car started to move. I slammed the door shut as Raksha took off. He was shouting at Chaya, "Seat belt, seat belt, seat belt!" and Chaya was crying harder and trying to put the seat belt on. She managed it, and I did too, dragging it across my belly as I begged him to stop the car. I was crying too. He didn't say anything else, just drove, racing toward the highway, toward Lake Shore Drive. I don't know what he was planning to do, where he thought he could go. I doubt he was thinking at all. He drove much too fast. Before we even reached the highway, we hit a piece of black ice; we skidded off the road and hit a tree.

We were all thrown forward, but the seat belts held Chaya and me. Raksha had never put his on.

Chaya started screaming, and I tried to undo my seat belt and get to her. The front of the car was crumpled and Raksha's head was slammed up against the steering wheel, completely still. I couldn't reach her seat belt release. I reached forward, unlocked her door, climbed out of the car and opened her door, undid her seat belt and got her out. I almost walked away from the car right then. We were on a deserted side street leading toward the highway. Nobody was there—and who would fault me, seven months pregnant and with a hysterical child, for leaving a grown man in a car that might explode? But I had to know if he was still alive.

He hadn't moved. I walked Chaya over to a tree and told her to wait there. Then I went back to the car. I must have run as well as I could, but I felt as if I were walking in slow motion; everything had been happening so fast, but now time had slowed until it was almost stopped. Chaya was safely away, and I had plenty of time to do whatever needed to be done.

Chaya, I could stop here. Or I could tell you that I found him dead there, tell you what the doctors said later, that the alcohol and the shock and his weak heart had combined to give him a heart attack and kill him at thirty-one. Maybe that's the truth.

I walked back to the car. I opened his door. I tilted him back in the seat, and I didn't know if he was breathing or not. His eyes were closed; he wasn't moving. My belly hurt and my legs ached, and I didn't know how to tell if he still lived. It didn't matter. Because what I did then was bend over my husband, shielding my actions with my body. I covered his mouth and his nose tightly with my hands and the folds of my sari. I counted seconds in my head. One one thousand. Two one thousand. Three one thousand. How long can a person hold their breath and live? I held my own breath until I had to breathe, until the air came rushing into my lungs in a great gasp, still counting. Seventy-nine. Eighty. Eighty-one. Eighty-two. He never moved.

I stood there until I heard another car pulling up, and then I stepped back and started to cry again. It was easy to cry. A white couple came up, all shock and pity and dismay. They herded me and Chaya into their car and drove us to the hospital, where we notified the police. The hospital sent an ambulance for Raksha. The family arrived soon afterward, and they were all around me when we received official word of Raksha's death. By that time the contractions had started, and

I was barely paying attention to anything other than my belly. Leilani had swept Chaya up in her arms; I knew she'd be safe there. Three hours later, Savitha was born, her birth so quick and easy I hardly noticed it. Savitha means sunlight.

What more is there to say? I didn't write in this journal again. I took the guilt on willingly. My life since then has been entirely for my daughters. I lost myself, buried myself, in caring for them. But they aren't children anymore. Savitha is married and gone away; Chaya is finally leaving too. At first I couldn't bear the thought, but lately, I've been waiting for her to go. I've kept her too close to me for too long.

I thought once that I would die when this day came, that I would fade away, a widow in mourning white.

I'm forty-nine. I have lived more than half my life unthinking, and the rest for my children. Now, shall I live for myself? Or should I turn myself in, pay for my crime? Chaya, when you read this, come and tell me what you think. I stole away your father, and you have never seemed the same. Silent instead of laughing. So serious. I did what I thought was best; I did it for myself, but also for you. Should I have done differently?

I wanted to be a good daughter, a good wife, a good mother. I am not sure that I succeeded at any of those, even the last.

Time to pull out all the threads and start over.

Interlude

Sins of the Father

Jaffna, 1977

VELU'S HAND SHAKES LIKE AN OLD MAN'S AS HE CROUCHES NAKED IN
THE DARK ROOM, A TIN BOWL OF WATER BEFORE HIM, A THIN WASH-
cloth in his hand. It is miserably hot, the worst of the Jaffna summer
heat, and he knows that by the time he walks from his house to where
the Tigers are encamped, he will be drenched in sweat. Still, he must
do what he can, and so Velu dips the cloth into cool well water, passes
it over his thin body. He has always been thin, but the deprivations of
the last several years have left him emaciated, his bones poking out,
sharp against loose skin. He rubs the skin fiercely, to compensate for
the lack of soap, to compensate for all that has happened—rubs until
his skin feels scraped raw, flushed and swollen. When the cloth goes
dry, he reaches for more water and overbalances, falling sharply onto
one bony knee, unable to catch himself with only one good arm. The
other hangs limp at his side, useless since the bullet caught it. He re-
sents it, and at the same time is grateful to it. Its obvious uselessness
saved his life the last time the army came through.

As he washes himself, he composes a letter to his cousin in America. It is a letter he can never send—so many factors conspire to keep

him from speaking as frankly to her as he would like. But for long years, ever since his cousin first wrote to him expressing her condolences over the untimely death of his father, Velu has kept up a secret conversation with her, in his mind. For every line that he puts down on paper, that he shows his wife, that is undoubtedly read by the Tigers or the government clerks before it finally makes its way across the seas, Velu writes a dozen more in the cavern of his mind, lines that echo there, pulsing with truths that cannot be spoken.

If he could, he would say this:

Kili, dear cousin, I do not know if this letter will reach you. Not because of the troubles—not yet. Letters are still going through; we are not yet to the days grandfather spoke of, when he would send letters to his daughter in Oxford, not knowing if they would ever be delivered. Shanthi left Colombo in an evil time, going to school in the midst of war. I was only a child, five or six, but I remember how our grandmother wept at the harbour. Did her father know what he sent Shanthi to, in 1942? Would he have kept her back, if he could have, safe by his side?

All he had were her letters, for that brief year before his untimely illness and death. He never knew that she married, moved to America, had six children. Perhaps I should send the letters to you, so you may know the girl your mother was. But I do not want to let them go; I find comfort in laying my fingers against the thin blue paper. I close my eyes and imagine America, imagine freedom, and prosperity, and peace. You have told me, over and over, that America has its own troubles, and I trust you are correct—but Kili, cousin, I must tell you that America does not know what trouble is.

Velu will not write that, of course. It would not be safe—and even if it were, he can hardly bear to think of his troubles, much less put them down on paper. As he rises from his body wash, he remembers the room he used to bathe in, as a boy in Colombo, in his grandfather's house. Hot running water in the silver taps, a marble tub big enough to sail small fleets across—and he had those fleets too, light wood boats carved by that same grandfather. He had sailed his boats in the tub, in the small pond in the gardens behind the big house. He had played tennis in the tennis courts, had taken meals at his grandfather's club, had enjoyed all the privileges of a young Tamil gentleman in Ceylon's capital city, both while the British ruled and after their departure.

He had been twenty-two in 1958, when the first riots erupted in the streets, Tamil and Sinhalese neighbors lifting hands and stocks and rocks to each other. Velu had not wanted to leave the capital, but his parents had insisted that they would all be safer in Jaffna—and besides, there was a girl there that they had heard about, a beautiful, respectable girl, a doctor's daughter, a very good match for their son. If he would just come north with them and meet her ...

In the end, Velu was a good son. He did as his parents wanted and went north. He met the girl, and she was indeed most beautiful. Velu married her within a year and settled in a nearby village. They worked, and talked, and sometimes laughed. They made plans to move back to Colombo in a few years, when things settled down. They were blessed with children.

It is photos of those children that Velu sees now, as he steps, naked, from one dark room to the next. A black-and-white photo on the dresser, two smiling faces. His son, Pugal, is seven in that photo; his daughter, Kamala, is only six. Their faces are so small.

Velu turns from the dresser to the bed where his clothes are laid out. His wife is not speaking to him, but she has pressed the clothes flat for him, as best she can. She knows he must look good today. A pillar of the community; a man of stature. Someone worth listening to.

If he only knew what to say.

Shall I hold on to these words? My wife does not want me to write to you. She has a myriad of reasons, and some of them are even good ones. She worries that this letter may fall into unsympathetic hands, that it might be used against the Tigers. She is also afraid that if the Tigers or the government read it, our children might be put in further danger. She believes that it is better to keep your problems to yourself, and that distant family, in America, family we have never even met, are not really family at all.

If my wife were writing to you, she would only tell you good things. Oh, she might go on at length about the injustices Tamils have been subjected to, here on this island where we, the minority, once ruled like kings. She would certainly bemoan the loss of my grandfather's fine house in Colombo, with its cars and chauffeurs, its marble floors, its Sinhalese servants, though she never lived there herself. She would speak of those few Sinhalese who were once our neighbors, our friends, in such language that makes me embarrassed to call her my wife. But she would not say one word against the Tigers, despite what they have now done to us.

Perhaps she is right, and they have done nothing to us. Perhaps we have done it all to ourselves.

Velu sits down on the bed, which creaks under his slight, sudden weight. He shrugs the shirt over his arms, pulls it closed against his sunken chest. He does not think about his limp arm; it has been years since the incident, and he has long since learned to cope, uncomplaining, with everyday life. Others may have praised his courage, his fortitude, in dealing with the injury, but Velu never saw much worthy of praise in his actions. In the end, it was not so big a thing, to lose the use of an arm. It was bearable. It would not break him.

It made life harder for his wife, though. Velu had rarely made love to her before, and after the incident, he had an excuse for avoiding such activity. She was too proud to ask, and so he became celibate. It was easier.

And of course, cousin Kili, my wife also does not want me to write to you because she is jealous. She has resented you since that first letter you sent. Although you and I have never met, I have enjoyed an intimacy within our letters that I have never found with my wife. When my marriage was arranged, I was pleased; she was a beautiful girl. And in many ways she has been a good wife, has taken care of me and of our children as well as she could, given the circumstances. But we have never learned how to talk together. We do not share the same beliefs.

She is bitter, my wife. She mourns the loss of our fine things; she grieves for the house that was promised her, the beautiful home she will never have. I decided my father was right to bring his family to Jaffna, to this Tamil stronghold. I thought that surrounded by our own people, we would be safer, and so I did not take her to Colombo when I could. And now, see—we are trapped. The fighting comes to us, and we have no resources to escape it.

Velu looks up from his shirt buttons to see her standing there, in the doorway. She is still beautiful, his wife. Her hair falls past her waist, dark and rich as a girl's. But he feels no pang of desire when he sees her—he is only reminded of their daughter, their Kamala, who has chopped her hair short. All that beautiful hair, which should by rights have helped win her a perfect husband. Velu hadn't asked for a rich man for his daughter—he had never cared for that. He had only wanted someone kind, someone patient enough to put up with her high spirits, her passionate ways. A husband who would cherish his daughter's fierce soul, would train it to worthy tasks.

There might have been a time when we could have left for America. You so kindly offered to send us money for the trip—it would have shamed me to accept it, but I should have, for the sake of my family. Since moving to Jaffna, I have tried one business after another, to support my wife and children, but I have not had much luck. I was never meant to be a businessman, you know. I was bred to be a gentleman of leisure, to read Shakespeare and the Ramayana, to argue the relative merits of each. I was once a fine batsman, the pride of our cricket team. I ate roast beef with horseradish for lunch, and an array of breads and rich curries for dinner. And now—now my wife eats plain rice for her single meal. She has grown so thin, my wife. Yet she always set some of her portion aside for the children.

They are so beautiful, my children. You should see them, Kili.

I would have gone to America, would have tried my luck there. But my wife did not want to leave her home. Her friends are here, her relatives. Having made one mistake, having kept her from comfort and relative safety, kept her here, trapped in this disaster, how could I have forced her again?

I should have. I know. It is a man's responsibility to make such decisions for his family.

I can hear you now, cousin, chiding me for my old-fashioned attitudes. Things are different in America. You yourself married a white boy, without telling your own father—and when he found out, he didn't even beat you for it. If my own daughter, my Kamala, had done such a thing, I would have considered myself within my rights to beat her to within an inch of her life. It would have been for her own good.

I know, I know what you will say. You don't need to say it. I would never have been able to do it, even if I knew it to be the right course of action. I have always been helpless where my daughter was concerned. I have spoiled her terribly; she has grown willful. You warned me.

His wife says nothing from the doorway, only stares, scornful, as Velu slowly stands, pulls on his pants. The pants and shirt have lain in a suitcase for years; he has become accustomed to wearing only a sarong, has grown dark-skinned as a field-worker here. But today he will wear pants, and socks, and shoes, despite the parching heat. He buttons the

pants, then sits down again, pulls on the socks. The shoes are more difficult—they have laces, and he has never needed to tie laces with one
hand. She watches him fumble for endless minutes, then, with quick
impatient steps, comes to kneel in front of him.

Velu leans back while his wife ties the laces on his shoes. He is surprised when, finished, she does not immediately get up. She leans her
forehead against his knee instead, her face hidden in a darkness of
falling hair. Velu tentatively rests one hand on her shoulder and finds it
shaking. His wife, his proud, unloved wife is weeping. In eighteen
years of marriage, Velu has never seen her cry. It is this that comes
closest to breaking him, in the end.

*Kili, may I finally tell you how I have sorrowed for your childless
state? Your words, so terse, when you told me that you had lost
another baby, that you did not think you would be able to bear a
child ... I went to church that very day and prayed for you. I have kept
you in my prayers ever since, though perhaps God does not listen to
those who are angry at Him.*

*I have been angry, I admit it. You have given me so much wise
counsel over the years regarding my own children—you deserved to
have children of your own. I could hear in your words, when you
asked after my son and daughter, the hunger you held. I could hear
the grief mixed in with joy, when you sent letters announcing the
birth of your sisters' children. It is a pleasure, I am certain, to be their
favorite aunty, but it is not the same. To know that a child looks to
you as their parent, that in your hands you hold all their hope and
trust—that knowledge is a terror and a delight beyond anything I
have ever known. I would that you had known it too, cousin.*

*If I had overridden my wife's objections, and sent the children to
you, to study in America, how things would be different now! My wife
was jealous at the thought of you raising our daughter and son; she
selfishly wanted to keep them close to her. I admit—I wanted that too.
I couldn't bear to let them go. And now see what has happened.*

I cannot send this letter with that news. I am thinking it only, imagining that I am writing to my beloved cousin, the friend of my heart. In this way I may tell you all I never dared to write down. I may admit that I have loved you for years, your courage, your strength, though I know you do not love me. I may tell you that I do not blame you for not loving me, considering what a failure of a life I have lived.

I have not provided for my family; I have not managed to love my wife; I have not even protected my children. I am the most futile, ineffectual man I have ever known. Perhaps it is better not to have children than to fail them so. Perhaps you are the lucky one after all—though I am certain that if you had been in my place, you, even as a woman, would have done far better than I have done.

Velu stands, pulls his wife up into his arms, holding her close. She is stiff against him but does not pull away. They stand there for long moments, taking what comfort they can in each other. It is meager sustenance, but they have been starving for months. They have learned to live on crumbs.

His wife is angry with him, he knows. Velu is angry with her too. They both blame each other for what has happened, and he does not know, at this point, who has the truth of it. Perhaps it is both their faults, or neither's. In some ways, it is easier, having someone safe to blame.

Others are not safe to blame. Others can destroy you in a single moment, at night, with loud knocking at your flimsy door.

Kili, my son has been taken. The army came and took him away on suspicion of being a Tiger. Can you imagine it? My gentle boy, always dreamy, always with his nose in a book. Can you imagine Pugal in the jungle, training as a guerrilla fighter? They wear suicide capsules on a cord around their necks, Prabhakaran's fighters, so that if they are taken, they may die before giving any information. They are a most perfect young army—they are not allowed to drink, or smoke, or have sex, or marry. They are united in their cause, to fight for a separate Tamil country, a Tamil Eelam, as they call it, to fight against the injustices.

There have been injustices, many of them. There have been tortures of Tamils, and rapes, and deaths. I could tell you stories—not rumors, but incidents that have happened to people I know—stories that would drive you from your comfortable Chicago home to cry out into the night. Young Tamil men with burning tires around their neck. Young women and old, raped, ruined, killed, and raped again. Aged fathers forced to watch while their children are beaten, shot, thrown from high windows.

It has been months now since they took him to Colombo, to that fourth-floor room we have heard of, from which none return. I have heard him screaming, every night since then, in my dreams.

He was only sixteen years of age, my son. So beautiful, so bright. Pugal wanted to be a doctor, like you, his admired aunty. Kili, I would have sent him to you, oh soon, soon. I would have told my wife to be quiet, would have taken your money and bought him a ticket, smuggled him out to the capital, to the airport, somehow. You must believe—I would have sent my boy to you.

It would soon be dark—Velu needed to go now, before it got too dark, too late. Before he lost his nerve. He released his wife, and she stepped back. She followed him as he walked to the door, handed him a walking stick as he stepped out. Stood in the doorway, watching, as he walked down the path with strong steps, heading toward the road, then to the jungle.

In this, if nothing else, she would support him. Finally, they were united.

My wife has been a fervent supporter of the Tigers, as are many of our neighbors, our friends. If she were younger, I think my wife would have gone and joined the Tigers herself. Would have lived in the jungle, would have done whatever they allowed her to do—bandaged wounds, carried messages, even learned to use a rifle. She would, without compunction, have shot to kill. Perhaps my wife would have been happier with them.

But even she cannot be glad that our little girl, our Kamala, has ignored our every protest, has snuck off in the middle of the night and gone to join the Movement. Kamala is mad with grief for her brother. She is sure we will not see him again.

Now I must do what I can for my daughter. I must go to the fighters, must plead with Prabhakaran himself. She is only fifteen, our Kamala. She is only a girl, and underage, so perhaps he will let her go, will send her back to her grieving parents.

If he does, then I will do one thing right, at least. I will beg and borrow, threaten and cajole—whatever I must to find her a ticket, to put her on a plane and send her to you. If I can only succeed in getting her back, then I will write to you, my dear cousin, will beg you to take her in, as I know you will.

I will send my remaining child away, that I might not fail her too.

I will write you a letter.

The Vallipurams

A Gentle Man

Massachusetts, 1979

"Let no one cherish anything, inasmuch as the loss of what is beloved is hard. There are no fetters for him who knows neither pleasure nor pain. From affection arises sorrow; from affection arises fear. To him who is free from affection there is no sorrow. Whence fear?"

—Gautama Buddha

SUNDAR WAKES UP HOURS BEFORE HIS FAMILY. THIS IS NORMAL, ALTHOUGH TODAY IS NOT NORMAL, TODAY IS A SPECIAL DAY. MOST days he makes tea, reads the paper, eats some toast without butter before going to work at his store. Sushila, his wife, never wakes until after nine. She likes to stay up late, talking on the phone with her friends. When the children were younger, he was the one who woke them, who ironed their Catholic school uniforms and put out milk and cereal. But now the children are able to wake themselves, and only Kuyila, his youngest, still sleeps at home.

It is Kuyila's birthday today. Tonight all of their friends will gather to celebrate his youngest daughter's seventeenth birthday. She has just finished high school and plans to start at the local community college in the fall. Not as smart as her older sister, no. His sweet Kuyila will never join Raji at Harvard. Just as well, considering what Raji is doing there, running around in public with white boys. It turns his stomach.

He drinks his tea, savoring the taste of cinnamon, cardamom, cloves, with shreds of ginger so fierce and strong. He's tasted the tea in American stores—weak, sugary brews. Diluted, adulterated. Pathetic. His wife claims she likes it that way, but she still makes his strong, the way they drink it back home. She knows that his standards haven't changed, that he still believes in doing things right. When she is with him, she drinks tea the way he does. But when she's on her own—who knows?

Sushila is still asleep; she has stayed up late, cooking for the party, making curries that will taste better the second day. She has made beef curries and pork and chicken for their friends, who are all Catholic like her; vegetables for him, the lone Buddhist. He has sometimes been tempted by the smell of her meat curries, but the thought of actually eating meat turns his stomach. He has not had meat since he was twenty, back in 1946. Two years before they married; thirty-three years ago. He has held firm to his convictions. If he ate meat now, it would make him ill.

He can taste already her brinjal curry, savor the spicy coconut sambol and the pungent pickled limes. His mouth is almost burning, though the fire is wholly imagined, and he takes a long drink of tea to soothe it. He chokes on a piece of ginger and coughs for a few moments, his whole body shaking. Then it's gone, swallowed down, and he is at rest again.

His wife is an excellent cook; none can deny that, at least, though he can guess what else they say about her. She won't be awake until eleven at least. But there is a lot to do between now and then. He washes the cup, dries it, puts it away.

HE CALLS THE STORE; NO PROBLEMS. HIS ASSISTANT IS A SOLID MAN, his cousin's friend, and reasonably trustworthy, although he wouldn't give the man access to the store's bank account. He knows that you can't really trust anyone here, in America, not the way you could back home, in Ceylon. It's just not the same; family and friendship don't mean the same things here that they did back there. He has learned that the hard way. Still, the man works hard, and the store takes a lot of hard work.

The store has fed and clothed him and his family; in it he sells saris, lengths of shining fabric in silk and chiffon with bright gold threads. Sundar started the shop with money saved up from work in Colombo, the capital, back when they were newlyweds. He had saved enough to bring his wife and young children to America, enough to buy a partnership in a new sari store, one of the first in the country, and then worked hard enough to buy the store outright a few years later. He's proud of the store, and it's doing well, but who knows for how long? When they first arrived, it seemed that their white neighbors shared their values, knew the worth of hard work, the importance of family, of decency. He'd thought it a good place to raise children, a place of opportunities. But in recent years, America has changed, changed completely. Nothing here is as it was, nothing lasts. In this country, everything looks bright and beautiful and substantial, but it is so often a sham, with nothing real supporting it. Not like back home.

Time to start cleaning. Sushila does the light cleaning—she looks lovely wandering around the house in a simple green sari, feather duster in her hand. But ask her to scrub the bathroom tiles, or even move the furniture to vacuum behind it . . . But he brought her here, after all, against everyone's advice. The first man in his village to go so far from home. It was his vision—America, land of opportunity, a shining bright future for his family. How could he have known that in America, you had to be fabulously rich to afford even a single servant? They are not fabulously rich, and his wife prefers not to think about the dirt that gathers in the corners, under the carpet.

He does not force it on her, though sometimes he is exhausted, coming home from the store only to find the house is so filthy that he cannot stand it. Sometimes he stays up late for nights on end, sweeping and scrubbing and mopping, while she talks on the telephone to her friends. She has so many friends, and they have so much to talk about. Sometimes he wants to take her face and push it down in the bucket of scummy water, just for a moment, just so she knows what she is forcing him to do—but he would never do that. He doesn't even raise his voice when he asks her what she has been doing all day long; he is not that sort of man. The Buddha counsels calm in the face of the vexatious, restraint when in the presence of troublesome souls. He tries to follow the teaching.

AN HOUR LATER, SUNDAR IS STILL CLEANING, BUT KUYILA HAS woken up. She comes down the stairs in her purple pajamas with sleep still crusted in her eyes, hair falling tangled down her back. How many times her mother has told her to brush it with oil and braid it before sleep? She always forgets, like a child. His little one, his delicate angel. She looks just like her mother did when he married her; much the same age as well. So lovely. They sent her to a Catholic girls' high school; both of them had agreed that it was best, after what had happened with Raji. But soon the boys will be swarming around her; even tonight, at the party, the sons of their friends will be drawn to her. His sweet innocent; if he could only keep her a child, safe, forever.

She wraps her arms around his neck as he bends over the bathroom sink, scrubbing at a stubborn stain. "Good morning, Appa." Oh, good morning, my daughter. Happy birthday. I hope you have a very happy birthday today . . .

Then she's off to eat cereal before starting to help with the cleaning. Dutiful child, not like her sister, who had always found some excuse to be out of the house when there was work to be done. Even today—where is she? Has Raji come home to help? No. She'll take the late train from Boston, waltz in the door at four o'clock when the guests have arrived and the work is done. And he'll have to count himself lucky if she comes alone.

So far, Raji has at least kept her shameful behavior with her at college, not brought it home to their house. He's not sure how much it matters, since she isn't discreet enough to keep it a secret. Running around in broad daylight, holding hands and kissing. All of their friends know what she does at night, when her mother calls at eleven o'clock and she isn't in her dorm room. One friend called them from *Australia* to tell them what she had heard—oh, how troubled she was, how concerned about their Raji. Sushila has pleaded with him to do something about it, has raged at him. But what can a father do? Raji has made her own choices. He will educate her, that is his duty; then she will be on her own.

THE HEAVY CLEANING IS DONE. NOW THERE IS JUST A LITTLE straightening left. Though soon Sushila will be up with an endless list of errands for him to run. He turns the sofa cushions in the family room, his fingers digging deep into the fabric, threatening to tear. She always has lists for him, and never mind what else he has planned; she never asks—that's yet another of his jobs, after all. To run around after his wife. He deliberately relaxes his hands, breathes deeply, releases the cushions.

He pulls open the curtains to let sunlight into the fading room. Sundar straightens the photos on top of the TV; so many of them. His beautiful wife, laughing at party after party. She likes parties, where she is always surrounded by her female friends. He can imagine the others not in the picture, the ghosts surrounding her. He is standing behind her, there to hold her up, catch her if she falls—the good husband.

There is Raji, so tall and straight and serious. His studious one, always busy alone in her room with her books and paper and paint. He had such hopes for her . . . all gone, now. And Kuyila, his angel girl, like a flower. Kuyila dancing, like her mother, a twirling burst of colored flame. After her Arangetrum, her graduation dance performance, she stood up on the stage so seriously, and thanked her teachers, her sister, her amma and appa most of all. You could see in her face her sweetness, her love for her family; it was clear from the light shining out of it. You can see it still.

There is a face missing from the photos as well, his son's, Raksha's—but the boy abandoned his family, and all the photos that contained him were thrown out long ago.

IT'S ALMOST TEN—TIME TO WRAP KUYILA'S PRESENTS. SUSHILA HAS chosen most of them. Pretty dresses, and one of them not to be wrapped, since Kuyila will wear it today. A white handbag. A dark green sari.

Sushila wore green the day after they were married. Sitting at the table with him, his mother, his sisters—he remembers how beautiful she looked in that green, how she smiled and blushed when one of his sisters teased her about the night before. His young bride.

He had been so nervous the night before. His friends had been full of coarse advice; he was the first of them to marry; they knew nothing. One of his aunties had pulled him aside—he can't remember now which one it was. She whispered to him: "The girl's more scared than you are." Then she stuck a chicken roll in his hand and went away. The older relatives never remembered that he had given up eating the flesh of animals two years before, when he became a Buddhist. But it was good advice. It had calmed him down and let him be very patient and gentle with Sushila that night. She had been so vulnerable, so sweet and still as he unwrapped her crimson sari. Afterward, he had fallen asleep with her small hand held tightly in his own. When he woke, it was still there. Sundar aches even now, at the memory of it.

His fingers continue wrapping, creasing the delicate paper, tearing it, folding it over each gift. Lipstick. Blush. Eyeliner. Small gold earrings. He does not approve of the makeup. His daughter does not need to paint her face to be beautiful. But it's not worth arguing with his wife. He learned that long ago.

The earrings are good; a girl should have some nice jewelry, for beauty and security. He has been saving money; a little here and there put into a special bank account. He started when Raji was born—money for his daughters' dowry, for their jewelry. Now who knows whom Raji will marry, if she ever does. Running around with American boys. Taking them back to her dorm room for anyone to see—and they run and tell her shamed parents, of course, and all their friends. Sushila screams at the girl, hits her, but it does no good. Violence never does. Raji will find her own path, away from her family, and the jewelry will go to Kuyila instead. It is just as well. A girl cannot have too much security.

One present left, but he will wrap it later.

AT ELEVEN, SUSHILA WAKES. HE BRINGS HER TEA AND SITS BY THE side of the bed while she drinks it. She has a list of instructions for him: buy chicken for the rolls, wine and beer, some large prawns; she's decided to make another curry. It will be expensive, more than they'd planned to spend, but he can work late tomorrow and make up the difference. She does not ask what he thinks.

She finishes her list and gets out of bed. Sushila wears a thin white cotton nightgown. Her heavy breasts show through the sheer fabric, her waist and swell of hips, the darkness at the juncture of her thighs. Her long hair falls thickly down her back. He stirs at the sight of her; he often does.

Kuyila is working in the front yard, trimming the roses, mowing the lawn. He can hear the roar of the mower through the open window, and knows that if he were to close the bedroom door and pull his wife back to the bed, Kuyila would not hear them. He considers it—if he did draw her to the bed, Sushila would not protest. She never protests; she is always willing, always available, the accommodating wife. But she will lie still beneath him, with her head turned away and her eyes closed. She will be still like a statue. It is the only time she is awake and not in motion—when he is moving in her, above her.

On that first night, their wedding night, Sundar had been so gentle with her but had not managed to coax a response from her. He had told himself that it would get better with time, that she hardly knew him, that he was a stranger to her. But it had not gotten better, and so only rarely had he let himself sink inside her. Once was a night when Sushila had gone shopping with her friends and had come back late—so late! Nine-thirty at night, and while it was true that the mall was open until nine, he had not been able to believe that she had only been shopping.

His anger had risen up in him then, and he had almost dragged her to their bed. He had wanted to hit her, wanted to hurt her, and he had come so close . . . Yet he had remembered the words of the Buddha and had restrained himself. He had taken her fiercely, but without causing her pain. He had stayed true to himself, to his beliefs, and she had never known how angry he had been. Sometimes he wondered if that anger had infected Raji, conceived on that night.

Sushila raises her arms, stretches, displaying the dark thatch of hair under her arms, and he bites his lip, drawing blood. He wants her. She is his wife, and he has every right to take her. But he knows that if he takes her back to bed now, she will not want him. She will not want him. He lets her go to her shower, undisturbed.

HE DRIVES TOO FAST ON THE HIGHWAY. HIS FAMILY DEPENDS ON HIM, he has a duty to them, and so he wears his seat belt—but he still drives too fast. A car speeds up, cuts in front of him, and he resists the urge to shove his foot down on the gas, rush forward and crash . . . that would be an extremely violent act.

Sundar forswore violence thirty-three years ago, and since that day he has not eaten fish or meat, not killed a spider or crushed an ant. He has never raised his hand to his wife or children, even though there was a time when Sushila begged him to discipline their son.

At sixteen, Raksha had taken to disappearing at night, climbing out windows and down trees, meeting with his friends. Eventually they'd heard about it, learned that the boy was spending his time smoking marijuana in a dark room with other teens, having sex with one girl or another, listening to music that preached revolution, revolution and sex, sex that they called love. Those children had no idea what love was, but they were everywhere that summer, smoking and drinking and running around late at night, singing. America had never seemed as alien as it did that year. Then came the rumors that Raksha had gotten a white girl pregnant, that she'd had an abortion or a baby, that she had disappeared or died—but maybe they were just rumors. No one seemed sure.

They had confined Raksha to his room, they had argued with him, his mother had screamed and wept—but for nothing. Raksha had grown sullen and silent. Finally he'd left, just disappeared into the night like a thief, without even a note. Sushila has never forgiven her husband for not being harsher with their son. She hasn't hesitated to discipline Raji, bringing the slim bamboo cane down on the girl's back, but it has done little good.

He has never hit anyone. He avoids harsh speech, and animosity of thought. All the Buddhism he knows he learned from a friend in school so long ago, and from what he can teach himself by studying books. He has learned at least a little after years of study, and knows that refraining from violent thought or action is essential if one wishes to reach the calm of enlightenment.

He removes his foot from the gas pedal. He strives for a peaceful state of mind, though he knows it will not come.

WHEN HE COMES HOME, SHE SCREAMS AT HIM. SUSHILA IS A WOMAN given to screeching, though he could never have guessed that when they married. He knew she had life and passion in her, but it seemed so joyous. She was sparkling then, like sunlight on water. Laughter bubbled out of her. She even got his littlest sister to laugh once or twice, ugly Mangai, who had never managed to find a husband. Mangai, who has ended up alone, living in a sad little house on the beach, battered by salty ocean winds, with only a maid for company. Without children.

Perhaps Raji will suffer the same fate, since she has apparently turned away from their society. Perhaps she too will end up ugly and alone. Once, the thought of his daughter in such straits might have tormented him, but he has been hurt too many times, betrayed over and over. His heart is closed to her; he cannot bring himself to care.

The first step to enlightenment, perhaps, to serenity. *When touched by happiness or sorrow, the wise show no elation or dejection; the wise become serene like unto a deep, calm, and crystal-clear lake.* He suspects that he will never find it, but he longs for that serenity.

Serenity is difficult to find when Sushila is shouting that he has bought the wrong kind of chicken. Does he do this to her deliberately? Is he trying to torment her? His neck is taut with tension, his shoulders tight, but she cannot see that—he is much taller than she is. He bows his head until she is finished. Then he goes out again, to get the right kind of chicken.

WHEN HE COMES BACK A HALF HOUR LATER, WITH THE CHICKEN, she does not thank him. She is busy cooking again, and two of his sisters have arrived as well to help. Their husbands are working and will arrive later. The women are laughing in the kitchen, gossiping and trading bits of cooking wisdom. They ignore him, but he is used to that. The house is clean; the food will be ready on time; she needs nothing more of him. He goes to wrap his daughter's final present.

He takes the photo from a manila envelope he's kept hidden in a drawer. He arranged for it months ago; his wife has no idea. It's a good photo. There is a frame for it as well, heavy silver. He slips the photo into the frame, attaches the back, tightens the screws. It will not slip away. For a moment, he hesitates. This is home that he is holding in his hands—but he has not been back in so long, and sometimes he hears disturbing news of strange events. There had been the riots, in '58. And since then, scattered violence, here and there. Even some deaths. His gut twists for a moment, but then eases again. The violence is transient; it must be. It will pass. He knows what home really is, and what it isn't. Sundar wraps the photo with steady hands in white tissue paper and places it in a box, wraps the box in shining red foil paper. It will glow from among the other presents in their decorous wrappings. Perhaps Kuyila will open it first—that would be a nice surprise.

Kuyila knocks on the bedroom door, calling to him—"Appa!" He is startled and calls to her to wait. Just another minute securing it with Scotch tape—there. It's done. He puts it with the other presents and goes to open the door. His daughter grabs his hand, drags him to the dining room window. "Look, Appa—it's raining!"

It's true. The rain is slanting down over the lawn, spattering against the circles of metal folding chairs; it will be a large party, perhaps a hundred people. Too many to seat comfortably all in the house. He had spent at least an hour mowing the back lawn and setting up the chairs yesterday, and now his daughter is panicking because they are getting wet.

"It's just a summer shower; it'll pass. Don't worry. Go get dressed; people will be here soon."

Raji would have argued, would have wondered if they should make plans to bring the chairs inside somehow, would have at least pointed out that it was still two hours until anyone was due to arrive and that their friends were always an hour late in any case. Raji had never agreed with him; she had always argued. Once, he had thought that was good, a sign of a strong spirit. Now he knows better.

Kuyila smiles in response to his words and says, "Okay." She goes upstairs to get ready; she trusts and obeys him. He would do almost anything to preserve that trust.

SUNDAR SHOWERS AND GETS DRESSED. HE HAS TROUBLE FINDING the tie he wants; Sushila has rearranged the closet again. He is looking for his favorite tie, the dark blue one with the thin white diagonal lines. It reminds him of river water, white foam on the darkness. He reaches back into the closet and pulls out a handful of old ties, ties that he hasn't seen in years. One of them is bright red, shockingly bright, even after all this time.

His son was fourteen that day, almost fifteen. Raji was only four then, and Kuyila was just two. Raksha had been born less than a year after their wedding; they had waited a long time for more children. Sometimes he wondered whether Sushila had actually wanted children, if she had been taking something to prevent them; motherhood had never really suited her. Maybe she had, and then had become careless as the long years stretched past, stopped worrying about it, and so he'd gotten his girls at last. She had her secrets, his wife. He'd never know the truth of it. Let it go.

Raksha had given him the tie on Father's Day. Such a bright boy he was, and yet already in trouble. Already running around with the wrong crowd, but they didn't know. His parents didn't know—how could they? Sundar was working seventy, eighty hours a week at the store in those days, and he was so tired at night. Sushila kept the family fed, and cleaned up a little, but she was busy herself with two young ones after so long without. She didn't spend much time on her son, who had already grown so tall. When Raksha had given him that tie, reached to hug him, had there been alcohol on his breath? Had there been marijuana smoke thick in his clothes? If so, neither of his parents had noticed.

When his grades started slipping, they had scolded Raksha, told him to try harder. Never doubted the boy when he said he was studying at the library late at night, trying to improve the grades. It had never occurred to the father to distrust his son. Adults could betray you, as he well knew, but children? Children were the light of life.

He should have paid more attention to the Buddha's example—the prince who walked away from his young wife and infant son to seek truth and an ending to false desire.

When Raksha ran off, they'd been frantic with worry, called the police, their friends across the country. The boy was found in Chicago, months later; he'd hitched his way across country. Raksha lived with white friends for a while, then eventually found a job, but refused to come home or answer their letters. He never told them why he had run away. They had given him everything, and he had thrown it all back in their faces. Finally Sushila, enraged, had demanded that they cut him off entirely, weeping with her frustration. He had quietly agreed. They were only acknowledging a separation that was already final.

They still received reports from friends in Chicago. Raksha had settled down eventually, had even married a Tamil girl from a good family, a professional family. Married above him, actually; he had always been a handsome boy. There had been some trouble, but it was eventually sorted out. Sundar has picked up the phone to call him, a hundred times, but every time he puts it down again.

Raksha has a daughter now, Chaya, a girl who will never know her father's parents. His son is lost to him. *For the sake of oneself, one should not long for a son, wealth, or a kingdom.* Sundar had never wanted wealth or a kingdom. He places the red tie back on the rack, finally finds the dark blue tie, soberly knots it around his neck.

SUSHILA HAS SHOWERED, IS DRESSING NOW. HE STRAIGHTENS THE bedroom, pretending not to watch her, listening to her talking nonsense. She slips her arms into a dark purple blouse and calls him to hook up the back. His fingers do not linger on the soft flesh exposed there; he is deft and quick after so many years of practice. Thirty years of marriage. He married her when he was twenty-two and she was seventeen; he is fifty-three now, a good age for a man to ease back, to rest in the comfort of his family's love and affection.

She tucks one end of her dark green sari into her half-slip, and he takes the other end in his hands, holding it taut as she folds the fabric in front of her, making the pleats that will allow her to walk freely, to dance later. She will call him to dance, and he will gently refuse, as always. He does not dance. She will dance with her friends, his sisters—not immodestly, of course. Only with women; never with men. But she will laugh freely, will be flushed with pleasure, will lean toward the women and whisper silly secrets in their ears, making them blush and giggle. Exuberant, yet unobjectionable, as always. But the public does not always reflect the private, and he has always known what really goes on.

Sundar is not sure when he first realized that his wife, his beautiful, innocent-seeming Sushila, was betraying him. The first clue was undoubtedly in bed, but he was so ignorant then; how long was it going on before he noticed? Before he realized that while she was willing, she was never eager for him? Before he realized that there was more than maidenly shyness in her lack of response to him?

In another kind of woman, perhaps that would have been normal, but not his Sushila, who laughed with her whole heart, who sometimes had taken the children out to dance in the rain, and who bit her lip and crossed her thighs as they watched the romantic scenes in American movies, the woman in soft focus, lips parted, clasped tight in strong arms. Somewhere in Sushila was a response, but not to him. Never to him.

He had never caught her at it. Never caught her sneaking out, or inviting someone in. He hadn't tried, hadn't wanted to. If he had caught her, he would have been tempted from the path. If he had caught her, he might have swung a heavy fist at her lying face, might have beaten her lover into a bloody pulp. And so he always called first if he was coming home unexpectedly early, or in the middle of the day. He had trouble sleeping at night, and took pills so that he would not know if she ever slipped out of their bed. Sundar had done his best to never know the truth. He had no real evidence; he had tried not to know—yet he was sure. He knew.

He would have done better not to love her at all, not to desire her. *Let no one cherish anything, inasmuch as the loss of what is beloved is hard.* But after thirty years, he has not managed it. Sushila is still his wife, and beautiful to him, and every night he fights his desire to reach for the woman who was the first to betray him.

She pulls the fabric from his hands; she is done pleating it. Sushila wraps it once around her body, and then crosses it up over her full breasts, over a shoulder to drape across her back and bare waist. He pins the heavy fabric in place at her shoulder, and she walks out of the room, still chattering about something, words he can make no sense of.

The rain stops, and he goes out with a dishcloth to wipe the chairs dry. No one has arrived yet—they will start arriving at four-thirty, four forty-five. They will eat the appetizers, they will drink the wine, they will have a roaring good time. Eventually, they will go away, leaving a scattering of presents behind, and then the family will sit down with Kuyila to open them. It will be late—maybe eleven, or twelve, or even later. Kuyila will be tired; they will all be. Their reactions will be muted, which is really a shame. He wants to see the looks on their faces as she opens his present. He wants it badly. He does not want to wait.

Maybe he won't.

BY FIVE, THE PARTY IS GOING STRONG—ALL OF THEIR CLOSE friends have arrived, and only a few more people are straggling in. Kuyila is lovely in a pale cream summer dress, with slim straps baring too much of her skin. The boys cluster around her, and she tilts back her head and laughs, delightedly, at what they say to her. What are they saying to her?

Sundar cannot wait any longer.

"Everyone—everyone, can I have your attention, please?"

His voice is not loud—it never is. But the word is passed along, and slowly the crowd turns to face him, gathering across the lawn, brown faces cheerful in the sunlight.

"I have an announcement—but first, I have a special present for my daughter." They gather closer, drawn by the word *present*, wondering what it could be. Everyone loves getting presents. Kuyila comes to stand next to him, and Raji and Sushila are near as well. Sushila looks puzzled, but not worried. Why should she be? He has never given her reason to worry.

He pulls the red foil–wrapped present out from behind his back, hands it to his daughter. The crowd murmurs. Kuyila smiles and takes it. She starts peeling off the tape carefully, slowly, and Raji shouts, "Just tear it!" Kuyila continues slowly, though, slipping the foil off and then letting it fall to the fresh-mown grass. She opens the box, slides the frame out of it, unwraps the tissue paper. Kuyila looks at the picture of the handsome young man, bewildered.

Her father raises his voice now, louder than any there have ever heard it before. He wants to be sure everyone hears this.

"You've come to celebrate my daughter's birthday, and I thank you! Now, please, join me in celebrating her engagement as well!"

The murmurs have grown louder, and Raji is looking furious. She knows that Kuyila has known nothing of this, but the crowd is not so certain. Surely they would have heard something of this before? Some rumor? But he is a very private man, after all, and the family has had such trouble in the past . . . maybe he wanted to keep it secret until it was all settled. But how nice to have the girl settled so young; how lovely! The whispers fly through the crowd; he keeps talking.

"She will not be going to school in the fall; instead, Kuyila will be traveling this summer to Ceylon, where she will marry Ashok, the son of one of my good friends, a cloth merchant in Colombo. Ashok is twenty-two, just the age I was when I married my own wife. I know he and Kuyila will be very happy—so please, join me in wishing them every joy and happiness!"

The crowd is caught up in his fervor, his excitement, and they begin to cheer, to press forward and congratulate Kuyila, shaking her hand, exclaiming over the handsomeness of the photo. The noise grows louder and louder, and he slips away in the confusion.

HE SITS ALONE ON HIS MARRIAGE BED, DRINKING A GLASS OF whiskey. It is the first taste of alcohol he has had in thirty-three years. He doesn't like it, but he drinks it down. His hands are shaking.

Later he will have to face Sushila, but he will convince her easily. Ashok's family is quite wealthy, and the boy is a very good catch. Kuyila would never have made a good student, and Sushila will be happy enough to be finally done with raising children, once she gets past the shock. Besides, all the agreements are made; the family is preparing in Colombo for the wedding. All that remains is to ready the bride and buy their plane tickets for the wedding. Sushila won't back out now.

Raji will rage, but she no longer has any power in this family. She gave that up herself. If Kuyila supported her, then perhaps, but otherwise...

The door slams open. Raji storms in, as expected.

"What do you think you're doing?" She is almost screaming, almost wailing. It is strangely satisfying to see so much emotion in her, to know that he has caused it. When Raji was younger, she was always bursting into the store, full of some scheme or another, but she has been distant for so long now, wrapped up in her life away from them. This is the passionate daughter he remembers.

"I'm doing what's best for Kuyila." He could chide her for her tone of voice but chooses not to. Why bother? It has been a long time since she has shown any respect for her father.

"What's best for Kuyila?! What's best for her is to go to school, to learn to support herself, to stop being dependent on you! Not to be packed off to Ceylon and married to a total stranger—she doesn't even speak Tamil!" Raji's hands are balled fists on her hips, and she leans forward, as if she longs to hit him.

He weighs twice what she does; he could flatten her with one slap across her insolent face. He sits still on the bed and keeps his voice calm. "She'll learn, and they speak English. She'll be well taken care of there." It's a good family; of course they'll take care of Kuyila.

Raji looks furious, as if she is about to explode. "She doesn't need to be taken care of, Appa—she needs to learn to take care of herself!"

For a moment he wonders if this is true, if he is making a mistake. Could Kuyila be happier with an education, with the ability to take care of herself? A few more years as a child . . . And yet, hasn't he seen what that leads to? If he doesn't take care of her now, won't she simply ruin herself and break his heart in the process? For a moment, he isn't sure—and now Kuyila is quietly entering the room. She stops by the door, looking so pale, almost white. He could have been wrong.

But Raji keeps shouting, "You're just tired of taking care of her— you just want to get rid of her. You got rid of Raksha, and you're happy to be rid of me. All you want is your precious serenity—all you want is to be left alone!"

What nonsense. Doesn't she know that he has always loved them more than he has loved serenity and wisdom? Wasn't that his first mistake, and his last? "Be quiet, Raji. You don't know what you're talking about." Suddenly Sundar is weary; tired of dealing with this child, this stranger. What has happened to his fiery daughter, the girl who used to stretch her arms wide and say that she loved him *this* much? This girl in front of him—she understands nothing. "If Kuyila tells me she doesn't want to go, of course she doesn't have to." He gestures, and Raji turns to see her sister in the doorway.

"Kuyila, you can't let him do this to you!" She is shouting at her sister now.

Kuyila sighs. "Raji, go talk to Amma, okay?"

"But—"

"Please?"

Raji looks like she wants to stay, but what can she do? She casts one more angry glance at him, and then storms out of the room. Kuyila stands still, framed in the doorway.

"Appa?" There is a question in her voice, but he doesn't know what she wants to say.

"Yes, Kuyila?"

She doesn't say anything. After a short silence, he beckons her to him. She comes to sit at his feet, leaning her head against his knee. He strokes her hair, brushed smooth and oiled so that it flows like dark water down her back.

"Do you trust me, Kuyila?"

She does not pause. "Yes, Appa." The others would have paused, at least.

"Will you trust me when I tell you this is for your own good, that I would never do anything to hurt you?"

"Of course, Appa. But . . ." She trails off.

"But what?"

"It's so far away . . ."

"Well. That's true. But we'll visit, and once Ashok gets established, you'll be able to visit us here. You've always enjoyed our summer trips to Ceylon. Do you remember—that summer when you were twelve, you said that you never wanted to leave. You'll see—you'll be happy there."

"Yes, Appa." She is a good girl. He had known that she would not fight him on this. They sit together, and he continues stroking her hair; after a little while, she presses his hand, gets up, and goes back out to the party.

She really will be happy there; he knows it. He would never hurt her, his sweet one, his darling daughter. He loves her more than is wise; he has never mastered the release of affection, of caring, that leads to true peace. He has to send her away, as far away as possible, perhaps to a place where she will not learn betrayal, if there is such a place left in this world.

The Emigrant

Colombo, 1979

THE HOTEL BATHROOM ONLY HAD TWO TOWELS. IT WAS SUPPOSED TO BE A FIVE-STAR HOTEL. KUYILA HAD NEVER ACTUALLY BEEN IN A hotel before, much less a five-star one, but she was pretty sure they normally had more than two towels in the bathroom. Maybe the standards for a five-star hotel were lower in Sri Lanka than in America. It was possible.

Her sister Raji had not only used one of the towels, but had also splashed water all over and then dropped her towel on the floor; it was soggy now, disgusting. Kuyila dried off quickly with the remaining towel and wrapped it around her, cold hair dripping water onto her neck, down her spine. She went out into the room and grabbed her underwear, avoiding her big sister's eyes. Raji sat on the edge of the bed, waiting for her to finish getting ready. Kuyila ducked back into the bathroom, removed the towel, and wrapped it around her head, tucking it up and back as she straightened, getting the mass of long hair tightly inside in a single swift motion.

She paused for a moment, contemplating her nude figure in the wide mirrors above the sink. Her body was slender, small-breasted.

Kuyila's skin was a light brown; she had always listened to her mother and worn sunscreen when going to the beach, or even just outdoors on a sunny day. Raji's skin was much darker—in the summer, she got dark enough that guys catcalling on the street thought she was black. Kuyila sometimes wished she had larger breasts, like Raji's, rounder hips and ass. Her body was more boyish than she'd like—it mostly looked fresh and healthy, in a seventeen-year-old sort of way, instead of sexy. Kuyila felt a brief shiver climb up her spine, wondering what her new husband would think of her body when he removed her clothes, her underwear. That thought was enough to make her pull her bra and panties on—white cotton, the only kind she'd brought with her, the only kind she owned. No one but her sister would see her underwear today, but she was still grateful for its pristine sensibleness. It reminded her of who she was today—a modest young bride-to-be, about to meet her fiancé and his parents for the first time. She couldn't have faced them if she were wearing black lace. That was more Raji's style.

The first time their mother had found a pair of lace panties in Raji's duffel bag, when Raji had come home from her freshman year at college, there had been a screaming fight. It had made Kuyila's head hurt, and she could only imagine how the noise level would have climbed if Amma had found the birth control pills that Raji kept in the side pocket. The fight had gone on for over two hours, and downstairs in the living room, Kuyila and her father had silently watched a soccer game on TV. Appa's forehead had scrunched up tightly, and Kuyila could almost see the new lines forming, the grey hairs sprouting from his head. There was nothing she could do for him then.

Kuyila loosened her hair from the towel and quickly blow-dried it—she wondered whether it was worth keeping the blow-dryer with her. Would there be outlets for it in the bathroom at her new husband's house? She braided it, a long braid reaching down the length of her back, past her waist; most of the girls she'd seen on the way to the hotel from the Colombo airport had had their hair braided. What about makeup—did she need it? Kuyila considered her face. Eyes, a little small. Nose, too wide, and lips, too thin. The cheekbones were all right—at least she'd gotten Amma's cheekbones, and she was careful about her weight, which helped her face. Kuyila had hardly eaten in the last week anyway, not wanting to put food into the churning pit that was her stomach. Overall, it was a pretty face. Only pretty, though; no one but her father would ever call her beautiful. Raji had inherited all of their mother's fine features, her lush frame, and even a few extra inches of their father's height—without trying, she turned heads in the streets, at parties. Kuyila had to work twice as hard and never looked quite as good. But soon someone would be looking entirely, only at her. She needed to look her best for him.

Her face looked a little pale. Pale was good—here, fair was beautiful. But too pale might be a problem. Amma had told her not to wear any makeup tonight, but perhaps a little powder . . . Kuyila was just reaching into her bag, pulling out some face powder, when Raji opened the door.

"You don't have to do this." Raji's voice was soft, but the intensity hit Kuyila like a slap.

"Raji, I'm busy." Kuyila kept her eyes fixed on the mirror as she brushed powder gently across her cheeks, her nose, her forehead.

Raji reached out and took her wrist, too tightly. "Kuyila—please."

Kuyila stood still for a moment and felt her sister's hand around her wrist; Raji wouldn't go away until she'd had her say. She turned toward her sister, tugging her wrist free as she turned. She saw them then, the pieces of paper in Raji's other hand. Plane tickets.

Raji spoke quickly, the words tripping against each other in their rush: "I got them before we left—there wasn't time to talk to you . . ." Kuyila was already tuning her out, knowing too well what her sister would say, eyes fixed on the tickets. It was so like Raji to do this, to make the grand gesture now, after all the transatlantic phone calls, the sari shopping, the commissioning of the thali necklace. After Kuyila and Ashok had exchanged cautious letters, after her family had flown halfway across the world. And now Raji offered this escape—to what?

Kuyila hadn't even gotten into a real college; no matter how hard she'd worked, Kuyila hadn't gotten more than a handful of As all through high school, not like Raji, who snuck out of the house, screwed around every night with boys, and still managed to win scholarships. Kuyila would never be a lawyer, an engineer, a doctor. Ashok, her soon-to-be husband, was a doctor. Kuyila would be a doctor's wife—a slender, pretty, perfect doctor's wife. That she could do, at least.

When she was just a little girl, she'd sneak out of bed and watch as her parents threw parties for her father's business associates; lying low behind the railing, she'd see Amma smiling, laughing, dazzling their guests. She'd be in one of her good moods, and when Amma was in a good mood, she was magic, like the princess Sita from her father's *Ramayana* stories. She could laugh and tell jokes and tease until you forgot there were worries in the world. Those good moods were painfully rare; Amma got tired, with the cooking and cleaning and taking care of Raji and Kuyila—and Raksha—until he went away. If they'd just stayed in Sri Lanka, Amma could have rested more. She would have had servants, and she could have simply stayed beautiful, laughing, perfect all the time.

Her sister had stopped talking, fallen silent. Kuyila turned back to the mirror, brushed powder across her face. "I want to do this, Raji."

Raji put an urgent hand on Kuyila's bare shoulder, startling her so she spilled powder across the counter. "You don't love him—you don't even know him!"

"I know enough. He's a good man, from a good family—Amma and Appa approve of him." Kuyila shook Raji's hand off her shoulder, then carefully brushed the powder into the sink, washed it away. She doesn't know how Raji can stand it, knowing their parents will never approve of the white boys she dates. "And you know what the aunties always say—'Love will come.' We'll grow to love each other, over time."

"Kuyila, you can't be sure." Raji sounded plaintive, lost, the plane tickets now forgotten in her limp left hand.

"Raji—enough. Okay? Just ... enough. Let it go." Kuyila considered her face one more time in the mirror, then put the powder down. She was wearing enough; any more would just look like she was trying to hide behind a mask. Kuyila stepped past Raji, out into the hallway, leaving her sister standing there still in the bathroom. Kuyila felt a pang of pity, or perhaps love. "Come on, sis—it'll all be okay. I promise. I'm going to live happily ever after." Kuyila wondered when she'd turned into the big sister.

Raji put down the tickets on the counter, but then just stood there, waiting, until Kuyila was finished dressing. Then she followed her sister out the door.

THE CEREMONY WENT BY SO QUICKLY. ONE OF KUYILA'S GIRLFRIENDS had told her that the wedding ceremonies were very long here. But maybe that was the Hindus or the Buddhists. It was a good thing that his family was Catholic, like hers—but maybe a slightly longer ceremony would have been better.

The dinner went quickly too, and the reception. Then Amma and Appa were saying good night, Raji was off getting secretly drunk in a corner somewhere, and Kuyila was smiling, hugging her parents goodbye. Her mother was crying. Ashok's mother came to lead her off, taking her to the bedroom. Other women, Ashok's aunts and sister, gave her advice she didn't hear, while fussing with her hair, her face. Kuyila kept smiling through it all, and Ashok's mother told her what a good girl she was. Kuyila hoped the smile was right—she wasn't sure if she was supposed to get upset, to cry. She could do that; it wouldn't be hard. But since she wasn't sure, she thought it might be better to smile. Kuyila bit the inside of her cheek, since she couldn't bite her lip, and smiled.

Then they were gone.

He came in, looking shy and scared, not quite looking at her. That helped.

"We don't have to do anything tonight." He said it so fast, she almost didn't understand him.

It was a gift, and one that made her like him more. Kuyila was tempted. She could put this off for the night, the night after, for weeks and weeks. But in the morning, someone would ask. Not directly, but with a hint, a look, a joke. She had heard stories of brides who refused their husbands—one aunt had confessed that she had hid under the bed for three nights running, and screamed when he came too close. Kuyila didn't want to be that kind of bride. So she smiled again and stepped forward. She tilted her head up, and when he still didn't kiss her, she raised up onto her toes and kissed him.

Ashok didn't taste like American boys, or at least not like Stephen, the only boy she'd ever kissed. Stephen tasted like mint and bubble gum. Ashok tasted like cardamom, like cloves. Strange, but not bad. They kissed for a while; then her legs started to hurt, and she came down from her toes. "Sorry—"

"No, no, I'm sorry . . ." he interrupted, still speaking too fast. "Please come, sit down." He led her to the bed, parting the white mosquito netting so that she could sit down. He sat down beside her, the netting falling closed, wrapping them in their own private world. Kuyila wasn't sure if she should kiss him again, wasn't sure what she should do after that, either. She'd seen the movies, but the furthest she'd gone herself was with Stephen in the shed last spring. It had been cold and cobwebby and pitch black except for a thin edge of sunlight around the door; Kuyila hadn't let him turn on the light. In the dark they'd kissed and kissed—then he'd unbuttoned her blouse and touched her breasts, but she had felt nothing. If Ashok was relying on her, then she was afraid they were in trouble. But then he leaned toward her, kissed her again, pulled down the sari fabric, and unhooked her blouse, his hands moving quickly now, just a little too rough.

It wasn't exactly like the movies.

KUYILA STOOD NEXT TO ASHOK AT THE COLOMBO AIRPORT, WAVING good-bye to her family as they walked through the door, down the stairs, across to their plane. They would be back in a year. Back home, lots of kids would be going away to college now, in September, and wouldn't come home again until June—that was almost a year. They would be homesick too, but they somehow coped.

The bathrooms were the worst. They had to live with his parents, though at least his dad was a doctor too and owned a large house with many rooms. It could have been a lot worse—in so many homes they'd visited, nice homes, the only way to go to the bathroom was to squat on the floor, your feet in their slippers placed in marked indentations. Ashok's family actually had toilets. But the bathroom vents, high on the walls, let in all the damp heat; the toilet seat was always wet, the walls were wet, and there were bugs everywhere. Spiders and chameleons and flying beetles and red ants and others that she couldn't even name. Kuyila hated bugs. She hadn't been able to stand them since the day with the ants. She had been seven or eight, sitting on the porch steps, waiting for the bus; she had put her bag down on the ground. Inside the bag, her juice had spilled. When Kuyila got on the bus, she put the bag in her lap. After a little while, her legs had started itching, and she looked down and there were ants all over her blue plaid skirt, her bare knees, her thick socks; ants had even crawled up under her skirt. She jumped up and started screaming, and couldn't stop until another little girl had managed to knock most of them off her.

In Sri Lanka, the red ants bit you, and the mosquitoes did too. Kuyila was allergic to mosquitoes—too many bites and her throat got tight, her chest started to feel squeezed, squished, as if a giant were sitting on top of it. At night, she lay awake under their netting, just looking up at the mosquitoes buzzing around, counting the chameleons that skittered along the ceilings. One, two, three, four, until the netting tore from the weight, came crashing down to smother them in crawling lizards, in stinging mosquitoes. That last part was only in her dreams, but even with the netting, Kuyila woke up most mornings covered in small red bites, which she desperately rubbed with the back of her hands, trying not to scratch them, trying to breathe.

THE HEAT WAS UNBEARABLE. KUYILA DREAMED OF AIR-CONDITIONED movie theaters, of wearing a tank top and shorts, watching an R-rated movie she'd snuck into with Jenny and Maria, complaining about how cold it was and about how they always over-air-conditioned the theaters. When they finally left the theater and went out into the summer heat, they'd get cherry ice cream and walk a few blocks over to the mall, and more air-conditioning.

Ashok said it would get cooler soon. They did what they could to stay cool, lying under the old, slow fan, staying very still, sending the servants for cold drinks. Kuyila was grateful that they had a refrigerator—so many didn't. She still couldn't just let water run in the tap until it got cold; she had to boil it every single time and drink it lukewarm. If she didn't, she came down with runs so bad that they were just disgusting, and then she had to spend more time in the damp, sticky bathroom.

Ashok's mother, Prema, kept trying to talk her into having hot tea instead, with milk and sugar, cooked on the stove. She said it made you sweat and that that made you cooler as the sweat dried on your body. Kuyila couldn't bring herself to do it; the thought of the drying sweat made her stomach churn. Instead she drank expensive cold sodas—Portello, black currant, or Necto, nectarine. They were tasty; she actually liked them better than Coke.

She loved the food too. Ashok's mother was a much better cook than Amma, and so happy to teach Kuyila. Her own daughter had no interest in cooking—she was a bookworm, like her brother, and always busy with her schoolwork. So Prema spent hours teaching Kuyila—she told Kuyila what she was doing while she cooked, and then had Kuyila try it, watching and offering advice. For every meal,

Ashok's mother always made at least one dish, and it was always the tastiest thing on the table. After only a few weeks of her teaching, Ashok looked up from dinner one day to casually compliment his mother—"Amma, this brinjal is very good." He was like that, thoughtful. Prema said, smiling broadly, "I'm glad you liked it, rasa, your wife cooked it." Ashok had looked so surprised—but then he smiled, and the smile spread across his face like sunshine. Kuyila flushed and felt warm all over, and even though cooking in the midday heat had made the sweat run down her back, pooling at the base of her spine, she found herself happy.

That night he held her close and ran his hand through her hair, over and over. Kuyila closed her eyes and pretended they were in Massachusetts, that the air conditioner had just broken down, and that soon they'd get up and take a nice cool shower together, then plop down on the couch in front of the TV. They'd pop a movie in the VCR, and then he would fall asleep with his head resting in her lap. She wasn't sure if she loved her husband, not yet. He was so often at the clinic, or at his export business, checking on the staff. But when he came home he brought fresh mangoes from the market just for her, and spoke to her gently, in his perfect (if accented) English, to which she responded in her still quite broken Tamil. Kuyila was growing fond of him.

That night, Ashok revealed his long-term plans.

"We won't stay here forever—there are opportunities in America. A few more years to establish the business, so we have some security; then I will apply for a hospital job. You can be near your family, and take me to your favorite places. You can have ice cream and air-conditioning ..." Ashok turned his head on the pillow, smiling down at her.

"That sounds nice," Kuyila forced herself to say; it was important to be supportive of one's husband. But she was surprised to find that she didn't want to go. Aside from learning to cook a dish now and then, she had no other responsibilities here, nothing she was supposed to do but sit with Prema, with Ashok's aunts and sister, listening to their gossip, improving her Tamil. They treated her like family, and Ashok himself treated her as if she were precious, a fragile flower imported from the far West. Here in Sri Lanka, she felt special, like a princess.

In America, she'd be just another housewife.

ASHOK CONTINUED TALKING OF AMERICA THROUGH OCTOBER, November—when the heat finally broke and a series of sweet, crisp, almost autumnal days lifted everyone's spirits. In late December, all plans to leave Sri Lanka soon were dropped—Kuyila was pregnant. She was seventeen. Prema told her that she had had Ashok when she was fifteen. Kuyila knew she should have expected this, but she wasn't ready. She wanted to go home then, wanted to go to her father, have him fold her into his arms and call her his rasathi, his little princess. She knew she should be happy—the household was ecstatic, rejoicing, especially after Ashok's grandmother placed her hands on Kuyila's belly and pronounced that it would be a boy. But instead she slipped out from under Ashok's heavy arm in the middle of the night, climbed out of their bed silently, out from under the white netting, and crept down the stairs, along the hallway to the kitchen, where she mixed oils and chili powders, syrups and milk—creating whatever repulsive concoctions she could think of and then gulping them down, without even noticing the taste. She did this every night for a week, until finally, finally she miscarried, doubled over the toilet for hours of bloody, painful cramps.

The family grieved as if they'd lost an actual child—Ashok's eyes were shadowed, and he looked older. Prema assured Kuyila that it wasn't her fault and told her not to worry. Young brides often miscarried—she had lost two herself. They would be more careful the next time. Kuyila agreed and tried to look sad, and hugged her secret to herself.

Ten months later, she was pregnant again.

THIS TIME, THE FAMILY WATCHED HER EVERY STEP. IT WOULD BE A girl, the grandmother announced, but Ashok seemed just as excited. Kuyila had no opportunities to try to lose this child, but she didn't really mind. She was eighteen now and had lived in Sri Lanka for a little over a year. Her family would be coming for a visit soon, and she wanted to have something to show for her year as a wife. Raji had been sending her long letters about her life in college, the parties she went to, the white boyfriend she was madly in love with. Kuyila knew it was petty, but she wanted to show her sister that she was happy, that she had made a good choice.

To be honest, she was also a little bored. Ashok's mother didn't really want her to cook much, and the servants took care of all the cleaning. Ashok's aunts were full of endless conversation, with talk of everyone in town—who should marry whom, whose business was booming and whose was failing. Kuyila didn't know those people. And her husband, despite his joy in the coming child, seemed busier every day, with less and less time for her. Kuyila was still waiting for love to come—she had grown to care for him, but she wasn't sure she loved him, or that he loved her. He never seemed passionate about her. Not like the boy in Raji's letters, who apparently declared his love every night over her sister's naked, unmarried body. Ashok was unfailingly kind to her, but oddly distant.

Maybe a baby would change that.

THEY NAMED HER MINAL, PRECIOUS GEM. ASHOK GAVE KUYILA A RUBY pendant the morning Minal was born: one large stone set in twenty-four-karat gold, on a slender chain. The gold was beautiful, softer than American twenty-two karat, richer in tone. The ruby was cut in many facets, so that every time Kuyila moved it caught the light. She never took it off, and with it resting against her skin, she felt like a queen, rather than just a simple princess. She felt she had earned it—the baby was big, and the labor had lasted almost two days. By the end of it, Kuyila had been convinced that despite all the doctors and the gleaming sterility of the Colombo hospital, she was going to be torn apart, was going to die for lack of American medicine. When Minal finally slid out, she did so with a last kick that tore Kuyila further. The pain made her pass out, and when she came back to consciousness, Kuyila promised herself that no matter what everyone said, she would never forget that pain.

People said a lot of things that weren't true—breast-feeding, for example, wasn't the wonderful bonding experience she'd heard about. Minal had a tough, strong, sucking mouth, and when she clamped down on Kuyila's tender, cracking nipples, a jolt of pain went through her. Still, when the light fell on Minal's face, tracing the soft curves of it, Kuyila had to admit that her daughter was beautiful. And Ashok was incredible with her—Minal fussed and fussed, but all he had to do was pick her up, swing her around, curl her into his slender arms and she quieted right down. Kuyila hadn't realized how much Ashok had wanted a child until Minal arrived; he had never said anything, almost as if he hadn't let himself believe she was coming until she was actually there, until he held her in his arms. As if he didn't think she would make it that far, and didn't want to love her until she did. But now that his daughter had arrived, he was head over heels. When Kuyila saw her husband's bright face, bent over the child, she felt a wave of emotion rush through her, like nothing she had ever known. She had finally found her role, her place in the world.

A FEW MONTHS LATER, ASHOK'S FATHER DIED. KUYILA HADN'T known him well; always busy with his patients and, when at home, buried in a medical journal. Only in the last few months, since Minal came, had he spent any time near Kuyila—and even then, it was only to spend time with the baby. His only grandchild so far. Kuyila was determined to give Ashok many children, more than one son. Not yet—her body still ached. But someday. She wasn't certain, but she thought the old man had been disappointed when the ultrasound told them it would be a girl. This wasn't a house of forced abortions, of dowry deaths and bride-burnings. Still, it would be good to have a son.

The old man had had a weak heart—it ran in the family. Minal appeared fine, but Ashok had it as well and could pass it down to other children. His family carefully hadn't mentioned that when the marriage negotiations were going on; Kuyila was glad they hadn't. Her parents would likely have pulled out, and every day she was growing happier with her choice, happy to take Ashok, weak heart and all. Since Minal's birth, he had been utterly attentive, a perfect husband. Kuyila thought he was really starting to love her now.

THE NEXT YEAR BROUGHT AN ASTONISHMENT, A MARVEL—RAJI CAME to Sri Lanka for a whirlwind arranged marriage herself. Apparently she'd caught her white boyfriend cheating on her—with another South Asian girl! In a frenetic fury she had sworn off white boys and asked Amma and Appa to arrange a marriage for her—she was here, married to a man called Vivek, and moved back to America with him before Kuyila could even ask her if Raji was sure this was what she wanted. Kuyila could only hope her big sister would find some happiness, the kind Kuyila was finding herself.

IN THE FOURTH YEAR OF HER MARRIAGE, KUYILA AND PREMA MADE a small pilgrimage, walking barefoot for hours, until they reached a sacred temple where only women went. Kuyila had been surprised by Prema's suggestion—they had both been lighting candles at the cathedral, saying their rosaries, asking for Mary's intercession to help Kuyila become pregnant. But Ashok's mother saw nothing wrong in praying at a Hindu temple, just in case. So Kuyila went.

No one bothered them: two obviously respectable upper-caste women on pilgrimage. But the roads were tense. Drivers of auto-rickshaws shouted at each other more than usual; bullock carts refused to get out of the way; more than one pedestrian was knocked down in their sight. And when the police came, they did nothing—or they made things worse, knocking down more people. Few women were on the roads, and when they reached the temple, few worshippers were inside. They made their offerings in silence, and then called Ashok to come with the car and take them home.

IT WAS JULY 25, THE DAY BEFORE MINAL'S BIRTHDAY. SHE WAS TURN-ing two, a little Leo, as fierce and proud as one. She loved being the center of everyone's attention. Minal was talking to her grandmother Prema, chattering away in a mix of Tamil and English, mostly Tamil, about big spider soldiers. Bugs didn't scare her.

The streets had become more restless, and Kuyila had started leaving Minal at home with the servants when she and Prema went to market. They were unlikely to see trouble at the house; they lived in the nicest part of town. But Kuyila was still concerned—in the rest of the city, it wasn't good to be Tamil.

Kuyila hadn't even known that she *was* Tamil until she was ten or so in America, and even though she'd now been living in Sri Lanka for four years, she still couldn't look at people on the street and tell if they were Tamil or Sinhalese. Ashok could tell by the line of someone's nose, by the way they shaped their vowels when they spoke English. She didn't really understand the cause of the current troubles—something about difficulty getting jobs, getting into good schools. Language laws, religious feuds. Ashok had told her there had been riots in the late fifties and might be again. He didn't want her to go out in the street alone; it wasn't safe for a Tamil woman to be alone in public.

Minal ran barefoot now across the wooden floor, playing soldier, shouting rat-a-tat-tat! Last night, Ashok told the gate guards to get the rifles out. In America, Kuyila had been in favor of gun control, of banning guns altogether, but now she found herself glad that they had them.

THERE WAS SOMEONE BANGING ON THE GATE. KUYILA COULD HEAR them faintly, shouting. There had been shouting and banging all day—gunshots in the streets. When Ashok came back for lunch, he ate quickly, telling them in between bites of the fighting that had broken out that morning, worse than anyone had expected. As soon as he'd finished eating, he squeezed Kuyila's hand, kissed Minal on the forehead, and then went running out the door. He was worried about the business, but at least his partner was Sinhalese, and the warehouses were in his name.

Tamil warehouses were burning, Tamil businesses were being looted, destroyed. Kuyila knew Ashok would want to go on to the clinic once the business was secure. But today was not a day for Ashok to see patients; he should leave that to the Sinhalese doctors; they'd understand. Kuyila sat in her cane chair, fanning herself, waiting for her husband to come home. A man had been shot yesterday, less than five streets away, just because he didn't pronounce a word as a Sinhalese would. Kuyila wanted Ashok with her behind the iron gate, the sturdy guards with their rifles.

The banging on the gate just wouldn't stop.

One of the gate guards came in, his rifle slung over his back.

"What is it?" Kuyila asked.

"A woman, with a child. She claims they're friends of the family."

"What's her name?" Prema asked.

"Himali."

Kuyila knew that was a Sinhalese name; she had learned that much, at least. "Do you know her, Amma?" Prema had insisted on being called that, but Kuyila had never gotten used to it. Her Amma was in Massachusetts, which seemed impossibly far away.

"Yes—her parents were old friends. Let her in, Raj."

Prema didn't look happy; her skin had paled, and she moved to sit down in her favorite chair.

"Is something wrong?"

"No, no. Nothing's wrong, kunju. Do not worry."

The guard showed her in; a woman who held hands with a young boy, perhaps nine or ten. Kuyila had been worried for a moment that perhaps this woman had been some old flame of Ashok's. She had braced for someone beautiful, but this woman was almost homely, dressed in a simple cotton sari, and she looked tired, old. Kuyila stepped forward to do her duty.

"Welcome, please. Come in. Can I get you some tea?" It was important, even in the midst of chaos, to be a good hostess, a proper wife. Kuyila knew that she had become a good wife; she had put all her heart into it in the last four years, and while growing to love her dear husband, she had grown to be the kind of wife he needed. A good cook, a pretty, gracious hostess for his parties with business associates. Undemanding, calm, friendly. Even in the midst of a civil war.

The woman looked shell-shocked; Kuyila wasn't sure she saw her, or Minal, at all. When she saw Prema, she froze for a moment—then she pulled the boy across the room, falling at Prema's feet, hiding her face against Prema's dark green sari.

"Where are your parents, Himali? Your husband?" Prema's voice was sharp, but her hand rested gently on the woman's greying hair.

The woman didn't answer—it was the boy who finally said, "They're dead, Aunty."

Kuyila's stomach twisted at the boy's words, and she picked up Minal and held her close. The woman was perfectly still, her face hidden. If she cried, Kuyila couldn't see it. The boy started crying then, and Prema reached out with a trembling arm, pulled him close. Kuyila wished desperately for her husband to come home.

WHEN ASHOK DID COME HOME, LATE THAT NIGHT, WITH BLOOD FROM the clinic still on his shirt, Kuyila finally understood. She didn't understand why, or how, or even when—but she saw the look in his eyes when he saw Himali, the way Ashok looked at her and at the boy, the same yearning hunger that Kuyila had seen when he first held their daughter. A look he had never turned toward herself.

She saw his eyes on the fleshy curve of Himali's back—the woman was turned away when he walked in, reaching up to turn off the ceiling fan; it had gotten unexpectedly cold. Kuyila understood then the discomfort in Prema's face. Himali hadn't even seen him yet; Minal ran to him, and he scooped his daughter up in his arms. Kuyila walked over slowly, steadily, until she was standing beside him. She was his wife; she should fight for him, for her place. Her chest was tight; she was suffocating. She should turn the fan back on; she should throw that woman out of her house; she should do something.

But she had lost this battle before she had even begun it. Even if she went down fighting, Kuyila knew from that look in her husband's eyes—it was over.

Mangoes with Chili

San Francisco, 1983

HIMALI WAKES IN THE SMALL ROOM SHE SHARES WITH ASHOK AND ROSHAN; WAKES UP LATE, OFTEN CLOSE TO NOON, AND LIES IN THE empty bed telling herself the story. She is twenty-six years old. Her name is Himali Manavalan. She is Ashok Manavalan's wife, recently emigrated from Sri Lanka. Her parents were both killed in the troubles, but her husband was able to take her and their son to safety here, in San Francisco, in America. Ashok is a doctor. They have a ten-year-old son, Roshan, who is doing well in school, despite everything. It is a sad story, but not an unusual one—many have lost family members to war, even in America.

When Himali has finished reviewing her story, she forces herself to climb out of the bed, to put her bare feet on the chilly wood floor. It is only October, but it is so cold here. Cold always, and no sun to light the room, to draw her early from her bed. Just the grey fog, chilling the hard floors, which never get clean. At home, her mother would rise, early each morning, and pour water across the dirt floors of their home, rinsing away layers of dust, dog hair, grains of forgotten rice. By the time the sun came through the open windows and open doors, the floors would be clean, newly made, soft and dry. Himali would be up by then, coaxing Roshan to take a little crab curry, some fresh hoppers the cook had just made—the boy was a fussy eater, and too thin. Her father would be at the store already, working hard, though he would come home for a meal and a little sleep in the heat of the day. They would tend to him then, but the morning was the women's time—once Roshan was fed, clothed in his white school uniform of shorts and shirt, and sent off on his bicycle, then it was time for a nice lazy gossip, with Amma and the aunties, while the cook prepared the midday meal.

There are no aunties here. There is only herself.

Himali opens the bedroom window. She puts her head out—it is wet today, not raining but thickly damp. "Good morning, Mrs. Manavalan!" the blonde girl calls from the courtyard below. She is often there, that girl, sitting cross-legged on the stones, not minding the damp, the chill. She is meditating, she says. When they first came to the building, the girl had invited Himali to join her. She had asked with enthusiasm, eagerly, as if she expected Himali to be as ardent as herself. Himali had refused, but it had been impossible to be anything but gentle in the face of such eagerness; now the girl greets her every morning with the same words, and Himali must call back her own, "Good morning!" though it is now scarcely morning, and she has long forgotten the girl's name. That is all right. After all, the name the girl calls her by is not rightly her own.

The real Mrs. Manavalan is Kuyila Manavalan, the woman Himali had shared a house with for two weeks. An impossible time, and an impossible woman. Despite Kuyila's brown skin, and her years living in Colombo, she was so very American. Arguing loudly with Ashok in those weeks, shouting at him in the middle of the night, so that his mother, the servants, everyone could hear them. Fighting a battle that was already lost, that Kuyila had lost before she ever met Ashok. Ashok's choice had been made years and years before, and if he had been kept from it for a time, he was no longer. *We are defined by our history*, Himali's father had liked to say.

Her father was referring to the ancestral history, to the great Sinhalese kings who had once ruled the island, lending legitimacy to those, like her father, who believed the Sinhalese had a duty and the right to rule it once again. Rule it democratically, but rule definitively. Her father was a good man, a decent man—he wanted to treat the Tamil minority fairly, as long as they didn't get too close. He had made that mistake once before, had let a Tamil family become neighbors, then good friends—and what had come of that? A daughter almost ruined, saved only by three sets of parents, working together. One Tamil boy, sent packing to medical school far away. One Sinhalese girl, quickly married to a respectable, dark-skinned, horse-featured Sinhalese man. It all happened so fast, who was to say that the child wasn't fathered by her new husband? But Himali always knew. Ashok knew too, when she came to his house, when he saw his son.

The phone rings, and she answers it. It is Ashok, of course—no one else calls here. He is calling to see whether she is up yet, and is happy to hear that she is. Some days, she doesn't get out of bed until Roshan comes home from school. Those are the bad days. Today she is up, and she tells Ashok that she has showered and dressed, has eaten, that she thinks she might go for a walk, maybe even go down to Golden Gate Park. He tells her that he will be home from the hospital as early as he can and hangs up, reassured. Thinking that it is only a passing sickness after all, the effects of grief and terror and even homesickness, that perhaps Himali is finally getting better. Thinking that he will finally have the wife he always wanted, the girl he has always loved. She can hear it in his voice, the painful hope.

Lies. She cannot get better. How can lies birth anything but more lies?

When Himali came to Ashok, made her way to him, from the house where her parents had lain bloody on her mother's clean floors, it all seemed so clear. A chance, finally. Himali knew he was married, of course, to some girl from America. Had heard that he had a small daughter now. But she chose to come anyway, bearing their son and the ghosts of her parents, carrying the horror she had seen into his house, knowing what he would do when he saw her. They were not children anymore, to let their parents choose their roads. And he had once loved her beyond all reason, had loved her despite knowing that he, a Tamil doctor's son, would never be allowed to marry a Sinhalese shopkeeper's daughter. Himali came to the house he shared with his mother, his daughter, his wife, knowing that Ashok loved her still.

She had done her duty by the husband her parents had chosen for her, had shared the man's bed and been grateful to find him lacking in desire, almost incapable. He touched her only a few times before it became evident that she was pregnant, and not at all after Roshan was born, seeming only grateful to have a son to call his own. He was a kind enough man, gentle with her, and Himali cooked and cleaned for him as her mother had taught her, until, when her son was almost eight, the man took sick. Himali nursed him through the wasting disease that pulled the flesh from his bones, and he seemed grateful. When he died, she took her son and moved back into her parents' house, finding an odd comfort in being treated like a child once again, with the burdens of wifehood lifted from her. She thought, briefly, of finding Ashok again—but he was married himself by then, with his own duties. What could she have said to him?

Himali goes to the tiny kitchen, sets a pot of water to boiling for tea. That is sufficient breakfast for her—Ashok eats cereal, cornflakes, and claims to like it, but she can't bring herself to eat cold food in the morning. She longs for her mother's hoppers, for pittu, for rice. Himali could cook them herself—but she doesn't have the right pans, the right flour, the right spices for the curry. Ground cumin at the store but no cumin seed, tamarind pods but no paste, and no curry leaves to be found. Ashok has told her there are Indian grocery stores where she can get many of the needed supplies, and Chinatown for fresh produce, for crabs almost as tasty as the ones back home. Chinatown isn't far from the Haight—just a short bus ride. When they came here in early August, Ashok took her on the buses, the trolleys, even the subway. Himali knows the way. And still, she can't bring herself to go. She will have tea now and make a cheese sandwich for Roshan when he comes home. Ashok will come home late, and then will go out again to pick up takeout from one of the restaurants down the street. The Ethiopian one has curries that remind her of home, though their bread is strangely sour. Or perhaps she will make spaghetti. Himali opens the cupboard and looks—yes, there are the long boxes of pasta, the jars of sauce. Spaghetti will be plenty for tonight. She can manage that, and it's Roshan's favorite food now. He loves spaghetti.

Himali walks from one room to another, waiting for the water to boil. She can't find a place to sit down. There are only three rooms—bedroom, bathroom, kitchen. Ashok has promised that soon they will move into a bigger place, once they've saved up a little money. They were only allowed to take a few hundred dollars out of the country—that and an advance on his hospital salary sustained them for the first weeks, let them rent this shoddy place. He says by January they can move, but Himali cannot imagine it. Instead, she pictures her mother's house, with its many large rooms and its high beamed ceilings. As a child, at night, she lay alone in her bedroom, with the white mosquito netting that made her feel like a maharani in a fairy tale, like Sita, Rama's wife, protected from the world. Her father came and tucked her into bed, kissed her forehead and called her kumari, princess, before letting down the walls of white. When she came back to her parents' house with Roshan, that had become her job, to do that for her son. Here, he sleeps on a thin mattress on the floor in a corner of their room, and she must be careful not to step on him when she wakes in the night, parched, desperate for water.

Maybe she will go out, after all. It is unbearable, the thought of staying here in this dank set of rooms, waiting for the rain that may or may not come. Himali does not shower. She dresses in a heavy sari, with one of Ashok's sweaters pulled over it, and a long grey coat. It is far more than anyone else on the street will wear, she knows, but she is so cold. She turns off the pot of now-boiling water, pleased with herself for remembering, picks up her keys, and walks out the door.

As Himali walks down the stairs, through the heavy iron gate, down the street, her left thumb plays nervously with the gold ring on her fourth finger. It is a bad habit, but she cannot seem to stop herself. She has been doing this since Ashok gave it to her, since the day he told her that he had the papers, the new identity papers he had purchased from a government official, certifying that she was Himali Manavalan, his wife, and that her Roshan was Roshan Manavalan, his legitimate son. The American had refused to give him a divorce. Himali admired the woman for that, for the spirit in her that kept fighting the lost battle. Kuyila remained the legitimate wife, and the little girl, Minal, remained the legitimate daughter. But Himali had the semblance of a marriage, and the body of the man. She had America too, if only by deceit, the country that woman had given up for her marriage, for her husband. Himali had almost expected Kuyila to go back, to go home to her parents, as Himali herself had done when she lost *her* husband. But the American had decided to stay in Colombo, to keep living in Ashok's mother's house, with his mother, and his little girl. Kuyila clung to what she could of her married life; Himali, cast adrift, could not blame her.

It isn't so far to the park, after all. Himali walks along a curving road, past a museum, a Japanese garden, walks until her feet in their heeled sandals start to ache. She hasn't worn heels, hasn't gone outside in days—or has it been weeks? Himali sits down on a bench and slips off her shoes, resting her feet in the cold grass. The damp chills them, but also eases the pain. The park is almost deserted—an occasional young couple strolls by, arm in arm, evidently so in love that the dismal weather, the now-approaching storm clouds, cannot infringe on their pleasure in each other.

Himali and Ashok walked like that, on the beach in Colombo, under the bright sun. She ran into the warm waves, came out again with her sari clinging to her body. Teased him with it, dancing away when he reached for her, laughing. They found private places in the great park, under spreading banyan trees. They climbed up into the trees, among the shrieking monkeys, and there she let him undo her blouse, cup her breasts in his slender hands. He pressed his ear to her bare chest, listening for her heartbeat. "Ah, yes, a strong heart," he said. "Are you sure?" she asked, turning her face up to his, so handsome in the leaf-speckled sunlight. "Oh yes," he answered, his lips coming to kiss hers, salty-sweet against her tongue. "I will be a doctor someday, and we understand these things."

Himali doesn't want to remember. She just wants to sit here, watching a little brown man push his white cart along the path toward her. He calls out something to her, but she doesn't understand it. Himali shakes her head, but he only comes nearer and repeats his words. "I'm sorry," she says, feeling helpless but not frightened. "I don't understand you."

"You not Spanish?" he asks, speaking with a heavy accent.

"No, no—Indian." It is easier to claim India than explain Sri Lanka, she has discovered. And India holds no memories to trap her with.

"Ah, India! The Indian ladies, so beautiful. You—you very beautiful," he says, smiling broadly at her. "Would you like to buy some mango?"

She is far from beautiful. Himali knows that, has always known it. Though Ashok too claims she is beautiful. Is that why she loved him, so long ago? She can't remember.

Himali should send this man away, but the thought of mango, sweet and tangy on her tongue, is irresistible. And the man is small, brown, and wrinkled—he reminds her of the sweets-seller in her parents' village. That man had just the same smile, the same way of telling you that you were such a pretty girl, you deserved something sweet to eat. Himali reaches for a coin—and realizes she has not brought her purse with her.

"I'm sorry—I have no money." It seems a betrayal, this unexpected thwarting of desire. Such a small thing she had wanted, a taste of mango.

"It's okay. Eat, eat." And he is taking a small white paper bag from his cart, one filled with bright slices of mango. "Chili? Salt? Lime?" He sprinkles each over the little bag, without waiting for her response. And then hands her the bag with one hand, a toothpick with another. She takes them from him and, after a moment, tries one.

Salt first, then chili burns her tongue, and Himali is a little girl again, leaning against her mother's knee as she makes a mango sambol, stealing bites from the bowl, being scolded. "Stop that, duwa! There won't be enough for your father!" Saying it fondly, though, so that the child knows that she is entirely safe in stealing another piece, and another. She eats the same way now, greedily, one piece after another in her mouth, not bothering with the toothpick anymore, just cramming them in with a sticky hand until the bag is empty. The sour lime lingers, but the sweetness of the mango prevails. The old man smiles and turns away, walking back to his cart.

"Thank you!" she calls after him. He doesn't respond as he pushes it away, down the curving road. Himali's mouth is tingling, alive in a way it hasn't been since the day she huddled behind a door with Roshan pressed up against her, not daring to breathe or let him breathe, terrified that the men with guns would find him there, discern that her child was half Tamil, fair game for their vengeful fury. Her father standing in the front door, defying them, denying them entrance to his house, berating them with all the strength and power of his years, his righteous indignation. *Is this how the descendants of kings should behave? What have we come to? You are not our sons! You are nothing, no one!*

A foolish old man, and so they turned on him instead, first beating him in the doorway, then, when her mother tried to intervene, shooting instead. Shooting them both in a blind frenzy while Himali huddled, smothering her son, trying not to breathe.

It is raining in the park now. No gentleness to this rain—an opening up of the heavens, a full-force pounding against her body, her face, running down her hollowed cheeks. Himali couldn't cry that day, couldn't let them hear her. She hasn't cried since—not when she finally came out to take up the bodies, not on the long road to Ashok's house, not even at the terrible look on that poor woman's face. Himali stole Kuyila's husband, just as surely as the rioters stole her parents away. And did so without remorse, with only a desperate need to take what she could, of what little was left to her. If she could, she would not change that choice.

Himali stands and starts walking back, through the merciless rain. She might still love Ashok, somewhere. Somehow. When she isn't angry at him for being Tamil, for giving her a son who brought killers to her parents' door. Angry at the language he speaks, the people he comes from, enraged by the very shape of his face.

She will try to love Ashok again. She owes that to him, and even more to the American wife, to the daughter who will grow up without a father. There has been enough sourness, enough bitter bite in what has been done to her, in what she herself has done. For balance, she must find something sweet.

Tightness in the Chest

Vermont, 1986

CHOPPING ONIONS IN THE DARK, WORKING BY FEEL; VIVEK HAS DONE THIS A THOUSAND TIMES NOW, ISN'T LIKELY TO CHOP OFF A finger. Working as quietly as he can, not wanting to wake her, to let her know that he is home, and hungry; let her sleep, keep her happy a little longer. Relatively happy. As happy as he knows how.

Raji's left food in the fridge for him. The remnants of her solitary dinner, cold pork chops and baked potatoes, ready for microwave reheating. She would have eaten hours before, with slices of white bread on the side, and ketchup on her baked potato. He did open the fridge, considered the food briefly. He always makes himself look at the food she's left for him, even though he knows that he will not be able to stomach it, not at this hour, after sixteen straight hours at the hospital. His head pounding, his stomach churning, craving coriander and curry leaves, chili and turmeric. A little chicken in a dark curry sauce, over a mound of plain white rice. Dal. Brinjal. He closes the fridge door, his husbandly duty done.

Vivek pulls small onions from a basket, chops them, almost as finely as his mother did. He fries the onions with a lid covering most of the pan, to keep the smell as contained as possible. He hung a drape over the kitchen archway, but still, sometimes Raji wakes. Wakes and lies there in the dark, until he's cooked and eaten, until he's come to bed. *Still hungry? No, I'm fine now—sorry I woke you.* In a few days they'll be moving to Massachusetts for his new job, moving into their first house. It's small, but the bedroom is on one floor, the kitchen on another. He's looking forward to it; they both are. She'll be near her family again.

His first week in America, Raji took him to a grocery store, a superstore, and laughed at his bewilderment. She took him up and down the endless aisles, the lights so bright they made his eyes ache, the vegetables smelling of floor wax, the meat locked behind glass. Vivek was content to be led, grateful for her guidance, and when they returned to their new apartment, he waited eagerly for his first American dinner, cooked by his new bride. Crisp green asparagus, grilled steak with a béarnaise sauce—delicious. He praised each slim stalk of asparagus, each melting bite of rare steak. She smiled and watched him eat, occasionally taking a bite herself. He took two servings, and afterward, she served him thick slices of hot apple pie. He ate until his stomach felt bloated, distended. But later that night, he found himself still hungry. Not just hungry. Starving.

After a week of such dinners he started cooking in the night, surreptitiously. A little curry, a little rice. Just enough to ease the cravings. After running short of groceries a few too many times, Raji couldn't help noticing. *I could ask my mother to teach me.* She tried to make him rice and curry a few times, but she didn't have the knack, the years of tasting that taught you when you needed a little less chili powder, a little more cumin seed. Vivek knew that she was happier eating spaghetti and meatballs, chicken parmesan, mashed potatoes. Raji called it comfort food. *Don't go to any trouble,* he told her. *I just want a taste, now and then. No big deal.* She served him smaller portions at dinner and started buying extra groceries for him to cook at night.

Marriage is based on compromise. His mother had told him that, and told him he'd have to make more compromises than most, given his choice of wife. He'd laughed at his mother, stroked her hair with affection and sadness, feeling the many coarse white strands mixed in with the remnants of silky black. *Don't worry, Amma. I know what I'm doing.* Had known when he saw the photo, so different from the studio portraits of the local girls. *She refused to sit for a picture; she doesn't like to be photographed; all I have is this candid.* Raji's mother, an old friend of his mother, had written that in apology, but he was grateful for the chance to see the girl like this. A young woman, actually—nineteen in the photo, a Harvard college student. Raji was swinging at the playground with her young cousins. A little too tall for the swing, her bare legs too long. Her head, her whole body tilted back and her hair falling long and loose behind her, almost brushing the dirt on the ground. Her face was turned slightly away—all Vivek could see was a profile, a single closed eye, a laughing mouth. It was enough.

Raji's mother had also written, her embarrassment rising off the page, that her daughter had dated, a little. He knew what that meant— knew that he likely wouldn't be her first, though she would be his. It didn't matter. He would be her husband; she would be his wife. That was what mattered. If there were problems, they would work it out, work everything out, and love would come. That was what his aunts always said, talking to their daughters about marriage: Love will come. He planned to be a good husband to Raji, a good father to their children. He imagined their daughter, in America, running through a big grassy backyard, riding her bicycle to school—a daughter with Raji's hair and eyes. Or perhaps a son, who played baseball instead of cricket. *Everything will be fine, Amma. You'll see.*

He had been so sure. From the first time he saw the photograph to the first time he saw her, standing so straight and still just outside the Colombo airport, among the weeping mothers, the eager children off to see the world, the inescapable hands of beggars. So sure, especially after the first time he touched her, in their marriage bed. She, regretting already whatever impulse that had brought her here, across the world to his arms, his bed, and he, with what felt like bird wings fluttering in his stomach, his chest, the knowledge that with one wrong move he could ruin this, ruin all the possibilities past repair. The rains had pounded outside the thin walls, monsoon rains thundering down in the thick, warm air. It had been difficult to breathe. But he had chosen rightly; his arms had enclosed her and she had opened for him, had, laughing and trembling, shown him how to touch her, how to please her. Vivek had come through the trial of fire, come to rest, to sleep heavily beside his smiling wife. Had fallen asleep thinking, *See, Amma? See?*

He had seen. The green card came a month later, the hospital job in Vermont. The plane flight had been long; the wind that greeted them as they left the airport was bitterly cold. But Raji took his cold hand in hers, rubbed it to warmth again. *Just wait until I get you home; I'll warm you up properly then.* And she had, and their bodies curving together, parting and rejoining in the night had been a talisman, a touchstone, a silent promise. He dissolved in pleasure, night after night; he lost himself and took her with him, both lost, lost together, joined forever at hip and heart. Or so he'd thought, until he woke one night with a churning stomach and found the bed empty. Vivek staggered down the hall to the bathroom to find his wife taking a packet of pills from her purse, a glass of water in her hand.

He recognized the pills, had prescribed them himself for more than one woman in the hospital. Three rows of blue and one of white. Impossible to mistake. *How long have you been taking those?* He had thrown the words at her, an accusation, his voice chilled and harsh. She had turned away, at just that same angle as in the photograph, her eye open this time, her mouth tight. *For many years. From long before I met you. Do you have a problem with that?* He hadn't known how to tell her what his problem was, hadn't known how to tell her how he had been watching her move through their apartment, watching her belly surreptitiously, spreading his fingers during sex across the skin above her mound and wondering if a child of his might be growing there already. Didn't know how to explain the cold ache in his gut, the mirrored cold in his chest. Could only say, *You don't have to hide them from me.* Raji stared at him, her eyes dark and wide, then gulped a pill down, dry, and went to bed. Vivek closed the door, then pushed up the toilet seat and knelt on the cold tiles, heaving up the contents of his gut until he was empty, drained dry, his mouth sour and his head dizzy. Six months of knowing her, six months married, and so much he didn't know. So much he was learning.

He spent too much time in the hospital, that first year in America. He had left his family behind, but the other doctors, working the same crazy hours, they understood. Their skin was white, but they were just like him underneath it. They understood how it tore at you, watching the patients come in at the end of your shift, and the hospital chronically understaffed, so you stayed, and stayed, for just one, one, one more patient. When you remembered, you called your wife, but too often she was already long asleep. Raji worked; she had a job at the college library, but it wasn't even nine to five, barely thirty hours a week. She hadn't finished college, after all; she had come to marry him instead. He was the doctor, and he was no dermatologist, no ENT, with regular hours and a comfortable office. He worked the emergency room, his gloved hands bloody, and no matter how many he saved, it was never enough. Only a few people had died back home, in the early troubles; he'd left home thinking it had been an aberration, that things were settling down. But the conflict was getting worse instead; now he crouched at the dining table in the early mornings, bent over the shortwave radio, pulling in the BBC reports reporting the riots, feeling an ache of guilt tugging at his chest. He wanted to save those lives, to close the gaping wounds. So medicine, long hours in the emergency room—and now, in America, he did save lives. The price was that he never saw his wife.

He thought Raji might have a talent; had seen it in the doodles by the telephone, in the quick, unthinking sketches scribbled at the end of shopping lists. He encouraged her to quit her job, to go back to school;

he made plenty for two, after all. Vivek had paid for the classes, so how could he say a word when she brought back the sketchbooks full of naked men and women, their bodies curving, muscles taut, almost hurling themselves off the pages, assaulting his eyes. He was an educated man; he should have known what he was signing her up for.

His wife, sitting in that class, her eyes following the lines of their bodies, pausing to shade in a nipple, to etch a cheekbone or the muscles of the groin. *How can you let her do this?* his mother-in-law asked him, shocked on the telephone, and Vivek only laughed, told her gently, *It's just art, Aunty.* And it was true, he saw naked bodies every day at the hospital, but those were different, were broken and fragile, wasted and suffering. Almost holy, in their pain, and he was only a sexless priest, witness to their suffering, able, occasionally, to alleviate the pain. The bodies his wife drew were healthy and whole, radiant with youth, with strength. Young art students, taking off their clothes to earn a few extra dollars themselves, and he didn't ask whether she ever took off her clothes for them, or even wanted to—he didn't want to know.

It was art, only art, and so he tried to ignore the twisting in his gut that reminded him that art was not necessarily safe, or sexless. Vivek kept silent, as she moved from sketches to paintings, to longer hours working under bright lights with nude, naked models. After a year of classes, Raji rented a studio space; their apartment wasn't large enough to work in. Sometimes he would go to the studio and stand outside the glassed door, quietly watching her, paint smeared across her hands, her cheek, her nose, eyes intent, lost in her work. She rarely even knew he was there; he came and went silently. She was happy there, and he didn't want to disturb that happiness.

Raji wasn't happy with him—or at least, not often. Vivek wasn't sure how often, to be honest. Perhaps she was happy enough. Sometimes, at night, usually after sex, Raji would roll over in bed, would curl her body against his back, reach around to hold him. Five minutes, ten, fifteen—he lay as still as he could, counting the minutes, counting their shared breaths, his heart pounding, happy yet afraid of the inevitable moment when she would squeeze gently, then pull away, returning to her side of the bed, leaving him abandoned, alone. In the early days of their marriage, he had tried to hold on after sex, taken her hand in his and tried to keep her longer. *I can't sleep like that, Vivek.* And he let her go, always let her go, hoping only that she would keep coming back to him.

He said nothing about the pills for one year, for two. His wife was young, after all—she'd only been twenty-one when they married. There was plenty of time. His mother called, the transatlantic connection weak and staticky. It wasn't even her phone; there was only one phone in the village, and it wasn't hers. She called to ask what was wrong, why there were no babies. She wanted him to bring Raji back to Sri Lanka, to see some village man, to see what was wrong. He hadn't lied to his mother since he was a little boy, stealing sweets from the market and denying it when caught. *Amma, don't worry. We've both been checked out, everything's fine. The doctor says we should just relax and give it time.*

On their third anniversary, he'd cooked for her. Biryani rice, tamarind shrimp, dark chicken curry, three vegetables, four sambols and chutneys. Enough food to feed both their families. Raji came home wearing a dark red dress, bringing flowers, candles for the table, and a painting of him. Vivek hadn't posed for it; she'd done it from memory. The figure was tall, imposing, dark. When he looked at it, he didn't recognize himself at all, but the man was certainly handsome.

He'd meant to wait until after they'd eaten, when her belly was full and she was comfortable, relaxed. But his mother had called again that day, and her mother as well, to wish them well, and as Raji was lighting the candles, the words came spilling out. *Do you want to start trying?* Vivek hadn't meant to ask yet, but as soon as the words were out he felt as if a crushing weight had been removed from his chest. Raji's face was completely still, bathed in flickering light. Beautiful. Then she said, *I'm sorry—I can't do this. I tried.* And she put down the lighted candle, carefully in the candlestick. Turned away, opened the door, and stepped out, into the night. He couldn't stop her, couldn't run after her. The weight was back, twice as heavy as before, and it was crushing him, bearing him down.

She was gone for less than a week; nobody else had time to notice. *Sorry, Aunty—she's still in the studio. Yes, working hard. A big project.* He barely went to the hospital, got people to cover his shifts. Vivek sat by the phone, in case she called, by the door, in case she walked in. Five days of this and then he had to take a shift. Five days, and when he came home that night, Raji was sitting at the table with the dinner reheated, the curry dinner that he hadn't been able to bring himself to throw away. He'd frozen it all, everything but the rice that wouldn't keep. She'd cooked fresh plain rice; she knew how to do that much. Cooked the rice and heated the rest, and when he came inside she said, *I'm sorry.* He had to ask. *Were you with . . .* She didn't let him finish. *No, no one. I was alone, in a motel. Vivek—I'm not ready to be a mother yet. I need a few more years of me, of us. I only went away because I needed time to think.* He sat down with her then, ate dinner. But he couldn't taste anything. He wanted to believe her. He didn't say, *You couldn't think here, with me, at home?* He didn't say, *Were you really alone?* She had had lovers before him. He'd known that before they married. He hadn't thought it mattered.

The next time she disappeared, he didn't even know at first that she had gone. He was leaving town himself, going to New York for a conference on a six AM train. She had set the alarm for him, and when he came out of the shower, he found her in the living room, struggling with their rickety ironing board, their temperamental iron, trying to iron his conference shirt—crisp, button-down, white. He wanted to stop her; he always did his own ironing, since she usually left creases in the clothes when she tried. But Raji was biting her lip, intent on the shirt, pulling it taut and carefully ironing every inch, paying attention as if her life, or his, depended on it. So he stood quietly in the doorway and waited, waited until she finished, setting down the iron, lifting the shirt, and carrying it carefully over to him. *Thank you.*

She stretched up on her toes and gave him a quick kiss on the cheek, then leaned against him, rested for just a moment, and he started to put his arms around her, careless of the shirt, wanting just to hold her—but then she pulled away. Her face was only half lit in the dim early-morning light, her eyes wide. *Have a good trip.* He stood there, holding the shirt, as Raji slipped past him, slipped away. She was only going back to their bed; he finished dressing and went to the train station. But when he came back three days later, he found her gone, and three days of newspapers sat in front of their apartment door. She came home a few days later, again without explanation.

The third time it happened, Vivek took the phone off the hook, so he could stop waiting for his wife to call home.

Raji always came back, but she could never explain why she kept leaving. He found himself wondering if it would be easier if, the next time, she didn't come home.

On their fourth anniversary, he didn't take the day off from work. He went to the hospital; he did his rounds, took care of his patients. He went to meetings, and at the last one, he couldn't concentrate on what the speaker was saying. Across the room, a blonde woman, another doctor, was staring at him, her blue eyes fixed and clear; she licked her pale lips when he glanced her way. This wasn't new; he'd ignored the woman for years; but that afternoon, after the meeting, she cornered him in the empty staff room. *So you're leaving in a few days, moving to Massachusetts.* He said *yes*, curtly, but she didn't back away. She stepped closer, spoke more softly. *I saw you, looking back at me today. I want you, Vivek. I want to touch your skin, want to see your body against mine. Don't you want that?* She leaned forward, pressed her small breasts against his chest. Her hair was cropped mannishly short, her body slender and fit, nothing like his wife's curves and rolls. Raji hadn't been thin when they married, and now she was noticeably plump.

That wasn't why he had sex with the blonde—he had sex with her so that he could tell his wife.

He took the blonde doctor in a supply closet, with her skirt pulled up and her legs wrapped around his waist. She whispered over and over in his ear, *God, I love your big, dark dick*. He wasn't listening. He didn't care.

When they'd finished, he'd gone home. He'd chopped onions in the dark, fried them, added cumin and black mustard seed, chili and chicken. Now he eats the curry over plain rice, soothing his churning stomach. Afterward he washes the pans, wipes down the stovetop by the light of the gas burner. Then he turns off the burner, walks down the hall, carefully removes his clothing, and climbs into bed beside his wife. His hands are still damp. She is awake; he can tell. Awake and waiting for him, silent. He can't stand the silence.

I had sex with another woman today. Vivek says the words, then waits, breathless, for her. Raji has gone still beside him, saying nothing. Then she rolls toward him and asks quietly, *Are you going to have sex with her again?* And he says, *No*. And she says, *Okay, then*. She says nothing else, just rolls away, moving a little further toward the edge of the bed, falling asleep.

Vivek lies there, very still, counting his breaths, wondering why it feels as if his heart is about to explode, the beats thudding in his chest, thundering like the monsoon rains that night, that first night, when it had still seemed possible that it might all go perfectly right.

The Children

Mint in Your Throat

San Francisco, 1990

YOU OPEN THE DOOR AND SHE'S STANDING THERE WITH GHOSTS IN
HER EYES. GHOSTS AND TEAR TRACKS; HER ARMS WRAPPED TIGHT
around her, fingers digging into the flesh of her upper arms. Standing
there in her short skirt, with dirt on her long legs and muddy bare feet.
She looks like someone who has forgotten how to speak.

*You stand there, with the words swallowed down so deep. He pulls you in,
gently. Asks you questions. You don't answer; you can't. Finally, he pulls you
into a hug—a long embrace, with arms protecting, cradling. His palms flat
against your back, your head tilted into the hollow of shoulder. Shaking
again, and he's murmuring reassuring words. The taste of mint in your
mouth. Dry, dusty mint. Tilt your head up, just a little, and he's looking down
at you, concern in his dark brown eyes.*

She's shaking, and you hold her tight in the circle of your arms,
trying to protect her from whatever has hurt her, trying too late. You
know what it must be. A mugger, a rapist, all the bad things, bad men
that your mom warned your sister about. Her head is buried in your
shoulder, her face pressed hard against your chest. You give up on the
questions, murmur soft, useless phrases.

He moved into the spare room a few months ago, and you don't know him and he doesn't know you, but he knows that you're not the type of woman to come home this late with dirt on your legs, with an inability to speak. You're not that kind of girl. You're not.

You're a smart girl—your father is a professor. You've been to college, to graduate school. You're in control of your life. You make your own choices.

His name returns to you. Joseph.

She looks up. She looks up for a long moment, and then she stretches up on her toes and kisses you. You have never been kissed before. Twenty-three and never been kissed. Another time, it would be almost funny.

You kiss him, hard. His lips taste like nothing, a relief. He pulls away.

"Shefali?" Startled, unsure. She kisses you again, her mouth open, her tongue pressing against your lips. You open your lips, just a little, and her tongue slips inside. Your breath catches; you can feel the blood running through your body, running out. You are leaning against her now; you are holding each other up. Her hands are clinging tight to your shirt, her nails digging into your skin.

You had been walking down Guerrero, exhausted. Class ran late. Missed the last bus and not enough for a cab, so you were walking home after eleven. Street deserted—pools of lamplight illuminating emptiness. Your father would have worried if he knew; he always worried. Since your mother died, he has done nothing but worry about you, his only child. But your father is in Chicago, thousands of miles away; he can't see you, and you have walked alone at night a hundred times. Backpack heavy on your shoulder and you wondering why the hell you decided to wear the damn heels to class. The sexy professor who noticed your legs yesterday was the reason. Stupid reason.

You've never been this close to a girl, for this long. All through high school and college too, everyone thought you were a ladies' man; nobody noticed that all the girls liked you and all the girls flirted but none of them dated you twice. They said, "You're such a nice guy," or, "I just don't feel that way about you," or, often, "Let's just be friends, Joe."

You smiled; you walked them to the door. Because you were, after all, a nice guy.

Your feet hurt like hell, and finally you stopped and took off the heels. Shoes in one hand, picking your way carefully along the concrete sidewalk, watching for broken glass. Unprepared for the swift figure out of the alley, his hand grabbing your arm, a pocketknife at your throat. Heels in his face? Scream? He dragged you into the alley, pressed you up against the wall. Just a pocketknife, but the blade was sharp.

Maybe sixteen, barely bearded and acne-spotted. White boy with dead-cat breath and a high voice.

"Hey, bitch. Bitch, you're gonna give me some."

Not wanting money. Visions of blood, and your legs were shaking. Glad of the concrete wall at your back. Cool. Calm.

"You want sex?" Your voice didn't crack.

He was confused. Maybe he'd expected you to scream.

"Yeah."

A nice guy, and you'd always figured that someday you'd meet a nice girl. Maybe a redhead, with green eyes and pale skin. You'd be friends first, and you'd fall in love, until one day, at a movie, you'd kiss her. And she'd kiss you back, and you'd know that she loved you.

Here was the test. "Blow job's fifty bucks. You wanna fuck, it'll be a hundred." Didn't let him see the fear. As if you did this every day.

So when one girl in college did sit on your bed, and lean against you, and started running her hand over your thigh, up toward your crotch—you pulled away. She smelled sweet and dark and musky, and you were so turned on you couldn't think, but you pulled away, because she wasn't the girl you were looking for. It might have been fun, but it wouldn't have been right.

"Where the fuck am I going to get that!" He was shaking. "I've got a fucking knife on you and you want fifty bucks?"

You sighed. A quiet voice screaming in the back of your head, ignored. "Look, whatcha got?" The knife against your throat; you imagined it piercing, the blood pouring out of you. That was how your mother died, in child-

birth, with her blood pouring out. What would it have done to your father, if you had died there, like that?

He shrugged. "Maybe ten."

"Okay. But you gotta wear a rubber."

He didn't move or speak. Sweat dripping down his face and the stink of fear heavy in the air.

Every semester, every year, you figured the right girl would come along. You graduated, and she still hadn't shown up. Then you were working, and there were no women in the programmers' basement. You started to get scared. Maybe you'd never find her. Maybe she didn't exist. After two years of that, you figured that you had to get out of Indiana, go someplace new, different.

He pulled the knife away from your throat, held it tight in his right hand. Fumbled in his pocket with the left, dragged out a crumpled five, a couple of ones. You took them, not touching his fingers. Didn't let your hand shake.

"Don't have a rubber." He was halfway apologetic, halfway belligerent. His forehead was sweating. Could have lost it right there.

You slowly reached back, watching his eyes. Watch the eyes, not the knife. Unzipped your backpack, stuffed the money in. In a mesh pocket, among tampons and spare batteries, found a single condom. Only God knew how long it'd been there. Handed it to him.

So you moved to San Francisco, moved in with a friend of your sister's. Shefali. Just for a few months, until you found a place of your own. She worked all day and took classes at night, so you didn't see her much, but didn't much mind. Pretty, but not really your type—too thin, too intense. A little intimidating. Your friends would have told you to go for it, but you'd waited so long already—you could wait a little longer.

He unzipped his pants, pulled out his cock. Got the condom on, with difficulty. Stood there, waiting for you, blinking.

You dropped to your knees on gravel. Muck on your legs. Spit on your hand and grabbed his cock. Rubbed it till it was hard. Then in your mouth, powdery-mint and latex. You almost gagged then but shoved it down. All down.

You were still waiting for your girl, and you thought you knew what it'd be like. After that first kiss, after lots of kissing, it would be slow and gentle. You'd talk a lot first, that first time, calming her nerves and yours. Then some kissing, touching, more talking. Slow and easy and gentle, just the way she liked it. If you were lucky, that would be the girl you married someday.

His hands tight in your hair. By the end, he was fucking your mouth, slamming into your throat. When it was done, he tossed the condom, zipped up, walked away. Tomorrow he'd tell his friends he got a blow job from a hooker for only seven bucks. He'd boast. He'd do this again.

You knelt there.

And then. You were running a program, trying to find the bugs. Lost in it, and you don't know how long it was until you heard the banging at the door. You lifted your head, confused. Shefali had a key. You went down the stairs, wondering what had happened. Had she lost her key? Maybe it was a neighbor? A fire? A shooting?

Once he was out of sight, the shakes took over. Deep shudders and still you were biting back the moan. Blankly you stood and started walking. Walking and walking. You circled your block three times before you walked up the stairs to the apartment and the door. Couldn't find your keys. You slammed your fist into the door until Joseph opened it, his eyes startled.

Now Shefali's body is long against yours. She's kissing you so hard, so fierce, like she wants to swallow you whole.

You can't help reacting to this woman in these arms, this woman who smells like night, this woman who wants you.

Your head is swimming and your muscles are tense. Her lips are traveling over yours, her tongue is entwining with yours.

She wants you.

Your hands balled tight in the fabric of his shirt, you pull him to you. You can feel him hard against you; he must want you. He has to.

This can't be right.

You take a deep breath and then pull back. You catch her hands in yours, her hands that are still locked on your shirt—as if she wants to drag you down or drag herself up.

You hold her hands and ask her with your hands, your eyes, your voice. "Shefali, is this what you really want?"

Such a kind voice, and you nod. Mouth yes, though your throat is still locked. Mouth please.

You don't know her—you don't even like her—but she wants you, she needs you.

You're a nice guy, and she needs you.

Can you say no to that?

He surrenders then, hands gentle on your back, lips moving against yours. He smells like open fields.

You release her hands. Her tongue thrusts into your mouth. She leads you up the stairs, to her room, her bed. Your hands travel uncertainly over her body, trying to erase the imagined touch, to replace it with warm hands, with care. Trying to be as gentle as possible.

But she is not gentle with you.

So slow, so patient, and you cannot stand it. You need speed, the rush of blood in your arteries and veins. He does not know how to give it to you, and so you take it, digging your nails into his back, biting down until you break the skin, riding him until you and he and the room and the world dissolve into light, into nothing at all.

Afterward, she cries. Shefali weeps, and terror rises in you and you wonder if you have done the wrong thing, if you have hurt her, hurt her worse, perhaps. You hold her close as she tells you everything.

Weep while he holds you, until the tears have washed a path down cheekbone and chin to opening throat. Tell him everything, every detail.

Your stomach churns, and you are glad that you did not ask her to go down on you. Not that you would have had the nerve, even if this had been a normal date, at a normal time. Not the first time.

He gets the seven dollars from your backpack and you throw it out the window. He puts you in a shower. You both go back to bed.

She is no longer shaking, and she smiles at you, and the ghosts seem fainter now. Maybe it will be all right. Maybe you did the right thing after all.

He holds you close and rubs your back until you finally fall asleep in his arms. Your last thought is of your father. He sent you a letter last week—on your next visit to Chicago, he wants you to have dinner with someone, the son of a friend. A nice Tamil boy, he says. He thinks you'll like him.

Shefali falls asleep before you, and you lie there in the moonlight, tracing the line of her cheekbone with your eyes.

This was not the way you had wanted it to be.

Challah

Philadelphia, 1998

GABRIEL'S FATHER, SAUL, STOOD WITH THE OTHERS OF THE MINYAN
AND RAISED HIS VOICE IN THE KADDISH, PRAISING GOD'S GLORY. IT
was the last day of the thirty; after this, he would only say this kaddish
on the Yahrzeit, the anniversary of his wife Esther's death. His voice
was strong; it did not falter in its praise of God, though his face was
weary and his hands shook.

"*Yitgodal ve-yitkadash she-mei raba be-alma divera chirutei, ve-yamlich
malchutei bechayeichon uveyomeichon uvechayei dechol beit yisrael ba-agala
uvizman kariv, ve-imeru: amein.*"

Gabriel said the words as well, and would for the next ten months,
the duty of a son. He was glad to be able to honor his mother's memory, but the words tasted like ashes. This was the god his father
claimed would cast him out for his love of men. Gabriel did not know
how long he could continue to believe in, or praise, such a god. But for
now, his thoughts were on his mother—it was for her that he raised his
voice. He was grateful that there was this ritual connecting him with
his father—they had barely spoken otherwise since she died.

"*Ye-hei shemei raba mevarach le-alam ul'almei almaya. Yitbarach ve-*

yishtabach, ve-yitpa-ar ve-yitromam ve-yitnasei, ve-yit-hadar ve-yitaleh ve-yit-halal shemei dekudesha, berich hu, le-eila min kol birechata ve-shirata, tushbechata ve-nechemata da-amiran be-alma, ve-imeru: amein."

After the ritual was completed, the circle of old men dissolved, patting Gabriel's back consolingly as they went, saying to Saul, "At least you have a good son, a comfort to you. And a doctor—it is what his mother would have wanted." They did not mention what Esther would have said of her son's homosexuality; it was the sort of thing that wasn't spoken of, though everyone knew it. Gabriel had come out many years before, and though his mother had wanted him to marry, to have children, she had tried to understand, to accept, as his father never would. Gabriel could still hear her voice in the hallway, remonstrating with her husband—"He is our son! Our only son, and a good boy. Look how hard he studies, Saul. He is not a child anymore; we must leave him free to find his own way." And his father's pained response, "But *this* way, Esther? This is not right. Even the rabbi says . . ." And then his father would be off, quoting the rabbi, quoting the Torah, and Gabriel would pull a pillow over his head, blocking out the words. When he had finished school, left his parents' house in New York to study medicine and then to practice as an intern, a resident, in Philadelphia, he had been both saddened and relieved. It was easier to withstand his father's reprimands, his mother's sad eyes, when he didn't have to face them over the dinner table every night.

The last of his father's compatriots left, leaving father and son alone together.

"So." His father said the word heavily, and then fell into silence.

"Do you need anything?" Gabriel asked. "Groceries?"

His father shook his head. "No, no—you know the widow Rabinowitz? Already she is sniffing around, bringing kugels, fresh lox and bagels, chicken soup."

"How are her matzo balls?"

"Heh. Not so good as your mother's."

"No. No, of course not." His mother hadn't been much of a cook, actually, but there were a few things Esther did well. She made delicious matzo balls, firm without being heavy. And her challah was astonishing, the envy of the neighborhood. She had taught Gabriel to make it as well, since she had not been blessed with daughters; she had been pleased with his interest. "So, there are good things to this *gayness* of yours," Esther had said. "An interest in cooking—and maybe you'll change your mind someday, and my challah will help you catch a wife?" Gabriel had only smiled and shook his head, his hands busy mixing the flour and water, kneading the dough, separating it into three strands and then braiding them together to form the loaf. Esther always did the last step, brushing the egg wash over the top. Now he would have to do that part himself.

"I'll come for Shabbat," Gabriel offered, as he shrugged on his coat.

"If you're busy at the hospital, don't worry about it," Saul said, turning away to find his own coat on the rack, pulling it on.

"I'll come." He patted his father awkwardly on the arm—since Gabriel had come out, his father had avoided hugging him. "Be well." Then he turned and went out the door, leaving his father standing there in the empty hall.

"I'M SORRY . . ."

Gabriel looked up from his patient notes the following Thursday to see another doctor standing next to the small cafeteria table. The man gestured out, to indicate the unusually crowded room; there wasn't an empty table available. Gabriel felt a brief flash of irritation—he had wanted to finish going over these files. But it wasn't the man's fault that the room was so full. Gabriel cleared away the notes, making a space where the man could put down his tray. "No, no—it's fine." And it *was* fine; now that his momentary irritation had passed, Gabriel was free to appreciate the man's good looks—his slender, tall frame and sharp-boned face. Gabriel couldn't quite place his ethnicity—

Hispanic? He needed a haircut but was otherwise neatly turned out, from his pressed white coat to his creased tan slacks. "I'm Gabriel. Pediatrics—I don't think we've met?"

The man sat down and smiled briefly, revealing a row of even teeth, very white. He really had a very attractive mouth. "Roshan— but I am only an intern." He had an accent, mild and pleasant, halfway between Indian and British to Gabriel's untrained ear. "General medicine for now."

"Well, welcome." The intern status explained the need for a haircut, and the dark circles under Roshan's eyes. Gabriel remembered his own intern year, four years previous. He had thought he'd never again get enough sleep. "Where are you coming from?" The new interns had been around for a few months, but work had been so hectic lately that Gabriel had been skimping on the requisite social functions. And then, with his mother's death . . .

"I am from Sri Lanka, originally, but most recently San Francisco," Roshan said, as he started to spoon Jell-O into that perfect mouth.

"Really?" Gabriel felt his interest piqued. There were plenty of straight boys in San Francisco, of course, but still. "Did you like it there?"

"I liked it very much," Roshan said seriously. Gabriel thought he could get to really like that serious tone, the formality of it. It was charming. And then Roshan smiled again. "But it was too close to my parents."

Gabriel laughed out loud then, because even with the recent loss of his mother, he knew exactly what that felt like. If Roshan was an intern, he was probably about twenty-four, twenty-five? Gabriel remembered that age very well. "Tell me about it."

After a brief pause, Roshan did.

THAT NIGHT, GABRIEL FOUND HIMSELF MARVELING AT HOW LITTLE contrast there actually was between their skin tones. He himself was swarthy, as his father and grandfather had been. Esther had been fair-skinned and blonde, but none of that had come down to him. Roshan said that he was unusually light-skinned for a South Asian; his mother was Sinhalese, her family originally from northern India. He had inherited her skin, the bones of her face.

"Your mother must be very beautiful," Gabriel said, as he traced his fingers across Roshan's bare and hairless chest. He could feel Roshan flush at the compliment.

"Actually, she isn't very attractive—a little heavy, and sharp-featured." He smiled. "But my father loves her very much."

"And does she love him?" Gabriel asked the question idly, but then found himself oddly curious to hear the response. Roshan paused a moment before answering.

"I think so. It's hard to tell with her; she's very reserved."

Gabriel thought, though he didn't say it, that that was something else Roshan had inherited from his mother. Roshan had been almost silent during the long hours of their lovemaking, though he had seemed to enjoy himself.

"You should probably get going," Gabriel said regretfully. He had been comparing their skin tones in the early-dawn light; they had been up all night, and Roshan was going to pay for it tonight; he was on call in the ICU. Two nights without sleep—Gabriel was barely thirty but already felt too old to handle that.

"Yes." Roshan rose gracefully from Gabriel's bed, sliding one slender hand along Gabriel's wiry body, patting his cock one last time before pulling entirely away. He started to pull on his clothes—he would shower at the hospital, no doubt, change into a spare set of clothes there. Gabriel lived on Lombard, only a few blocks from the hospital, which made life much easier; he walked in every day. Philly was a good city to walk in, and the hospital was in the old part of town, with its cobblestoned streets. It cheered him up every morning, just walking to work. There was so much history in those streets, so much sense of place.

Gabriel watched Roshan dress, then asked, from the safety of his bed, "Do you want to hook up again sometime?" It was never easy, asking that, no matter how many men he had brought home to this tiny, cluttered apartment. It would be nice, not to have to ask that again, to have someone he could take for granted, could rely on to be there. Since his mother had died, he'd been wanting that more strongly than ever before, wanting an anchor he could hold on to.

Roshan hesitated before answering, and Gabriel felt his own skin flushing. But before he could get too embarrassed, Roshan said, "I would like to see you again. But there are . . . complications."

"Oh?"

"I am not . . . out. At the hospital. Or—at all, really."

"I see." Gabriel felt a flash of disappointment—he always found it exhausting, pretending to not be involved with someone, being careful to not touch them in public, not hold hands, not say anything that might be incriminating. That was why he had come out in high school, so long ago; he just got so sick of lying. But Roshan would hardly be the first closeted man he'd dated. Sometimes, they changed their minds. "I can cope with that. If that's all . . ."

"It is not." Roshan sat down then, on the edge of the bed. His hands were opening and closing, unconsciously, as he sought the words he wanted. The words ended up being simple, in the end. "I am married."

And now that flash of disappointment expanded into a burning anger. "You didn't think that was worth mentioning? What's your wife going to think now? Are you going to tell her you had to spend an extra night at work?" The man didn't even have the consideration to call his wife—Gabriel hadn't left his side for the last twelve hours. "You're not going to stay closeted for long if you keep pulling tricks like this!"

"It is not like that, Gabriel . . ." He rose again, took a step back toward the door.

"Look, I don't care what plan you have for getting around your wife. I don't give a damn about her—but you could have told me before you fucked me. You don't even wear a ring!" Gabriel was careful about that; he had dated a married guy once before, when he was very young, and it had just about broken his heart into pieces when the guy refused to leave his wife to be with him. Gabriel had sworn that he'd never get in that situation again. And now here he was, and fine, he wasn't in love with Roshan yet, but he'd been headed that way. The guy was so hot, and smart, and, okay, exotic, strange, different—it had definitely been a turn-on, learning Roshan had grown up in another country, had only come to the United States after he'd turned ten. Gabriel already loved the way he talked, the formal speech patterns, the accent. And the perfectly groomed fingernails, the painfully white teeth—and the contrast between all of that and the few whispered obscenities Roshan had let out in the darkest hours of the night, when Gabriel was riding him, hips pressed hard against Roshan's sweet ass . . . But the man was a liar, a cheat. "I think you'd better leave." Gabriel pulled the sheets over his naked body, searching for a slender thread of dignity.

Roshan frowned and dug his hands into his pockets, looking bewildered, frustrated. "I do not know how to explain—wait, here!" He pulled out his wallet, and for a brief moment Gabriel thought that the man was going to offer him money; he felt his anger swell to an incandescent rage. But instead, Roshan rifled through and pulled out a slip of paper—it looked glossy, like magazine print. "Please, read this." Gabriel didn't reach out for the outstretched paper, and Roshan finally put it down on the chair by the bedroom. "Read this, Gabriel—then page me, if you are willing to talk. Please." He turned away then and walked out.

Gabriel stayed where he was until he heard the heavy front door close, locking with a firm click. Then he got up, went to read the slip of paper. It had obviously been cut from a magazine, creased and worn as if it had been sitting in that wallet for months. It said:

*Sri Lankan female, straight but not into serious relationships,
looking for gay South Asian male for sham marriage. Let's make our
parents happy. You know you want to.*

—*shefali@upenn.edu.*

He couldn't see Roshan that night, in any case—he had promised
his father that he would come for Shabbat. Gabriel left the city early,
took the train from Thirtieth Street Station to Penn Station; he normally found it a pleasant ride, and would often catch up on journals on
the way. But today he just stared out the window at the towns rumbling past. It was raining, the way it had been on the day they buried
Esther. When he got into the city, instead of changing to the subway
that would take him to his father's apartment, Gabriel climbed into a
cab and rode it out to the cemetery where they'd buried her.

There was grass growing on her muddy grave, but no flowers
planted. Gabriel felt a sharp pang of guilt—he had not been here since
the funeral, and he was sure his father hadn't been either. It had seemed
too hard, to come out here where her cold body lay, slowly decompos-
ing. He had wanted to cremate her, but Saul had been horrified at the
idea. So here she was, her bones slowly blending with the soil. Maybe
that was better; he could come here in the spring, spread flower seeds.
Esther had never been much of a gardener either—she hadn't been a
very practical woman at all. But she had loved flowers; Saul had always
made sure she had fresh flowers for the Shabbat table. Flowers and
song, bright colors and soft fabrics—anything beautiful, Esther had
loved. She hadn't liked rain; she would have been cold and unhappy in
weather like this. He hated to think of her out here in this weather.

"What do you think? Should I call him?"

Gabriel wasn't surprised to find himself talking to his dead
mother—she had always been easy to talk to. When he had come home
from high school senior year, head over heels in love and burning with
the desire to tell someone, it was his mother he had confessed to, terrified and exhilarated all at once, tears in his eyes. Esther had gone very

pale, her blue eyes even bluer against the whiteness of her face. But she had pulled him into a hug, had held him when he burst into tears. She had stood up to his father, had even gone out and bought him condoms, slipping them to him that night with a whispered injunction to *be safe, be happy.* More than a mother should be called to do, surely. And Roshan was beautiful; she could understand that.

But is he beautiful inside, my boychik? *That is what is important.*

She had known that—the beautiful Esther had married his father, after all, surely one of the ugliest men on God's green earth, almost a caricature of a stereotyped Jew with his massive nose, shrunken torso, fierce, squinty eyes. But a good man, an upright man of the community who had cherished his wife and had even tried, on occasion, to understand his wayward son.

Gabriel couldn't answer that question, he just didn't know. He stood in the rain a little longer, until he was quite thoroughly soaked. Then he heard his mother scolding him to go inside, go, even a big doctor can catch his death of cold. So he left the cemetery and got back in the cab.

HE HAD STOPPED ON THE WAY TO HIS FATHER, BOUGHT FLOWERS for the table. Nothing fancy—just some white carnations, fresh and simple. His father had grunted approval when Gabriel arrived with them clutched in a wet hand. "Your mother would have liked that." The rest of the meal was silent, except for the prayers. They had eaten store-bought bread, the widow Rabinowitz's soup, her chicken and kugel. Neither had eaten very much—grief was thick in the room, weighing heavy on their stomachs. When they finished, Gabriel washed the dishes while his father blew out the candles, put away the remaining food.

"I should get back," Gabriel said. "I have work in the morning." Work, and a decision to make. To call Roshan or not? He still didn't know. He wondered what his father would think if Roshan were a woman—would he be upset that she was brown-skinned, wasn't Jewish? Gabriel just didn't know.

"Yes, yes, of course."

Gabriel ached to see Saul like this, his face so lined, so old. "I'll be back next week, Dad. Call if you need anything." He pulled on his coat, still damp.

"Son." His father's face was abruptly stern. "You must not keep coming up here, every week. It is too far."

"I don't mind."

"No. I am telling you, no. I will be fine—there are more than enough people to pester me here. If the widow Rabinowitz doesn't drive me up the wall with her nagging, your mother's sisters will manage it nicely. You, stay there."

Gabriel felt a pang of bewildered grief—was his father rejecting him outright now? But then Saul reached out, took his son's head in both hands and pulled it toward him. He kissed Gabriel's forehead, then released him. "Go, son," he said gently. "Be safe. Be happy."

"You're sure?"

"I am certain." His father opened the door for him, said, "Come back in a month or two, tell me then what you've been doing."

"All right, then. Good night." Gabriel stepped out the door, heard it close behind him.

He started walking to the subway stop, still not sure what had just happened. Those had been his mother's words, the words Esther had said to him, the words she had undoubtedly said to his father. Gabriel didn't know what they meant. But he knew one thing—he would be calling Roshan after all, would at least let him explain what was really going on. Roshan deserved that chance at least, the opportunity to step forward, to tell the truth.

After that . . . well, after that, they would just see what happened. See if there would be an opportunity to find some happiness after all.

It was what his mother would have wanted.

Bodies in Motion

Chicago, 1999

CHAYA WASN'T SURE HOW SHE'D ENDED UP AT THE DUKE OF PERTH, SIPPING SCOTCH WITH DANIEL OWENS, WATCHING THE APRIL RAIN fall steadily through the foggy window of the pub. The sequence of events was clear enough: the e-mail arriving at the department, from Jenny, who had been her roommate in grad school. Inviting her to apply for a tenure-track job at UC Davis, with a possibility of preferred access to the big telescope at Keck Observatory. His interruption of her reading the letter, her explanation of her dazed state; his congratulations and offer of a celebratory dinner. She'd accepted and let him take her across town, to eat alone, together. That was strange enough. And now she was on her third shot of single-malt Scotch, which was unheard of. The events were clear, but her motives were opaque. She had sat mostly silent through dinner, letting Daniel's friendly babble fill the empty space.

When she finally spoke, her words dropped into a stream of his chatter, like heavy stones.

"I don't know if I should apply."

"But it sounded like she was practically promising you the job..."

"That's not it."

Daniel's mouth started to open again—she could practically see the flurry of words resting on his tongue, eager to leap out. But he closed his mouth, trapping the words behind his teeth, his firm lips. Daniel laced his fingers together under his chin and sat there, waiting. He had nice hands, with long, thin fingers. Chaya had noticed them before. Two more glasses of Macallan arrived, and she took one in her own hands, staring down into the clear liquid.

"I can't leave my mother." Twenty-nine years old, and she couldn't leave her mother? She didn't owe Daniel an explanation, but the words were whispering in her throat, wanting to come out. She couldn't say them to anyone else—she'd had a few friends in grad school, but hadn't really made any at UIC. Why not Daniel? He was there, after all. And a live band was playing at the front of the pub, not too loud, but loud enough. No one else would hear.

"My father died when I was eleven. It was a car accident. Black ice on the road, a winter storm. We were driving home after one of my piano recitals, and we just skidded off the road and slammed into a tree." There was more to the story than that—Chaya remembered leaving the recital, her father pushing her into the right front seat, her mother crying, climbing quickly into the back before the car started and raced away. No one had ever told her what was going on that day, why everyone was acting so strangely. After the accident, she hadn't asked. She had felt, obscurely, that it was somehow her fault, though she didn't know why. After the accident, she hadn't talked about her father at all. "My mother was eight months pregnant, but she was barely hurt. None of us were, actually, not by the impact. Just thrown around a little, and my mom went into labor early. But my father had a heart attack, from the shock, and died."

Chaya had never told the story out loud before, and she was surprised at how calmly she was telling it now—eighteen years made a difference. It had all been a long time ago.

It was only when Daniel wrapped his hands around hers that

Chaya realized that she was shaking, and that she had spilled Scotch all over her hands, all over the dark wood of the table. She felt a brief desire to pull her hands away from him, but she forced herself to leave them. He was steadying her; it felt good. It helped her keep talking. Chaya was fighting waves of nausea, though perhaps those were from the thick fried smell of fish and chips, wafting past their table, trailing a waitress loaded with plates.

"So my mother, who was only twenty-nine—that's how old I am now—my mother was left with an eleven-year-old daughter and a premature baby girl. My mom's parents helped us, but they died a few years ago. My dad had been estranged from his family; I don't know why. They've never spoken to us, I never even met them, though my grandmother on that side did send some money for the funeral.

"My aunts, my mother's sisters, all helped raise us, but they have families and careers of their own. Savitha, my sister, got married this year—she married a cousin, actually. They moved away a month ago, without saying a word to anyone. They sent one postcard from the road just telling us that they had gotten married—no address, no phone. She hasn't written again or called since she left."

Her voice dropped a little, so that Daniel had to lean closer to hear. "So that leaves me. My mother—she's not strong, since my father died. I can't leave."

Chaya expected Daniel to try to persuade her to go—but he just kept holding her hands, safe in his. His eyes were fixed on their hands, pressed against the scarred wood with its unsteady lines carved by legions of sloshed patrons. When he finally spoke, he didn't look up.

"I'm sorry to hear about your father, Chaya, and sorry for your sake that you won't be going to California. But I'm not sorry that you're planning to stay here for a while longer."

Daniel looked up then, and Chaya was startled to find that she wasn't surprised by what she saw in his face. It wasn't love. But there was concern, and desire. She wasn't surprised—maybe she'd known for months, since she first met him last August. Had he been watching her? Had she really not noticed? But he'd always respected her boundaries, kept a friendly professional distance.

Chaya shook her hands loose from his. She dried them slowly on her napkin. Part of her wanted to just run out the door, disappear into the rain, dissolve. But she liked Daniel. He sent her almost-funny astronomy jokes culled from the Net; he liked to stop by her barely open door, pushing it open further to share a tidbit of department gossip. He had bright green eyes; Daniel seemed happy with his life. Somehow, those had never seemed good enough reasons before; she wasn't sure what had changed. Had anything changed?

Starting with the spilled liquid, Chaya wiped the table clean, meticulously. Daniel watched until she finished. Then she carefully, precisely, put her hands out again, and he took them in his. He leaned forward, and so did she. When they finally kissed, it was the very lightest brush of lips.

CHAYA BURST OUT OF HER MOTHER'S DOOR, HER BOOTS SLOSHING through puddles—it was still raining almost every day, though the calendar now claimed it was May. Her mouth was pressed tight, her head tucked down. From the door, her mother called out to her, "Don't be so sensitive!" before letting it slam closed. Behind that door, the conversation of her mother and aunts would continue, the endless conversation. Chaya wrapped her arms tightly around herself and continued to march down the sidewalk. She circled the block, her thoughts running in circles too.

Every time Chaya went home, all four of her aunts came by the house. Every single one had to hug her, kiss her, pinch her waist, and say she was putting on a little weight, wasn't she. Well, to be fair, Leilani Aunty usually didn't participate in the poking and squeezing; she preferred to lean against the kitchen counter and watch the show—but she was a poet, unmarried and strange. The others would tug at her hair, checking if it was still strong, still thick, until Chaya felt like a horse being readied for sale. Her mother would even come pry her mouth open and check her teeth. "Brushing every morning? Every night? Flossing?"

Chaya would endure, would bite the inside of her cheek until it bled, would wash the salt blood away with her tongue, telling herself they meant well. But this last year, her visits to Oakbrook had grown less and less frequent, though it was only half an hour away from her Greektown condo.

It wasn't as if she were pretty like her sister, Savitha, who would sometimes indulge her mother and be slim and fair and beautiful in pale pink saris. Chaya always refused to wear them; she wore sensible slacks and Gap button-down shirts. She had a good postdoc now, had published a few papers. She was reasonably confident that she could find a tenure-track job in the Chicago area in a year or two, if they would just leave her alone to work in peace. Some of the aunts were academics—they should have understood. But they never talked to her about her work; it was always marriage, marriage and babies.

She could have told them about Daniel—he wouldn't even be the first white boy in the family. One of the aunts had scandalized everyone by marrying a white boy, decades ago. But it was all so new, so fragile. Chaya couldn't bear to put him under their lens.

After circling the block for the third time, she finally stopped at her car. Chaya unlocked the door, climbed in, pulled her seat belt on. She was fanatic about seat belts. She put the key in the ignition and started the car. She bit her cheek again, closed her eyes, opened them, deliberately released her sore cheek, and then smoothly pulled out. It was late, and she was teaching tomorrow morning—Chaya knew she should go home. But she could never sleep when she was feeling this crazy; work was the only thing that would help her. She could work all night, teach in the morning, and then sleep. Daniel would understand.

She drove at precisely fifty-five on the highway all the way back to her office.

SHE'D WANTED TO BE UNDER THE STARS FOR IT, HAD WANTED EVERY-thing to be as perfect as she could make it. Chaya had gone to the doctor, gotten a prescription for the pill. Daniel had suggested condoms, and maybe it was silly of her to prefer not to, but he didn't complain. In some ways, condoms would have been easier, would have kept a distinct separation between them. But separation wasn't what she wanted. As they waited the weeks until the pills took effect, the weather warmed. It seemed the perfect conjunction in late May, when it was finally safe, and warm, enough.

The hardest part had been letting him touch her. Hands were relatively easy. She had had to shake hands often. But anything more was almost impossible—she'd endured so many embraces. *Poor fatherless child*, they said, clicking their tongues in sympathy, reaching to pull her into their sticky, smelly arms. She'd been lost in folds of shifting silk. Her mother had clung to her, pulling her around by the arm like a rag doll, making Chaya sit on her lap when the baby was asleep. Chaya had closed herself away, placed her secret self in a deep chamber of her heart, and only when she was alone did she let it come out again. When she climbed the long flights of stairs to the roof of her apartment, lugging her homemade Dobsonian, the telescope she'd built herself, bundled in layers of thick wool, suffering the cold because if she plugged in a portable heater, any heat would rise, obscuring the view—she saw the stars, and they saw her.

Chaya endured her family because she had to, but until Daniel, she let no one else touch her.

She was learning to take pleasure from his touch. Chaya didn't invite him to her apartment—that was her place, her sanctuary. Even her mother wasn't allowed there. But she spent hours in Daniel's bed, where he slowly persuaded her to open her body to him. He didn't talk much in bed, and she was grateful. It meant she didn't have to talk either, which made it all easier. She closed her eyes and let him touch her, closed her eyes while he unbuttoned and removed her shirt. Music often played on the stereo, something sweet and Scottish, and Chaya lost herself in it, smothering her worries deep enough beneath the music that she could continue onward.

They spoke with their bodies, with leanings and touchings and gentle fingers. Daniel kissed patterns along her body, points of light that connected in strange and shivering nets. The first time she came, with his mouth between her thighs and her fingers tangled in his red hair, their bodies covered in sweat, Chaya felt herself an exploding nova, racing outward, expanding furiously, and then, slowly, coalescing again into inert matter.

In late May they drove north, over the border to Wisconsin, and hiked through the woods until they were nowhere near anywhere or anyone. The stars were bright and unblinking, a brilliant profusion, far away from the haze of city lights. It was in an unnamed field, a cow pasture, that Daniel entered her. Chaya lay below him, looking up at the luxuriant night sky. If the grass was itchy and the air cold, she didn't notice.

"TALK TO ME."

Daniel's voice was soft, and Chaya knew it would remain so, but she could hear the frustration underneath. Only a month had gone by, but they had already had this conversation too many times.

"There's nothing to say. Come to bed." She lay beneath the white sheets, waiting for him. He paced up and down by the window, and she watched his pale muscles moving in the moonlight.

"Something's wrong, and you won't talk about it!"

Chaya didn't know what he wanted; she didn't know what to say. "Daniel, come to bed." In bed, she could talk to him with arms and legs, with soft moans and hurried breaths. Couldn't the opening of her body be the answer to his questions? "Nothing's wrong, nothing's changed."

He stopped pacing and stared at her. "That's right. That's exactly it. Nothing changes, Chaya. I don't know where I am in your sky, but it's impossibly distant, and I can't move closer to you." Daniel sank down on the edge of the bed and took her bare feet in his hands, squeezing gently. "All we do is have sex. I want you to talk to me. Tell me about your family, your childhood. Tell me your dreams—or hell, your nightmares. Anything! This silence—it's driving me crazy. Don't you get it?"

Chaya shook her head and her hair swung loosely. She was growing it because Daniel liked long hair. He had never said so, but his fingers reached for her hair and tangled happily there during sex; she could tell he'd like it longer. How many times had her mother told her to grow her hair, and how many times had Chaya ignored her? And now she was growing it for Daniel—couldn't he see how she felt? She wore earrings now, gold hoops, and sometimes even bangles on her wrists. She tried to be beautiful for him.

She was good with math, good with small, precise calculations. If Chaya added this to that, then looked over there, in exactly the right place—she'd find the hidden star. A tiny bit off, subtraction instead of addition, a misplaced decimal, and it would be lost to her sight, lost in the expanse of constantly moving celestial bodies, and the vast spaces between them. But she rarely lost a star. She didn't know words— bodies in motion, that was what she knew. That was all she knew. He was an astronomer too, so why wasn't it enough for him?

Daniel sighed. He continued to hold her feet, and after a time his fingers started to caress them, tracing the instep while Chaya tried not to jerk them away. Eventually, his hands moved up her legs, and she gratefully parted them for him. As he bent to kiss her, he said softly, "Talk to me . . ."

JULY WAS BLAZING THAT YEAR. CHAYA SPENT MOST OF HER TIME IN her air-conditioned office, and when Daniel came by, she was always too busy running analyses to talk. His apartment wasn't air-conditioned, so they weren't having much sex. Once or twice, they used the upholstered chair in the office Daniel shared, but his office-mate was often around, even at night. It wasn't very comfortable in any case.

By the end of the month, Daniel was stopping by less often than he had been. Chaya's hair was still growing, but she wasn't sure why.

THE END, WHEN IT CAME, WAS NOT UNEXPECTED. THE HURT, BEWIL-dered look in Daniel's eyes had faded, and Chaya had no trouble read-ing the pure frustration that replaced it. The night he chose to break up with her, she watched him pace around his living room, building up his nerve while she turned the pages of a book she wasn't reading. Her heart twisted, and she decided to make it easier for him. Chaya closed the book and said, "We need to talk."

It went quickly after that. She said that she was sorry, but this wasn't working. He politely protested, but not for long. Daniel said he'd always care for her. She didn't say that her chest felt as if it were being pierced by long, thin knives, that her throat felt like it was being choked of air, strangled by a Thuggee's silk cord. Daniel gave her a long hug, and she tried not to go stiff in his arms. Chaya kissed him once, gently. He offered to drive her home, and she said she'd rather walk the twelve blocks.

"Are you sure?"

Chaya nodded. He walked her to the door, and she went out into the night.

The stars were shining brightly, in a sky unnaturally clear for that time of year. It didn't seem appropriate; it should have been a cloudy night. But at least it meant that she didn't have to stay home in her empty apartment. Chaya picked up the Dobsonian, loaded it in her car, and drove north until she found a good cow pasture, wide and open and relatively free of cows. She watched the stars all night, counting them, naming them, the way she had as a little girl, sitting on the back porch and leaning against her father's strong arms.

He had introduced her to the constellations, had traced the outline of Orion's belt, his scabbard. Her father hadn't been a scientist, or even an intellectual. But he had loved the stars, had talked about how he'd like to take her on a rocket ship and go out there someday, just the two of them. Go out and visit the moon, or Mars—and just keep going, out and out. Leaning against her father, Chaya had always felt as if she knew exactly where she was, and where she was going.

When Daniel had held her in his arms, she had felt just a little of that feeling again.

SHE WENT OFF THE PILL. THERE SEEMED NO REASON TO CONTINUE with it after he left. Chaya knew she should date, should try to meet someone else—but why? The gaps were too large, the spaces unbridgeable. No matter how precise your calculations, people never moved along the expected paths—she hadn't dated anyone before Daniel, but she had always known that was true, had felt the certainty buried deep within her, where logic couldn't reach. She had not known how to warn Savitha before her sister married and moved away. She had never known how to say this to her mother, how to say it without reminding her of Appa.

Her mother knew nothing of Daniel's presence, then absence, in her life. Her mother still said to her, "Chaya, what about this one? Dr. Singh's son—medical school at Northwestern, so close, and handsome too."

"Not right now, Amma. I don't have time to take care of a husband."

Her mother sighed. "You're getting so thin, Chaya; you're not eating right. Just settle down with a nice boy—let him take care of you! No wonder none of you modern girls are getting married; you're too self-sufficient. You think you don't need anyone."

In mid-September, Daniel knocked on her door. It was bright and sunny that day—one of those brief warm days that come to Chicago in September. Yet he looked cold. Maybe that was why she let him in. Daniel hated the cold; he did all his viewing from inside insulated control centers, protected by thick layers of glass. He should never have become an astronomer.

"Nice place," he said.

"Thanks."

They stood there for a moment with the door still open, and then he stepped forward, letting it close behind him. Daniel stepped forward, and Chaya stepped into his arms. He bent his head down and took her face in his hands; he began kissing her. Fierce, hard kisses, oddly contrasted with the gentleness of his hands. He lifted his head for a moment to start to talk, "Chaya . . ."

"Shh . . . ," she said, and went up on her toes to kiss him again. Her lips were aching for his.

They didn't make it to the bedroom—they slid down to the floor. Chaya didn't know what to say to Daniel, whether to tell him to stay or go, but her fingers were unbuttoning his shirt, unbuckling his belt. His hands slid under her shirt, caressed her spine, unhooked her bra, and cupped her breasts. Their bodies knew how to speak to each other. His mouth was on her skin and her mouth was on his skin.

Very quickly they were both naked enough on the scratchy carpet, and he was whispering her name as he slid into her. Was it then that she remembered? Was it then that Chaya said softly, "No . . ."—while her body strained up to meet him? There was no time to explain the why of it, almost no time at all between his first feverish, frantic entry and their mutual explosion. Just time enough for confusion to taint it all, and afterward she lay with his face against her neck, his mouth still whispering her name.

She didn't explain. Daniel started to say something about missing her, needing her, wanting to work things out. Chaya pulled away and dressed again. She asked him to go.

After Daniel left, she climbed into her old rocking chair, pulling her legs up to her chest. Chaya started to rock; as she rocked, she replayed the scene in her mind, the moments when he knocked on the door, the kiss, the undressing, the entry, the protest, the conclusion. Or was it the protest, the entry, the conclusion? Or even the entry, the conclusion, with no protest at all? Chaya didn't know. She did not know what she had said with her atrophied mouth, and the language of the body had betrayed her.

Tomorrow she would go to a clinic, minimize the consequences. And after that—she didn't know.

CHAYA DIDN'T KNOW WHEN EVERYONE LEARNED ABOUT THE NEW woman. She only knew that she was the last to find out, in the bitter cold of late November.

She learned from the silences. Colleagues would either fall silent as she walked into a room or turn and heartily greet her: "Chaya! So, what are you working on these days?" She hadn't even realized that they had known about her and Daniel—Chaya had thought it was private, their own secret, but clearly her colleagues had known. Oh, everyone was very kind, very tactful. If they had been less so, perhaps she would have found out sooner, and been saved some embarrassment.

Daniel was engaged. What was worse, as Chaya discovered, was that he had started dating the woman, a young poli sci professor, in August. Chaya didn't know whether it had happened before or after they'd broken up, and she wasn't going to ask Daniel. But it had started before the incident at Chaya's apartment, which raised unpleasant questions of what else Daniel hadn't told her. The questions spun in her head, tracing new elliptical paths. Chaya had almost decided, at the end of October, that she should call Daniel. Had almost decided that she should trust him, had been persuading herself to try to forgive him for that day, for what had happened, *if* it had happened ...

Chaya had stared at the phone, cursing her indecision. She had almost called a dozen, a hundred times. She was lucky she had not.

Perhaps she should tell him that.

She wasn't getting any work done anyway. Hadn't accomplished anything productive in weeks. In a few days she'd be flying to Tucson for some time on the big telescope at Kitt Peak. The time had been scheduled months ago; Chaya had been so pleased when her proposal had been approved, with three whole nights of observation. Enough time to gather the evidence that might actually prove her latest theory. But now she couldn't bring herself to care; lately, Chaya hadn't even been going up on the roof. She just sat in her office, stared at the computer, and stewed.

On the first day of December, Chaya cut her hair, so short that the ice wind bit at her ears. Windchill put the temperature at minus fifteen, with worse to come. She didn't care.

CHAYA KNOCKED ON DANIEL'S DOOR.

He opened it, and Chaya stood there in the doorway, looking in at the place that was achingly familiar. The white couch with the pillows arranged just so. The tidy bookshelves and desk. The soft grey rug. Daniel was a neat man—that had surprised her when she first came here. She had expected something more chaotic. There were a few changes now; bright paintings hung on the walls, cheerful abstracts in orange and red. The poli sci woman.

"Is she here?"

"No, Laurie's out of town for the week. Conference." Daniel stepped aside, and Chaya came in.

Chaya wasn't sure what she was expecting. Daniel, to his credit, did not immediately try to make love to her once the door closed. That argued well for him; perhaps he hadn't been dating Laurie yet when he came to Chaya's apartment that day. Daniel didn't even step toward her. Chaya didn't know why he did, or didn't, though. *Why* had become important.

"Why didn't you stop?" She said it abruptly, with no prelude—if she'd worked up to it, she wouldn't have been able to say it at all. That was how words so often behaved; fine in her head but choked in her throat, smothered in her mouth. So this time Chaya simply spit them out, without thinking about it.

"What?" Daniel looked completely confused.

"That time, at my apartment"—her voice rose in volume with each phrase—"why didn't you stop when I asked you to? Why didn't you stop when I said no?" Chaya was shouting. She had prided herself on never shouting in a family of frequent screaming fights. Chaya had always been the calm, contained, quiet one, but now, if she didn't shout, she would cry, and crying was unacceptable. "I trusted you!"

Daniel looked blank, bewildered, even a little angry. He didn't say anything at first, though—he just looked at her. Finally, he sank down onto the couch and started to speak. "Okay, I think there's some confusion here. Could we just go over this slowly?" He paused, but Chaya said nothing.

Daniel continued. "I'm sorry that I left when I did. I'm sorry that I started sleeping with Laurie right after we broke up. I'm sorry I didn't come after you sooner. I'm sorry I didn't talk to you first when I did come after you, and I'm particularly sorry that I didn't tell you about Laurie then." He paused again, but Chaya still didn't speak. Daniel went on, slower. "I meant to talk to you, but I had missed you so much. When I saw you, my body just took over. I'm sorry that I just let you send me away that day, that I didn't stay, or at least come back. Maybe things would have worked out differently." He shrugged.

Chaya's shoulders had relaxed a little, and her arms loosened. As she started to open her mouth, Daniel held up a hand. "Hang on. I wasn't done. I'm sorry for all of that, but you weren't exactly clear with me either. And more importantly, I also don't know what you're talking about, when you ask me why I didn't stop. I thought you wanted it . . . and Laurie and I had only slept together a few times at that point . . . and we'd been using condoms, if that's what you're worried about. I didn't put you at any risk." Daniel sounded almost indignant now.

"I wasn't on the pill."

Daniel hunched over slightly, as if his stomach hurt. "Jesus. I didn't know."

"I know that." Chaya's face was completely still. "That's why I said no, why I told you to stop."

Daniel's pale face grew even paler. "You didn't. I swear it, you didn't say anything at all. You just kissed me, and pulled me down, and took off my clothes. You didn't say a word. You never do. Trust me, if you had said anything, I would have noticed!"

Chaya stared at him, just stared, while her mind went back to that day in September. Had she actually said it at all, or had she simply thought it? Chaya bit her lip, wondering if she had ever really believed it, or if she had just convinced herself that she did, so she would have an excuse, a reason to be angry with him. What was wrong with her?

Daniel asked, in a voice suddenly rough, "Did you really think I could do that to you?"

Chaya shook her head, realizing that no, she didn't really believe it. She started to cry. Tears welled up, as if the ice in her chest were melting, as if she were flooding, drowning. She walked over to Daniel and, shaking, held out her hands to him.

"Hey . . . ," he said, and pulled her down to the couch, into his arms. Chaya huddled there, with her face pressed against him, sobbing until his shirt was soaked, her fingers digging into his chest while he slowly rocked her, whispering soft reassurances.

Chaya's head was pounding by the time she stopped, her eyes aching with soreness. She had to breathe through her mouth; she couldn't seem to clear her nose. Daniel still held her tight, and she felt oddly safe, almost as if she were cradled in the limbs of a tree, so solid and deeply rooted that it couldn't be shaken. When she was finally still, breathing slow and deep, his arms tightened around her. He said, "You're not...?"

"No." His arms relaxed. Relief, plain and clear in the body whose language she had once spoken so intimately. That hurt too.

"So, you're engaged." Daniel nodded, his chin against the top of her head. "Do you love her?"

He didn't hesitate. "Yes. I know it was fast, but yes. I love Laurie very much."

Oddly, that wasn't as painful as Chaya might have expected. Did she still love him? Had she ever?

"We've got lots of talking to do," Daniel said quietly.

Chaya took a deep breath. She pulled back a little—just enough to talk, but not enough to let go. Not yet.

THEY KEPT TALKING, MOSTLY ON THE PHONE. DANIEL MADE HER A deal—for every story he told her about his life, his family, Chaya had to tell him one of hers. Laurie wasn't thrilled, but she apparently believed in being civilized about such things. The wedding was still on schedule. Chaya thought she was actually glad of that.

It was hard at first, getting the words out. She tried closing her eyes and pretending she was talking to herself, but the words still stuck in her throat. Finally she took to typing the words on her laptop, and then reading them back to him on the phone. It was ridiculous, she knew. But it worked, and after a few conversations, she didn't need the laptop anymore.

They talked for hours, until Chaya's ears were actually ringing, until her neck ached from holding the phone. Words came spilling out of her like waterfalls from the rocks, and she was giddy with the pleasure of it. She had never thought that talking could be so intoxicating.

Work improved—the time in Tucson went very well, and the analysis of the data went even better. She presented a preliminary talk on it at a conference over the holiday break. In mid-January, Jenny called. The position at Davis was still open, very much so, and they were excited about her current line of work. Chaya told Jenny she'd think seriously about the job.

IT WAS EARLY FEBRUARY WHEN HER MOTHER CONFRONTED HER.

"So. You're going to California?" Her mother talked loudly over the whirring of the mixer; she was making caramel pudding.

"What?" Chaya flushed. Maybe she should pretend she hadn't heard that. She had almost decided to go, but she wasn't ready for this conversation, for her mother's threats and complaints—she hadn't prepared . . .

"It's warmer there," her mother continued, relentlessly. "And you can keep an eye on your sister."

"Davis isn't so close to Berkeley." Chaya turned away from the stove, where she was toasting almonds.

"Not so far either. Don't burn the nuts. I'm worried about her—she isn't sensible, like you. Maybe if you settle down there, you'll find a husband. And with both you girls out of the house, I can finally take a vacation. I've never been to Sri Lanka myself, you know. Not in all these years."

Her mother's voice was firm, calm. She didn't seem worried at all—and since when did she think Chaya was sensible? The impossible suddenly was becoming possible. Chaya turned back to flip the nuts. If her mother didn't need her now—had her mother ever needed her?

Maybe Chaya had just wanted to be needed, to have a clear place and purpose, even if it had meant going nowhere.

DANIEL THOUGHT SHE SHOULD GO TOO, THOUGH HE SAID HE WOULD miss her. Chaya stopped trying to argue against it when she realized that three drafts of letters to Davis now sat on her computer, and that she was already thinking about what to take with her, and what to leave behind.

It would be something new. Something strange, and different—a shift away from her fixed orbits, a chance to leave these endless circlings and chart her own unique path.

The morning of the day she was leaving, Chaya went to the cemetery where her father was buried. She still didn't know what had happened that day of the concert. She didn't know why her mother, her aunts, had always refused to talk about her father. There were secrets in her family, things unspoken; it was the way things were, the way they had always been. But as she bent to lay roses on her father's grave, Chaya made a silent promise to him—that she would do things differently from now on. That she would tell her own story, at least, without hesitation. And she swore that the next time someone trusted her with his body, his heart, she would trust him back. Before it was too late.

Minal in Winter

Chicago, 1999

Dear Raji Aunty,

I hope you and Vivek Uncle are well. How is the painting going? The painting you sent on my birthday—of the women bathing at the waterfall—hangs over my bed. I think my mother would be shocked, but my roommates are very impressed that I have an aunt who paints such things. The women in their bright saris remind me of home ...

All my letters to my aunt start like that, and never finish. I have written twenty or thirty of them in the last week. Words and lines and paragraphs of politeness, all true and all lies. I cannot write what I am really saying. I cannot write that I am in terrible trouble, and I don't know what to do. I cannot write that I want to leave here, leave school, leave Chicago and flee to her in Massachusetts, that I want to hide in her guest bed with the covers pulled up over my head until it all goes away. I cannot write and ask her to fix everything for me. I cannot do anything but write and write and write these letters that say nothing and that I crumple up and throw away before starting again.

Dear Raji Aunty,

I hope you and Vivek Uncle are well. I am not. How is the painting going? The painting you sent of the practically naked women, with the water coursing over the bared necks and pointed breasts and arched backs, makes me think that maybe you might understand and be able to help me. Didn't you have a scandalous youth, once upon a time? The aunts always fell silent when I entered the room, but I heard bits, fragments, perhaps just words I wanted to hear. A scandalous youth, and a white man for a lover—but now you are married to a nice Sri Lankan man. You are married married married. How can I talk to you?

MINAL BARELY NOTICES WHEN HER ROOMMATES COME BACK, WHEN they ask her to join them for dinner, when she shakes her head no, when they leave again. The snow is falling outside their window, and she takes her unfinished letter to Rose's bed, to sit near the window and watch the snow fall on the highway and the lake, watch the waves crashing up and down, higher each time, the wind whipping them up until the white ice of them crashes up and over the thin strip of snow-covered park, reaching to the deserted highway. It is terrifying. The monsoons had been hard and fierce at times, had uprooted trees and drowned the fields—but they had never been so cold.

She has been cold for months.

She had arrived in September, fresh off the boat from Sri Lanka, with a full scholarship for the sciences and plans to be a doctor. Her mother had insisted Minal wear the warmest clothes she had, so she had sweltered in the layers of heavy sari and warm sweater on the long plane ride, and still, when she stepped out of the airport and into the brisk wind, she had instantly been cold, chilled through. Her mother's sister, Raji, had flown from Massachusetts to Chicago to get her settled, had taken her shopping for more appropriate clothes, had made sure that she drank hot tea and soup and even fried samosas for her in the dorm kitchen—and Minal was still cold, deep inside. The chill had deepened when her aunt left, leaving her alone with her roommates, who seemed nice enough but who were so terribly pale and alien.

She wore a turtleneck, shirt, heavier shirt, sweater, stiff new blue jeans, two pairs of socks, and a thick wool coat. She shivered in the unforgiving stone buildings that wore the artificial heat like a thin blanket over grave-cold bones. Calculus class, high on the third floor of a grey Gothic building, was the coldest. The first weeks she spent huddled in on herself at her desk, only raising her head long enough to copy down the equations on the board. Minal would practically race back to her dorm afterward, to strip off all the clothes, turning the water on with shaking hands and chattering teeth, waiting until the tiny bathroom was full of steam before taking off the last layers, stripping to the skin and climbing into the blessedly warm water.

The water covered her toes, her feet, her ankles, her calves—and then she sank down into it, so that it covered her stomach and ribs and small, pointed breasts, lay back in it, so that her hair was soaked in water, spreading out around her like a night-black fan, lay back until only her nose and mouth lay on the surface of the water, disembodied. Steam filled the room, her bones warmed, she was happy—but eventually, always, the hot water would run out, and she would have to climb out of the tub, dry off, wrap her thin body in a robe and step out into the chilly air that hit her face like a slap.

Sometimes she thinks that if it hadn't been for Diego, she would never have warmed at all, just slowly frozen into a thin icicle of a girl, so cold and hard that even when they shipped her back home, she would not melt, not even when her mother's tears rained down on the ice.

Sometimes she thinks that would have been better.

Dear Diego,
I need to talk to you. I have something to tell you. Meet me downstairs
at Cobb, tomorrow, at . . .

I don't get further than that. I can write the words that I know will frighten him, insert the place, the date—all it needs is the time and my signature before I slip it under his door, down the hall, just four doors down. He's waiting for it. Our notes have become something of a joke on the floor, but a friendly one. When I first admitted to my room-mates how we'd gotten together, how I'd written him a note and slipped it under his door, like a schoolgirl, they'd laughed and laughed. But eventually Rose decided it was just too romantic, and Karly had agreed, and soon it seemed the entire floor had adopted us as their very own storybook romance.

Romance, hah! If they had seen how my hands were shaking all that night, how I tossed and turned, how little I slept, waiting, expecting him to sadly but firmly shake his head no, with a little hateful pity in those coriander-green eyes . . . well. They probably would think that romantic too. Idiots.

I admit, I had grown fond of the notes, these last three months.

Minal, meet me for breakfast?

Diego, I'll see you at 8:00.

Minal, do you have time to visit the museum on Saturday?

Diego, I'm skipping calculus this morning—join me?

We never wrote anything that seemed of importance in those notes—and yet I kept every one. I knew what they didn't say, what they didn't need to say. They didn't say, "I'll give you a dozen kisses if you get up early to eat with me." They didn't say, "Let's skip the electricity exhibit and go neck in the statue garden." They didn't say, "Rose and Karly are going to *their* classes, so we have an hour—join me in bed?" They didn't need to say any of that—we knew.

And if I send him this note, if I finish it with a time and sign it and slip it under his door, he will think he knows what it means. He will think it means that this is the end, that I have grown tired of him, or that I have decided this was a mistake after all. And he will be wrong, but he will also be right.

This is the end of something.

OCTOBER. MINAL SITS IN THE LOUNGE PAST MIDNIGHT, STRUGGLING with equations. Tea water is heating on the stove, heating, boiling, boiling over, hissing, and she swears as she jumps up, grabs the pot handle and lets go again, grabs up some of her skirt to help her hold the handle as she lifts the pot off the range and clunks it down in the sink, spilling boiling water everywhere and just missing scalding herself again—"Goddammit!"

"I've never heard you swear before."

"What?" Minal swings around, her long black hair swinging with her, straight and smooth like a waterfall, and he bites his lip.

"I don't think I've ever heard you swear. Do you need help?" He is leaning in the doorway to the small kitchen, taking up space—taking up so much space. Minal loses his name for a moment, then finds it again—yes, Diego. A second-year from four doors down. She has a little trouble understanding him; he has an accent. And his eyes are very green.

"Why would you know, or care, whether I swear?" She turns back to the sink, lifts the pot, pours the hot water into the mug with the tea bag waiting. She puts the pot back on the stove and turns off the flame.

"I've been watching you."

She is startled but will not look at him. The words could have sounded menacing, in another mouth, but from him they sound sweet, and slightly sheepish. She takes down sugar and pulls out a spoon, and milk, before answering.

"Really." She does not know how she means that—challenging, inviting? But it must have come out wrong, because he is pulling away, stepping back out of the doorway so the light comes spilling back in, walking away.

"Sorry. I should really get to bed. Good night."

And he's gone. Damn.

SHE WRITES HIM THE FIRST NOTE THAT NIGHT AND SLIPS IT UNDER his door, and doesn't sleep until almost dawn.

Diego,
I'm sorry if I snapped at you earlier. Would you like to study together tomorrow night?

When tomorrow night comes, they share a table, and she helps him with his calculus. His hand brushes hers. Her hair falls across his leg as she leans in over his papers. His breath quickens. She feels it on her cheek. She turns, or he does. He leans, or she does. Their lips meet and hold. Their tongues, tentatively, dance.

October 18

Amma,
Yes, my studies are going well. I am working hard, and getting all As. Do not worry. You asked what my days are like, here in America. I get up in the mornings and have breakfast—a bagel, which is a kind of bread, and cream cheese. I go to classes all day. I have lunch and dinner in the dining hall. If you could send some of your curry powder, then I could cook curries sometimes. The food here is very bland. There are Indian restaurants, but I do not have a car, so it is difficult to get to them, and besides, they are too expensive. The food is filling enough. After dinner, I study until bedtime. I spend many hours in the dorm lounge, working. If I am not in my room when you call, it is probably because I am in the lounge or the library, studying.

And kissing.

NOVEMBER. SHE RECITES POETRY TO DIEGO. IN SRI LANKA, SHE HAD escaped the endless rounds of family gossip, the sisters tearing into each other and the aunts nagging, by reading her books. English books too, of course, but also the ancient Indian poets. She tells him the *Ramayana*, in pieces, in between calculus problems. It is a reward when he solves a particularly difficult one. Minal recites translated poems until he knows them too and can recite them back to her.

I CANNOT COUNT THE CLASSES I HAVE MISSED FOR KISSING DIEGO.

He is from Puerto Rico. He whispers Spanish words to me while he kisses me. He starts at my toes, *mis dedos de los pies*, and works his way up, kissing and whispering, so soft I can barely hear it, barely feel it. *Te quiero; tus pies. Tus rodillas. Tus caderas.* Then he stops and moves to the top of my head, and starts working down. *Tu pelo, tu nariz, tus orejas.* The first time he licked my ear, I felt a shock run through me, not so different from the time I stuck my finger in an unshielded outlet as a little girl. But now I am greedy. I do not want him to stop at my ears. My hands are on his hips, on his back, on his shoulders, pushing him gently, urging him down.

Te quiero; tu garganta, tus brazos, tus muñecas. Tus uñas, tu estómago, tu cintura. He would linger at my waist if I would let him, would play with my belly button, but I do not allow it. I urge him onward— quickly, hurry hurry! We have only twenty minutes left, fifteen, ten be- fore Rose and Karly return. And they are lovely roommates, such nice girls, and if they come back before you finish, I will kill them, and then you. So hurry, hurry, *por favor*, my darling.

DECEMBER. THEY HAVE SETTLED DOWN A LITTLE. THEY HAVE STARTED going to classes again, and her professors are relieved. The leaves have all fallen off the trees—Indian summer is long gone—but Minal is no longer cold.

She is blazing so brightly that she is amazed that others cannot see it. She is feverish with heat. She sits in class with her legs crossed and her coat tightly closed. She has slipped an arm out of a sleeve and with it caresses a breast, squeezes a nipple. She pulses the muscles of her crossed thighs, there in the large lecture hall, with Rose to her right and a stranger to her left, taking notes with one hand, though her eyes are almost closed and her ears are filled with the thundering of her own pulse and she is on fire. She will blaze up like a goddess, she will strip off all her clothes and burst into flame and dance along the desktops, with a dozen arms spread wide and one on her breast and one between her thighs—she will roast all of these pale-skinned people with her heat until their clothes turn to ashes and their skin turns to burnished gold and then they will jump up with her on the desktops and dance!

She takes a deep breath. Minal releases her breast, smooths down her sweater and shirt, with slight awkwardness slips her hand into a sleeve. She relaxes her thighs. The professor is making his closing comments.

Minal resolves, again, to pay more attention in class.

MAHADEVIYAKKA LIVED IN THE TWELFTH CENTURY AND LEFT AN arranged marriage to become an ecstatic devotee of Shiva. Did she believe that the god came down to her, that he pierced through her, giving her the courage to abandon everything?

ON HER DECISION TO STOP WEARING CLOTHES
Coins in the hand
Can be stolen,
But who can rob this body
Of its own treasure?

The last thread of clothing
Can be stripped away,
But who can peel off Emptiness,
That nakedness covering all?

Fools, while I dress
In the Jasmine Lord's morning light,
I cannot be shamed—
What would you have me hide under silk
and the glitter of jewels?

Would they have stripped her of her clothes and dragged her through the streets? Would they have proclaimed her shame to the village, to the kingdom, to the world? What did her mother think? Did she lead the procession?

MINAL GOES ALONE TO THE WOMEN'S CLINIC.

She tells them about the broken condom—it is hard to say the words. They want to discuss the situation; all she wants is for them to be silent and to please just give her the pills. Finally, they hand them to her, and a woman who does not believe that Minal speaks English repeats the directions over and over and over. Two with a meal. Two more later. She goes back to her room and takes off her coat. Removes her boots and places them carefully at the foot of the bed. Lies down, eyes open. Stares at the digital clock as the minutes click by. It is two hours until dinnertime. It is surprisingly cold in her room today, but the blanket is at the foot of the bed, too far away.

Twenty minutes before dinner, Rose runs in and out again, in a flurry of words. Among them, "I grabbed your mail too—looks like a letter from your mom! Here y'are! Gotta go!"

My darling Minal,
I have such news! Your aunt is a miracle worker! Your father's eld-
est sister, Bharati, has arranged such a match for you! A doctor
from Delhi, the son and grandson of doctors, with a big practice of

his own—now you do not need to become a doctor! Your grand-
mother says it is too early, that you should finish your studies, but
I married when I was your age, and I never regretted leaving school
behind me. So much better to be a doctor's wife, with servants to
cook and clean and fan you and take care of your babies. A life of
luxury! Bharati Aunty says he took one look at your picture and
said, "This is the girl for me!" No need to finish out the year—come
home, we will have such a celebration. And we need to start shop-
ping for the wedding saris, for the jewelry, for the shoes—I hope you
have not put on too much weight eating that terrible greasy
American food...

AND SO, I WRITE LETTERS TO MY AUNT THAT I WILL NOT SEND. I STARE
at the now useless pills, left too late because I am a confused, weak-
willed fool. They are enshrined in a small green glass on my desk, a
testament to stupidity. I write notes to Diego and tear them up
again. I look at the photo my mother sent. He is not bad-looking,
this doctor. His skin is fairer than Diego's. Maybe I should write to
him and ask him what I should do. Maybe he will volunteer to perform the operation himself, and then we will be married, and all
will be well.

At least I have learned something out of all of this. I have learned
that while I like Diego very much, and I like his body even more, I do
not love him.

Amma,
His skin, Amma, is like your milk toffee with almonds, creamy and
soft. His eyes are a startling green, coriander green, except when he
is tired, and then they are the dusky darkness of curry leaves. His
body is tall and strong, like a young palm tree, firm and unmarred.

His fingers are supple, and his tongue is skilled, and when he touches me, I become water falling, a river coursing down the tumbling rocks, down into the waiting arms of ocean.

Amma, the poets spoke truly.

Amma, why did you not tell me that such pleasure existed? Why did you not warn me that it would turn my brain to water? You should have spoken clearly, sharply, like a knife, telling me exactly what would happen when he first breathed on my neck, when he cupped my chin in his hands and tilted it up, when he cupped my breasts in hands so broad that I disappeared into them, when I lowered myself onto him, and he thrust into me, like a young god.

How could vague whisperings of shame and family disgrace compare?

Amma, I do not even love him. Though for a little while, I thought I did.

THAT NIGHT, WE WERE DOWN AT THE LAKE, CLAMBERING ACROSS THE shattered rocks at some hours past midnight, dodging the spray as the waves came crashing up, laughing. I don't remember being cold as we danced on broken stones.

Diego was standing quite still when he did it, though. He stopped still on a rock and I stopped, facing him. He caught my hands in his and tipped his head back and shouted into the night, "I love you, Minal!" A great shout—his voice was usually so soft—I hadn't known he had such a sound in him. And a blaze of warmth in my chest, and I was shouting too, shouting like an idiot into the night, shouting that I loved Diego. Laughing and then running across the rocks, chasing each other until he slipped and fell and bruised his side, and it could have been so much worse, there on the sharp, slippery rocks. That sobered us.

We went quietly back to the dorm, and down to the empty piano room, the only public room in the dorm that could be locked, and there we made love, very carefully at first, and then less so, burning in our fierce desire.

That night.

SHE PUTS DOWN THE PHONE, SLOWLY. THE CLINIC HAS TOLD HER that they can do nothing right now. That she must wait until late January, at least. That she should come in and talk to a counselor. That they can schedule the appointment now, if she's sure. That there are other options. She was polite to them, though absent. It seems that some part of her brain is accepting the data, processing it, even though she cannot think about it at all.

It startles her a little, how competent she has been about it all. The pharmacy, the purchase of the little box, the ripping open of the packaging, the careful following of directions. The disposal of the final, damning results.

It is Friday. Exams are over and her roommates are gone. Diego leaves for Puerto Rico tomorrow. She leaves Sunday, to spend Christmas in Massachusetts. Raji Aunty has written, saying it is not nearly as cold there as it is in Chicago, and that there will be another guest at the house as well. That almost shook her resolve, but surely there will be a time when the guest is away, out Christmas shopping perhaps. Minal will talk to her aunt then. She will ask her what to do.

ONE MIGHT THINK THAT UNDER THESE CONDITIONS I WOULD BE LESS fond of sex.

This is not true.

Was it greedy of me, not to tell him until morning? To take one last night, with his hands between my thighs, stretching me open for his tongue? To spend hours licking every inch of his body, yes, even those inches shyness had kept me from before? My mother always said I was a greedy child. I took more than my share of caramel pudding, of milk toffee. Well enough. I do not regret that last night. I will remember always the surprised look on his face when I took him deep in my mouth, the groan he gave, the tensing muscles beneath my digging fingers. I will remember his hands, above his head, clenching the pillow as he arched. I will remember later the way my head fit so perfectly in the hollow of his shoulder, the slowing beat of his heart, his hand stroking my hair. Poor Diego.

In the morning, I told him I was leaving him. I think he had expected it. I hope so.

I didn't tell him the rest. Perhaps I am a terrible person. Perhaps I will write him a letter.

Dear Diego,
You may soon have a son. Or a daughter. Sorry I forgot to mention it earlier . . .

Perhaps not.

MINAL WAITED LONG HOURS IN THE AIRPORT, THROUGH ONE DELAY, and then another. She paced, up and down the carpeted halls. The heating wasn't working very well—despite the crowds of people, she felt quite cold. And when she finally got on the plane, her neighbor insisted on turning his air jet so it hit Minal too. Her right side slowly froze. She asked for a blanket, but there weren't enough. She used her coat as a blanket and unbuttoned the top of her long skirt, sliding her fingers inside. It only warmed her a little.

When she finally arrived, past two AM, her aunt bundled her quickly into bed, with a hot water bottle for her feet and extra blankets. There was no sign of the other guest, but Minal was too tired to talk. The morning would be soon enough. Her aunt patted the blankets one last time before she left, turning out the light as she went. Minal curled into the blankets and quietly cried herself to sleep.

❧

I HAVEN'T BEEN IN MY AUNT'S HOUSE BEFORE. IT'S EMBARRASSING. I know my mother would want me to write and tell her all about it, but what do I say? That my uncle's medical sketches of the human form are hung up right next to my aunt's lush oil paintings? That while either might be innocent separately, they are clearly lascivious together? That when I sat in the kitchen drinking my breakfast tea, waiting for my aunt to wake up, a nude reclined before me, a brown-skinned woman basking in the sunlight, her sari a discarded crimson puddle around her, her face caught with an unmistakable smile? Oh, Amma would love that.

Raji Aunty comes down, Vivek Uncle behind her. Is his hand on her back, or her buttocks? Is that faint scent perfume, or her own musk? Must I see sex everywhere? Is there something wrong with me? He says it is good to meet me, and that he is sorry he has to rush. We'll talk at dinner. Then it's a kiss, a long kiss, for his wife, and it's off to the hospital. That's it—I'll ask *him* to perform the procedure. That's perfect—just keep it all in the family!

Ah, one of these days I'll say the wrong thing and get myself into real trouble.

There is no sign of another guest. I ask my aunt when they'll be arriving. She tells me, with a little smile, that the guest was already here. She's pregnant, it seems. She had been having a little joke with me. They just found out. The baby is due in July.

If there are gods, they must hate me.

RAJI AND MINAL SIT AT THE KITCHEN TABLE, SIPPING MORNING CHAI. Raji's eyes are sharp, focused on Minal's face. Minal is sure she is noting each new line, realizing that it has only been a few months since they last met.

"Are you well, Minal? You look a little tired."

Minal bites her lip before responding; it has been bitten raw. Her fingers tap the table, click click, click click. "Well enough." She tries to smile but does not manage to pull it off.

"So. Your mother has written to me, about this doctor. A brilliant match, I hear." Raji's tone is careful, inquiring. Minal's lips purse, just slightly, but enough. Raji nods and says, "Your mother . . . she's a passionate woman. But she isn't good at admitting when she's made a mistake. Ever since she moved back to Sri Lanka, she's become more Sri Lankan–than–thou." She pauses, but Minal says nothing. Raji continues, gently. "Maybe it's the right thing for her; she does seem to love it there. Even your father's behavior wasn't enough to bring her back home. But maybe you aren't ready for marriage, or at least for a traditional arranged marriage; maybe Sri Lanka isn't the world for you . . . ?"

Minal's fingers tap, but her eyes are fixed on the tabletop, and her lips stay shut.

Raji falls silent as well. They continue drinking their tea, and after a while, she reaches out for a pen and a long pad, starts to scribble on the paper—a shopping list. Cauliflower, eggplant, fresh chilies, more paper, Cadmium Blue. She asks, "Do you think we need anything else?" Minal hesitates, then takes the paper away from her aunt and writes something on it. She pushes it back, and Raji reads it. Pickles and ice cream. She laughs. "I haven't been craving either of those, but thank you for the thought." Minal doesn't laugh. She says, quietly, "I have." Raji stops laughing. They are silent for a while. Minal counts to a hundred in Spanish, and then back down again. She wishes she'd learned more of it. Her chest is aching. *O, mi corazón!*

Then her aunt leans forward and whispers, "Pickles and ice cream? Really?"

Minal starts to laugh. "No, not really."

"Well, good. That's something, anyway." Suddenly, they are both laughing. This may turn out all right.

They compare dates. Minal is perhaps three days later. They agree that that's something, at least, though they're not sure what. Then a little silence again, and then Raji asks the dreaded question.

"What do you want to do?"

I COULD DRAW A CHART. THE BRANCHES: TELL MY MOTHER, OR NOT; go back to Sri Lanka, or not; have an arranged marriage, or not; have a baby, or not; be a doctor, or not; tell Diego, or not; marry Diego, or not. Some options exclude others. I don't really think I can have a baby *and* an arranged marriage. And I'm not even sure I can tell my mother *and* have an arranged marriage. There are many things I'm not sure of, but there is one thing I do know, sitting here with my aunt the painter, looking at her nudes beside her husband's medical sketches.

"I don't want to be *just* a doctor's wife."

Raji Aunty nods. She knows what I mean. I want to stay here and study, which means no arranged marriage back home, which means I'll have to write my mother. Amma can't make me go back, not with the scholarship supporting me here. Small blessings.

"And I don't want to marry Diego." That part is also clear, and has been for some time. He is sweet and kind and lovely in bed—but I don't want to marry him.

"School?" she asks. I nod. Definitely school. Only two choices left to make. This is going faster than I'd expected. I feel a little dizzy—or perhaps that is the baby.

"If you want . . ."—She says it slowly—"I could help you raise the baby. You could transfer to Yale, and I could tell people I'd had twins, at least at first, if you wanted."

"That's too much." It is too much, and yet I know she'd do it. Family. She was family, after all. Even if she had had an arranged marriage, even if I hardly knew her.

"Or, I could ask Vivek to recommend someone."

"No!" I couldn't stand him, a stranger, my uncle, knowing.

"Or I could take you somewhere myself." She waits, patiently. I get up and start pacing. Back and forth, back and forth. I can put this decision off for another month, if I want. If I said so, she would pick up her shopping list, and we'd go off, and nothing else would be said, and nothing would be decided. I think I could love Raji Aunty very much, but right now, I almost want her to be more like my mother, just to have someone who would tell me what to do. Finally, I stop pacing and face her.

"You want your baby, don't you?" I ask her quietly, knowing what she'll say.

"Very much. We've been trying for a while." Her dark eyes are steady, and I know that she knows what I am about to say. I bite my lip, then speak.

"I don't want this one."

"Okay, then. I don't see any need to tell your mother. I'm here to take care of you." Her voice is firm, decisive, and with that last decision taken out of my hands, with everything over, finished, I sink down into one of her kitchen chairs and bury my face in my hands, and do not cry.

Dear Amma,

I am very sorry to write you like this, but I must tell you that I do not want to have an arranged marriage right now. I am busy with my studies, and still have many years of school before I become a doctor. Please thank Bharati Aunty for me, and send my regrets to the young man in question. I will visit you this summer, but do not plan to set me up with anyone then either. Raji Aunty will be coming for a visit then too, so you will get to see us both at once . . .

❦

I AM MODELING FOR MY AUNT UNTIL THE HOLIDAY ENDS. THIS IS A LITTLE strange, but she promises that my face will be turned away in the picture. The family in Sri Lanka knows she paints, but nothing of the subjects. They undoubtedly think it is a pleasant hobby for a doctor's wife, and that she paints wildflowers, or sunsets. She will be exhibiting her paintings in New York next month. I will be in one, with my body thin and bare, with my arms outstretched, with the snow surrounding me. She is painting me a tree in winter, barren and brown, waiting for spring. It isn't as cold in Massachusetts as it is in Chicago. It is easier to believe, here, that spring will come.

I can stay quite still while she paints, but the muscles get tired and eventually start to tremble. The trembling is interesting.

I am glad that she does not need to paint me and the snow at the same time. Her studio is warm and steaming, and there is always hot tea on the kitchen stove. My uncle knocks before entering, so that I have time to dress in an enveloping robe, and we have been having some very interesting talks about medicine, about muscles and sinews, electrical synapses and rushing blood. I think I am going to like being a doctor. Bodies are fascinating.

I will talk to Diego when I return. He deserves to know. He probably also deserves to have a say in this, but I don't think I am strong enough to give him one. Hopefully he will be all right. I'd like him to be happy.

Perhaps I can set him up with Rose. She likes him, I know.

As for me—the world is wide, and there are many possibilities.

Snow falls outside my aunt's window, quietly blanketing the ground, lacing the trees.

It's really quite beautiful.

Wood and Flesh

Berkeley, 1999

SAVITHA TEASED HER COUSIN THAYALAN EVERY TIME HE CAME TO VISIT WITH HIS PARENTS. SHE SAT WITH HER KNEES APART, SHE BENT over to pick things up, she blew kisses at him with wet lips as he was driving away. Thayalan wrote her long letters full of the small details of his life, slipped them into her books at school. Savitha didn't write back, but he was patient, and faithful. It wasn't hard not to look at other girls, not with a cousin so reckless, strange, and endlessly fascinating. The pale blondes who occasionally let their hands rest on his strong arms held no interest for him.

The first time the cousins had sex was when they were both fourteen. Savitha was a few months younger than Thayalan. His mother was visiting her mother; Savitha's sister Chaya had moved out by then, gone off to grad school. Savitha took him up into the attic; Thayalan was trembling with uncertainty, eagerness. He had heard the rumors by then; the boys all knew about her.

Thayalan was fascinated by her slim, light-skinned beauty, by the air of danger that surrounded her. He had written Savitha a love letter on his mother's pink stationery, had slipped it into her locker at school.

That day, Savitha closed the door, led him to a sheltered corner where her mother had piled old blankets and sheets, neatly folded. She pulled out a sharp knife—the big butcher knife that her mother used to chop chicken bones in half before dropping the pieces into the bubbling pot of curry. Thayalan's eyes widened, but he didn't say a word. Savitha told him that he had to swear a blood oath, to tell no one what they had done—and that he had to promise to love her forever, to always be faithful to her. Thayalan was silent for a long moment, and Savitha almost turned and left the attic then. There were plenty of boys who would have done exactly as she asked, without hesitation. But something held her there as he gazed at the knife. Finally Thayalan nodded his head in agreement, holding out his open palm for her cut, his eyes open and steady. Savitha found herself glad that he had waited until he was sure.

Afterward, they lay down together on the old blankets. She pulled her clothes off, quickly, and he followed. His bony hips moved against hers; his hands pressed hard against her small breasts, her flat stomach. Thayalan's bloody palm left blurred lines on her brown skin.

Savitha didn't touch him again for years. When she came to him and asked him to take her away, he was ready. He'd been waiting.

THEY FOUND A HOUSE OVERLOOKING THE BAY, FACING WEST TOWARD the ocean. Just the two of them there, though it was large enough for a real family. The yard was overgrown, overtaken by wildflowers, crabgrass, one corner swallowed in a fierceness of blackberry bramble. When they first moved in, Savitha went out to attack the bramble, enthusiastic, armed with a sharp pair of clippers. Hours later, Thayalan found her kneeling there, arms scraped bloody and the mass of bramble still overwhelming. Savitha's eyes were bright and wet, but she was hacking away, blindly determined until he knelt down, wrapped his arms around her, stilling her. *Later*, he promised her. They'd deal with it together, later. Thayalan took the clippers away, led her inside to wash and bandage her arms.

The house itself was barely furnished—desks and PowerBooks, bookshelves and a bed. Even after two months, they hadn't bought pots and pans. Neither had ever learned to cook. They bought mediocre Indian takeout instead and added raw red chili powder to make it palatable, eating one-handed, hunched over their computers. Savitha programmed for a small gaming company; Thayalan was writing a historical novel about Sri Lanka, set in the early 1950s, right after the British left. He hadn't sold it yet.

In early summer, Thayalan asked her to see a doctor. She was sure it would be useless, but agreed. Savitha chose a doctor recommended by an online referral service; she specified someone older. He turned out to be kindly, patient. He examined the suppurating sores on her belly; he was sure that he had seen this sort of thing before. The doctor prescribed bland food, less work. Savitha nodded politely and thanked him. She didn't say that the work was what kept her sane. She didn't mention that the sores had been with her since childhood. He gave her soothing cream, ice packs for the sore tendons in her arms. He sent Savitha home with a cherry lollipop and told her to call if the condition persisted or worsened.

The condition had improved since their arrival in Berkeley, but it did sometimes worsen. Those nights, she almost cried from the accumulated pains of the day. Savitha would curl in on herself, naked under the pale sheets, and Thayalan stroked her hair, her shoulders, until finally her muscles loosened and she fell asleep. He cried then, silently, for her. His body was long and loose on the bed, his face peaceful, and the tears slid down the line of cheekbone, pooling in the curve of ear, soaking into the sheets. Savitha would wake and kiss the tears away, licking the salt skin dry.

SHE HAD NEVER CRIED MUCH HERSELF, THOUGH HER CHILDHOOD had been complicated, full of pain. Falls and scrapes, bumps and bruises. Savitha had forever been injuring herself—cuts on her elbows and knees, sores on her back, along the column of her spine, a bloody gash on her forehead, two inches of raw abraded flesh on her upper arm. First bicycles were forbidden, then climbing trees, then running. And still the wounds kept appearing. On her twelfth birthday, Savitha woke to blood on her sheets, cramps in her belly, and a raw sore across her stomach, another on her right thigh. She washed her own sheets that morning and all the ones after, rising often before sunrise, hating the sun, the dawn, the morning—everything that wrenched her from sleep. She washed the sheets because she had no choice, until the day Thayalan took her away from her mother's house.

Savitha tried to talk to her sister about the sores, once. But Chaya was going to be a scientist, like their grandfather; she believed there were rational explanations for everything. Chaya was certain that Savitha was doing it to herself—cutting herself, scraping herself, rubbing her own skin raw in the deep hours of night. Chaya pointed to the blood under Savitha's fingernails; she dismissed Savitha's explanation that she had woken and instinctively felt for the new wounds, pressing her fingers into the scrape, feeling the welling beads of blood. Perhaps Thayalan believed that as well, that his wife was secretly injuring herself. Savitha couldn't prove otherwise, not even to herself. But she didn't believe it.

At least Thayalan didn't try to convince her of that theory, if he did believe it. He kept his own counsel and took care of her as best he could.

SAVITHA CAME TO HIM THE NIGHT SHE TURNED EIGHTEEN AND SAID, *Take me away.*

He asked, *Where?*

She said, *As far as you can.*

A friend of Thayalan's helped them rent a U-Haul, and while her mother was out, they loaded the van with the carved bed frame, with black trash bags full of the pale shimmering saris Lakshmi compulsively bought her daughters, though they never wore them. They filled the van with blue jeans and T-shirts, with their computers, wrapped carefully in old blankets from her mother's attic. They left Chicago on a Monday, and by Saturday they were in Berkeley, and married.

It was true that he was her first cousin, but that wasn't so unusual, back in Sri Lanka. It seemed better than the alternatives.

SEX STARTED IN FIFTH GRADE, THOUGH HER MOTHER REFUSED TO believe it. When Savitha asked Timothy to meet her in the gym, up on stage, near the light board, he went. They skipped lunch and created a nest out of old stage curtains, frayed blue velvet. Her muscles were taut, her body was aching; perhaps he could give her body what it wanted. Savitha didn't dare remove her uniform—just helped Tim push the blue plaid up, out of the way, pull aside her cotton panties, far enough so that he could sink first fingers, then penis, inside her. It hurt just enough, just exactly enough. It quieted her.

After the first time, they brought their lunch to the gym, ate quickly just before the bell rang. Tim lasted almost a month. She spent the next two years with Tim, with Bobby, with Matthew, with Jeff. They did what she told them to, gave her exactly what she asked for. They would have given her anything. In seventh grade, Katharine Swenson told her about condoms. Savitha found out later that two girls in her class had had abortions by then.

She didn't sleep with South Asian boys, though there were a few in her class, and more in high school. That would have been much too dangerous, even though none of them were Sri Lankan. Savitha didn't bring any of the white boys home, either. She met them in the gym, under the bleachers, in the basement music room, in their parents' houses, in their parents' beds, in the woods, and once, actually up in a spreading maple tree. Her spine pressed against the broad support of a branch, her skirt pushed up to her waist and her legs wrapped around Jeff's sweaty waist. Two things grounding her—the bark scraping against her bare back, and the pleasure sheeting through her, pulsing waves from her center, a sharp incandescence. For those few minutes, Savitha knew exactly where and who she was.

That was one of the few times she climbed a tree and didn't fall out of it.

BY OCTOBER, THEIR FAMILY HAD TRACKED THEM DOWN. HER MOTHER wept on the telephone, her words a blur of Tamil and English, sliding back and forth, swift castigations, entreaties. Savitha listened for half an hour, forty-five minutes, an hour, her eyes fixed on the computer clock, watching the numbers shift. She took as much as she could, then handed her husband the phone. Thayalan listened patiently, murmuring softly. *Yes, Lakshmi Aunty. Yes, I know. Don't worry. She's fine.*

It was the first call of many—several times a week, Savitha's mother called. She asked if they were eating well, if they were healthy, if they were sure they didn't want to come back to Chicago, to the family. *No, Aunty. No, not yet. Maybe for Thanksgiving, Christmas, in the spring.* Savitha's mother asked if she can come to visit them, at least. Thayalan looked at Savitha, who shook her head. *Not yet, Aunty. Later.*

Savitha didn't like to leave the house. Thayalan did leave, though— he went out into the world, he met people. He signed up for evening classes—wood carving, rock climbing, sailing. Thayalan had always learned things quickly; he was used to being effortlessly good at almost everything he tried. He was good at making friends too—though Savitha was paid well enough, the only way they could afford to sublet the house was through friends Thayalan had made online, friends who knew of secret rent-controlled houses, leased to generations of students, passed down in the dark through grubby hands.

The only thing he was not good at was healing his wife, though he did as much as he could.

Thayalan coaxed her outside at night, and they walked the deserted streets of Berkeley. From their house on Solano, they headed down to University, then east to Shattuck, down to Dwight, east again, as far as Telegraph. They wandered the campus, silent beneath the moonlit shadow of the campanile. When Savitha tired of walking, Thayalan took her sailing under the stars, out on the bay in a tiny Sunfish. The expanse of water was huge, and dangerous. It calmed her.

Once, Thayalan persuaded her out in the early afternoon, but that was too much for her. The sun was too bright, and she fled to their little house. Savitha wished then that they had curtains, so that she could pull them closed and shut out the world.

SHE TOOK A KNIFE TO HER BELLY WHEN SHE WAS NINE—CAREFULLY. She wasn't stupid.

Savitha knelt in the bathtub with her father's pocketknife, her small face intent as she planned her design. There was a sore just below her belly button, a little to the right, an oozing eruption of pus, slightly smaller than her palm. Savitha was tired of washing and bandaging and had decided to try something new—she would make it into a flower. The stem was easy enough, a single clean line, cut just deep enough to break the skin. It almost didn't hurt. The petals, though— she managed two curving petals around the flower's rough center before her hand started to shake, her determination wavering. Savitha rested, cut one more, and decided it was enough. Already, in the cutting, she knew—this wasn't going to help.

The flower faded long before that first boy, Tim, would have discovered it.

THEY BOTH WORKED HARD MOST DAYS, WORKED UNTIL THEY WERE TOO tired to think. Savitha turned to computer games after work. She built elaborate cities, beautiful gardens, systems of water pipes and sewer lines. Cities linked together to form countries, entire civilizations. She added element by element, building to a crescendo, a climax of beauty and harmony—and then tore them down again. Savitha lost herself in the games for hours, days, but in the end, they did not satisfy. Eventually, always, she deleted her constructed worlds and went back to work.

Thayalan walked away from his computer instead. Most nights, he read history books, thick tomes on India with perhaps a single slim chapter on Sri Lanka, research for his novel. When he grew tired of reading, he turned to carving. Thayalan went alone to the kitchen for a sharp knife and sharpened it further on a smooth stone. He pulled out a piece of wood from a pile stacked by the door. He opened the back door onto a night heavy-scented with jasmine; the owners of their house had planted jasmine vines by the kitchen door, trained to climb over the trash cans. The sweet scent of the flowers couldn't quite cover the smell of rotting garbage. But it helped.

He sat down in the doorway and started to carve. Thayalan liked the sharpness of the knife, the careful pressure he had to exert. Too little and the cut was weak, ineffectual. Too much and the wood was sliced through. Although even then, he could usually turn it to something else, find something of grace in the mauled fragment.

Thayalan carved small animals, flowers, fish. What he liked best was the long history of the art, the sense that men had whittled forever, since knives were first made sharp enough to cut through wood, coaxing beauty out with clever hands. He had learned a lot in a few months of practice, but sometimes he still sliced through his finger or palm, staining the wood a darker brown. It was the price he paid for learning, unavoidable.

THEIR BED FRAME WAS CARVED AS WELL, THEIR ONLY TREASURE. Tree branches climbed up the tall pillars, leaves and flowers, heavy fruit in impossible combinations: mangoes, bananas, coconuts, jackfruit— all on the same tree. Birds nested in the canopied frame; small creatures hid in the dense foliage of headboard and footboard. Elephants thundered along the base of the frame, and monkeys chittered just above their heads. It was a cacophony of nature, unbearable in its liveliness. Savitha had loved it her entire life, although at times it overwhelmed her. It was once her grandmother Shanthi's bed; Grandfather had ordered it for her when they settled in Chicago, had had it shipped all the way from Sri Lanka. Savitha knew her mother would never have given it to her—Lakshmi had never learned to part with anything. So Savitha had stolen it from her mother when they left Chicago.

When they slept in it, sheer white draperies enveloped them, like mosquito netting. Neither one of them had ever left America—in fact, before now they had never left Chicago. But they imagined what it must have been like in Sri Lanka, the mosquitoes buzzing around the curtains, the world shut out of their small white enclosure.

It would have been practical to keep the bedding simple: barren, dark. Instead, the drapes enclosed many soft pillows, a lush duvet, and cotton sheets in the pale colors Savitha loved: mint and ivory and ice blue. The sheets were washed daily, replaced as needed. New sores sometimes developed on her body during the night. Thayalan did all of their laundry, the sheets as well as their T-shirts, jeans, socks. Savitha did what dishes there were, took out the trash, and tried not to think about the soiled sheets.

She asked him to tie her to the carved bedposts, with beautiful lengths of sari fabric: rose pink, sea green, gold embroidered. Thayalan had no desire to hurt her, but he made love to his wife that way, bound, with his hands tight around her thin wrists. He bit her neck, her breasts and nipples. He dug his strong fingers into her flat buttocks, hard, until Savitha was finally wet for him, open and arching. Thayalan closed his eyes as he sank into his wife; he imagined that he was touching her gently, feather-light.

THE FIRST NIGHT OUT OF CHICAGO, THEY STAYED IN A MOTEL NOT far from the city and had sex for the second time, his second time ever.

They celebrated their escape the next morning with greasy sausage biscuits and drove ten hours west. That second night, Thayalan woke in the dark. His body was curled around hers, spooned, his arm wrapped tight around her shoulders. His hand was cradling hers, nestled between her small breasts, sticky and wet. Thayalan almost pulled away, forced himself to hold still instead. Savitha had woken already, had lain there in the dark, aching, waiting for him to wake. When she realized that he wasn't going to pull away, wasn't going to run screaming into the night, she started to relax.

Savitha told him everything then, the long history of sores, of wounds opening on her body, slowly healing, only to open again. She told Thayalan everything she knew, everything she guessed, everything she believed. It wasn't much. There were mysteries in her family, secrets that went unspoken. Maybe if Savitha had stayed, had been a good girl and married a boy they chose for her, maybe the aunties would have revealed all. That was how it was supposed to go—girls were kept innocent until they married, or at least everyone agreed to keep up the pretense that they were. It was only after marriage that the women spoke freely, pulled out all the dirty laundry, discussed it over the plates of steaming rice, the endless curries.

Savitha hadn't been willing to take that route, hadn't been capable of it. She had never been interested in innocence, or pretense.

BY THANKSGIVING, THEY HAD TIRED OF TAKEOUT FOOD. THAYALAN bought a cookbook, started teaching himself to cook. He didn't attempt curries. They contented themselves with simple American dishes. Spaghetti and sauce, hamburgers, mashed potatoes—all with extra crushed red pepper sprinkled on top. Savitha helped with the chopping, but didn't understand how Thayalan could take so much pleasure in preparing food. The tasks seemed dull and repetitive to her, but he claimed he enjoyed watching the meal come together from so many small parts.

Savitha enjoyed watching her husband move, the muscles of his arms flexing as he lifted pots or poured cream into a bowl. The curve of his back as he bent to taste a sauce, hot from the pan. She got into the habit of sitting at the kitchen table watching him stir and sauté, her mouth wet. Savitha asked him, *Is it ready yet?* Thayalan said, *Soon, soon.* Sometimes he paused in his cooking to bend over, spoon in hand, and kiss his wife. Savitha kissed back, eagerly, her hands coming up to cup his face, pulling him to her until, laughing, he pulled away, turned back to the pot, saying gently, *Later—do you want me to burn down the house?*

She ate everything he prepared, asked for more. Thayalan learned to make other dishes—rich cream sauces, roast beef, chicken pot pies. They didn't try to work while eating those meals. They sat across from each other and talked instead. Talked about family, work, the future. The sores had been appearing less frequently; a week or more would go by without an incident. Savitha had moved on instinct, running away, bringing him here, hadn't known if it would help. But recently, she had started imagining a future.

After eating those heavy dinners, she felt satiated, bloated. After one such meal, Savitha announced abruptly that she was going to go for a run. She had no appropriate shoes, but Thayalan didn't try to stop her, too startled by the decision. She was out the door before he could protest, running barefoot in the chill of evening, running along the streets where they had walked together. She ran all the way to the campanile and stopped there, gasping, feeling small knives piercing her chest. Her stomach churned and her legs seemed about to dissolve— but Savitha felt good. Felt strong.

The next morning, she joined a gym and started lifting weights.

HER FATHER HAD DIED IN A CAR ACCIDENT BEFORE SHE WAS BORN. Her mother raised two daughters alone, with an overflow of wet kisses and too-tight embraces. Not entirely alone, of course—Savitha's horde of aunts had come and gone without warning or apology. The uncles had hovered in the background somewhere, drinking sweet milky coffee on the porch, talking Tamil politics in low voices.

Her mother had talked and talked and talked, had always been willing to talk of everything, except her dead husband. Once, when Savitha was twelve, she had asked her mother yet again about the father who had died before she was born. *Tell me a story about Appa.* Her mother had ignored her, stirring a large bowl of cake batter with a heavy wooden spoon. Savitha asked again, louder, and Lakshmi turned, angry, the spoon in her hand coming down heavy against the side of Savitha's head, leaving wet batter stuck to her daughter's hair. *Be quiet!* Lakshmi said, and turned back to her bowl, stirring the batter once again with the same wooden spoon. It was the only time Savitha could remember her mother hitting her. She didn't ask about her father again.

Her aunts mentioned him, occasionally, in the midst of a flood of other talk. Savitha stood in the hallway outside the dining room, pressed up against the wall for hours, listening. The aunties talked about folks back home, cousins and second cousins caught up in the fighting. Houses that had burned down in the bombings. They sat over their meal, over a table full of curries, rice, noodles, uppuma, and talked about the shocking scarcities of sugar, of rice, back home. Soldiers on the beaches, on the roads—narrow escapes. Her relatives talked more about what was going on in Sri Lanka, a land Savitha had never seen, than they did about their own lives here, in America. They were obsessed with history.

Savitha couldn't understand why they cared so. Her skin was brown, but none of the white boys had ever seemed to notice or care. When Tim's hands had moved on her body, it was just him and her, in their own private world. Nothing else had mattered.

THAYALAN GAVE HIS WIFE BOOKS THAT CHRISTMAS. THE WINTER rains had started—three months of Berkeley rain, not unlike monsoon season on the island, but gentler. He gave her *History of Sri Lanka*, and *Sri Lanka in Change and Crisis*. He promised more, if she liked these. Savitha resisted them at first, ignored them, played computer games instead. But eventually she picked one up, started reading.

Ancient stories of kings and wars, along with chapters and chapters on irrigation. An island surrounded by salt water good only for fishing. Water had been terribly important—even in the current conflict, the politicians invoked the ancient king whose chief accomplishment had been to build the great freshwater tanks, the irrigation channels. Savitha imagined streams of cool water, sluicing across her body, washing away the blood and healing the bruises. She finished the books, asked for more.

It had grown too windy for sailing, too cold for midnight walks. Savitha still went to the gym, had even started taking dance classes there. Beginner modern, beginner jazz. She delighted in the growing strength in her limbs, the slow gain in precision, control. When she spun in a pirouette, Savitha felt as if she were flying. But she grew tired quickly, and then the books soothed her body's aches. Savitha nestled beneath the white drifting canopies, a small figure in the pale sheets of their carved mahogany bed; she read compulsively.

As the winter progressed, she started reading Tamil newspapers too, in translation; Savitha couldn't actually read Tamil, or speak it, or understand more than a few common words. The translated stories were compelling. Web pages by militant Tamil groups told horror stories of Tamil girls being raped by Sinhalese soldiers. Savitha lingered over these stories, closed her eyes, tried to imagine the scenes. She had never been raped, had never had a man do anything to her she hadn't asked for. No one, other than her mother with that single strike, had ever treated Savitha roughly at all.

Reading the stories made her own pain easier to bear. Though it seemed like it should be the other way around.

BEFORE SAVITHA HAD BEEN BORN, A RELATIVE HAD COME TO JOIN them—her second cousin Kamala, adopted by her aunt Kili. Kamala was sent to them by her parents, sixteen years old, sent across the ocean against her will. Savitha remembered her, a slender woman, who would sometimes play running games with her, chasing Savitha through the rooms of her father's house. Kamala played, but didn't laugh—she always seemed angry. She had moved away again, disappeared, when Savitha was still a little girl. When Savitha was older, the aunties would occasionally comment on her resemblance to Kamala— *How alike they are!* But Savitha couldn't see the resemblance. She had done nothing with her life, and Kamala had been a soldier in the war. In that war, girls fought too.

Young men and women now needed green cards, were being shipped off to India in a hurry so they wouldn't join the Tigers, wouldn't leave school to learn to shoot and kill in the jungle. The aunts discussed young women in America that the boys might marry. They even occasionally mentioned Savitha—but it was too soon for that, too soon even to talk about it. College first, of course, for both the girls. Let the poor fatherless children get a good education, be able to support themselves.

Savitha's grandparents had both gotten advanced degrees; all of her aunts had finished college, and most had gone further. Savitha's mother had been the only one of the girls not to go to college directly from high school. She had married young instead, an arranged marriage, and unfortunately to a drunkard. Savitha had learned that much about her father; he had been an alcoholic—sometimes cleaning up for a year or more, but inevitably going back to the bottle. Neriya Aunty, whose husband had killed himself, said more than once that it was God's will and God's blessing that had taken Lakshmi's husband away, though she never elaborated on why. The conversations that mentioned him always switched tracks abruptly, shifted away, elsewhere.

IN FEBRUARY, SAVITHA CALLED HER MOTHER. THEIR CONVERSATION was brief—Savitha was firm about saying good-bye after fifteen minutes and putting down the phone. But it was pleasant nonetheless.

So, you're cooking?

Thayalan is. But I'm eating.

Good, good.

And I've started studying dance.

Bharata Natyam? Your grandmother was quite a dancer as a young girl, you know. If she hadn't gone away to school, she might have become famous.

No, no—I've been studying American dance. Just beginner stuff. I didn't know she ever danced.

She was really something—or so she said. You should try Bharata Natyam; it is so beautiful. You would be good at it, rasathi. I never studied myself, and I've always regretted it.

I'll think about it, Amma. No promises, though.

There were possibilities in that conversation.

THERE WAS MORE TO HER FATHER'S STORY, SAVITHA KNEW. WHEN she was growing up, there was always something unsaid, something that hovered in the air around her. Leilani Aunty in particular always watched her and her sister, too carefully. Her mother often smothered her against her large breasts, sometimes bursting into tears for no reason. And when Neriya Aunty finally found out what Savitha had been doing with the white boys, what she had been doing for years—when she confronted Savitha and her mother in the kitchen, Lakshmi said it wasn't true, couldn't possibly be true. She turned away, turned back to the stove, stirring the onions too hard, so they flew out of the pan and spattered hot oil across the stove, across her bare arms. She'd screeched then, dropped the spoon and ran to the sink to run cold water over what would later become many small circles, a host of scars. That conversation was effectively derailed, and if she ever again discussed Savitha or her daughter's sex life with her sisters, she didn't do it where Savitha could hear.

Lakshmi had always been good at keeping silent on the important matters.

SPRING CAME TO BERKELEY, AND THAYALAN TOOK TO LEAVING SMALL carved gifts for her beside the computer. His single flowers grew into garlands, gardens. The miniature animal faces now had bodies attached. He got better and better, and sometimes, Savitha couldn't help smiling at the lovely curves of the petals, even laughed at the silly monkey faces. Thayalan started talking about making chairs, tables, sofas. They could have an entire forest of furniture, a carved wilderness within their four walls.

It scared her when he talked like this. If she allowed it, they would be doing more than simply existing; they would start putting down roots, trying for something better than a minimum of pain. Savitha didn't know if it was safe, what he was offering. But she didn't want to tell him no. She was stronger now, and she wanted that dream. Though sometimes, Savitha couldn't help wondering—if she weren't in pain, would Thayalan still find her beautiful? She had shaped herself around the memory, the endurance, the anticipation of pain. She didn't know who she would be without it.

Sometimes they drove down the coast, to Half Moon Bay, and went sailing on the ocean itself. In the coolness of evening with the sun going down, Savitha always urged Thayalan to go out, go further and further west. Further than was safe. She was terrified of the deep water but couldn't help herself. She kept urging him to go out, out, out, to where the waves would rise up and overwhelm them, where they would drown in the unknown waters. Thayalan always went only as far as he thought safe, and then stopped and turned for shore. Savitha knew that no matter how much he loved her, there was a point beyond which she couldn't push him, a point where he would simply stop. His love was not entirely blind. It was the reason she chose him—not because Thayalan was her cousin, familiar. But because he wouldn't let her throw herself off the boat, into the salt sea. If he lost interest, walked away, she wasn't sure she would survive it.

THAYALAN KNEW THAT HE WOULD NEVER LOSE INTEREST—HE FOUND his cousin, his wife, endlessly fascinating. Savitha thrilled him, led him closer to the edge than he would have ever dared to venture on his own. What he would never tell her was how often he was tempted to go further, to just follow her blindly, right off the world's edge.

Often, it was a very close thing.

SINCE HER OWN FAMILY HAD REFUSED TO DISCUSS HER FATHER, Savitha had tried writing to her father's parents, not long after she turned fourteen. She sent a long, polite letter to her grandparents and received no response for weeks. Finally a letter arrived, a single sheet with a few brief lines from her grandmother, saying only that her husband would prefer that they not be in touch with their son's family. Savitha had heard that her father had, for some unknown reason, been cut off by his family, but somehow, she hadn't expected that they would rebuff her as well. She burned her grandmother's letter and stopped trying to eavesdrop on the aunties. Whatever her family's secrets were, they were too good at protecting themselves. Savitha wasn't going to hurt herself any longer trying to fight through to them.

A few days later, she found Thayalan's letter in her locker.

THAYALAN BEGAN TALKING ABOUT TAKING A TRIP IN THE SUMMER, OF going to Sri Lanka. It shouldn't be too risky, as they were both

American citizens—not completely safe, but if they stayed in the south, safe enough. Thayalan had a longing to see the massive stone carvings at Sigiriya, a desire to run his fingers along their curves and angles. Savitha was afraid that the trip might disrupt the fragile equilibrium she had gained in the last year, might bring sores back to the surface; she was afraid that her skin would erupt, explode. Savitha wanted to stop, to freeze them here, in this bearable space. But at the same time, her curiosity had reawakened. If the immediate past was closed to her, perhaps the further past was not.

She had relatives in Sri Lanka—many on her mother's side, of course, but some on her father's side as well. Her grandparents had brothers and sisters. Savitha knew the name of at least one of her great-aunts, Mangai, whom she believed was still alive. Her father's father was Sundar, who didn't speak to their family, but Sundar's sister, Mangai—perhaps she might. Savitha could write to her, could visit. Maybe Mangai would tell her about her father. And whether or not she was willing, or even could—Savitha had a newfound longing to see the land where the kings once reigned, to trace the paths of the old irrigation canals, where the fresh sweet water fertilized the parched fields. Perhaps Savitha would study there. Perhaps she would learn to dance.

The newspapers made it clear—even in the middle of a war, children were being born there, life was going on. Without sugar, sometimes without even rice—going on anyway, despite the grief and the pain. Sometimes, the blood on the sheets was only from a bridal night. Sometimes, there was celebration, there was pleasure, there was joy.

Epilogue

Monsoon Day

Colombo, 2002

SHE COMES HOME, ROWING THE BOAT WITH STRONG ARMS OVER THE
BREAKWATER, JUMPING OUT TO DRAG IT UP ONTO THE SHORE.
Mangai was once a curiosity, and beggar children gathered to laugh, to
point, to stare at this strange woman in her widow's white, this old
woman who went out alone to the sea, every day, in her battered fishing boat. But familiarity breeds comfort as well as contempt, and they
have long ago grown used to her, this strangeness, this madwoman.
They have heard her story from their sisters and brothers, their parents, and now no one bothers to tell it. They leave her alone, for the
most part. They let her fish.

Most days she trades much of her catch. She wakes up long
before dawn, goes out for cold hours in the boat that she has learned
to care for, to watch over. Comes back with enough fish to trade for
her other small necessities. Rice and lentils. Her goat gives her milk;
her chicken lays an occasional egg. It is not much, but she is not as
hungry as she used to be, these days. Once the fish are gone, she
sleeps away the afternoon. In the evening she walks on the beach;
she sits on a particularly large rock; she watches the waves coming

in, going out. Since the servant woman died, two years ago, she has lived alone.

Some days are different; this is one of those days. It is monsoon season; the rain has been coming down hard for weeks, working its way through her not quite sealed roof, sending quiet trickles down the walls of hardened clay. There are days in the monsoon season when lentils and rice are no longer enough, when the insistence of memory overwhelms her. Those days, she stands on a teetering stool to reach the highest shelf; she pulls out her hoard of spices, from dust-brown fenugreek to crimson saffron threads. The rain stopped for a few hours this morning, but now it starts coming down again. She walks through it to the village center, her white sari plastered to her slight frame. There she trades smoked fish for rich coconut milk, ghee, fresh vegetables. The other women look at each other, and then tell their daughters: "Mangai Aunty is cooking. Go. Watch." As Mangai slowly walks home, limping, the girls trail behind her, eventually gathering under the spreading banyan tree that guards the door to her small house. The monsoon rain is pouring down, slamming hard into the ground, and the children jump as they go, squishing mud between their toes. Mangai walks blindly, eyes unfocused, nose deep in the scent of fresh mango rising from the full string bag she carries. Her arms should be aching, but on days like this, she doesn't notice.

She enters the clean kitchen, clears a space on the table. She takes her large knife in hand, sharpens it carefully on a stone. The girls have crept up to the sides of the house now that she is safely inside; they peer in through cracks, over windowsills. She waits until they are settled before she begins to cook. It is another part of the unspoken bargain that brings her harmony with her neighbors; the bargain has kept her safe with them for decades; she is not about to break it now.

Mangai starts slowly, but then catches the angle, the rhythm of it, and moves faster. She puts down the sharpening stone, places three onions on the table. Cuts off the top and bottom of each. Cuts them in half, lengthwise. Peels the skins off, being sure to get each bit of brown. It is not a day for being careless, for being just good enough. When she is satisfied, she rinses them in cold water, and then begins to slice them. Her eyes tear up. It is part of the price she pays for this indulgence. Paper-thin slices, from a hand swift and skilled with long practice. She has been cooking since she was eight? Ten? At least sixty years now. Her mother would come and pinch the extra flesh on her arm, hard, when she did not slice thinly enough. Punishing her for two sins at once—for being too clumsy, too fat. Probably for being too dark as well, though Mangai truly could do nothing about that. If her mother had lived to see her now, perhaps she would have at least conceded that Mangai is no longer fat. She has become a rail-thin woman, wiry and strong from the hours on the ocean, slender from endless meals of rice and lentils. Two cups of each will sustain her in a normal day.

She slices each half-onion, holding it firmly, keeping its shape—then turns it ninety degrees and dices it crosswise. For this first dish, she needs a small dice, pieces that are less than a quarter the size of her thumb. When the onions are finished, she slides them into one of her large Teflon pots. Her brother in America, Sundar, has tried to send her money; she refuses it, over and over. But one Christmas, he and his wife, Sushila, sent her a beautiful set of Teflon-coated pots and pans. Those, she kept. She imagined Sushila in the store, choosing each pot with her delicate hands; Mangai found that she couldn't bear to send them back. And besides—she loves the way the food slides right out of the pan, the fact that she can just rinse it and be done. She has no interest in the gadgets they send as well; one corner of the kitchen holds cardboard boxes full of unused kitchen toys: lemon zesters, garlic presses. Mangai sent back a television recently; she doesn't know what her brother was thinking. These days, it would only bring news of the fighting in Trincomalee, in Colombo. Young men dying, and now women too. Mangai suspects Sundar has sent money to the guerrillas. He has tried over and over to convince her to join him in America, but this is her home, and she is old. Sundar worries endlessly over her, and the war. Mangai sees no purpose in dwelling on what she cannot help. But the Teflon—that, she likes.

She sautés the onions in ghee, adding black mustard seed, cumin seed. She chops three tomatoes while she waits, chops them small and juicy. When the onions are golden, she adds a teaspoon of raw red chili powder. As it cooks, the smoke rises and makes her cough. That's her cue to add the tomatoes, a few tablespoons of vinegar, a little sugar, and a mix of dry-roasted spices, dark and fiercely aromatic. As the tomatoes cook down she quickly peels and chops three large potatoes; this first dish is a potato curry, because that takes longest to cook. Into the pot. She stirs hard, turning up the rich blend of onion and spice, coating every piece of potato. She lowers the heat on the gas range (another gift; she remembers cooking over an open fire), covers the dish, and turns back to the cutting board.

One of the tricks to cooking a feast is to think about the timing of it as you plan the dishes. If you are making hoppers, soft pancakes with high, crispy sides, then it is important to remember that they are best eaten entirely fresh—that you will have to make them one by one and serve them to your guests. So you can't expect to have ten or twenty minutes before the meal in which to make an array of sambols and chutneys. You must make those in advance, or do without. Certain flavors go together, but so do certain timings. If the timing is off, the entire meal may be ruined.

When Mangai was sixteen, Sundar had married. Her mother, along with several aunts, had prepared the wedding feast. The bride and groom had stayed at their home for eight days, before taking the train to Colombo, to his parents' home. Mangai's mother had had her making the midday meals during the week following the wedding as well. Mangai had never cooked for so many before, and while she made enough food, there was always something wrong with it. After every meal, one of the aunts would point out, kindly, that Mangai really had to be careful not to put too much tamarind into the fish curry, or too little salt in the sambar. After all, with her looks, it was important that she be a good cook. None of those meals came out perfectly—somehow, she always managed to ruin them. Secretly, she was glad.

But now she has been cooking for sixty years; she has become better than a good cook; she is the best cook for miles around, and everyone knows it. That is why the children huddle in the rain, why young Rani, fifteen years old, peers boldly through the window. The girl is eager to catch the police chief's son, and Mangai's cooking skills would be a potent lure. Mangai could tell the girl that this kind of cooking is not learned by watching, or even by teaching—that it is only the passage of time that grinds the lessons into the muscles and bones. But she cannot be bothered.

Mangai pauses before starting the second dish. She undoes the top of her sari, pulling the loose end of the fabric back over her shoulder, down across her breasts. She tucks it into her waistband, leaving her upper body covered only in her thin white blouse, less constricted. It will be easier to cook this way, though that is not why she does it. She chops three more onions, chops them finely this time. As they sauté, she sets eight eggs to boiling; they will be ready when the sauce is finished. Timing, again. Cumin and mustard seed, but this time only turmeric and salt are added. The onions cook gently, caramelizing, filling the room with their sweet scent. Nothing to make her choke; eggs should be sweet and slick, they should slide down your throat as delicate and ephemeral as honey. She had made eggs for those bridal breakfasts; she watched Sundar's bride swallow them greedily, the muscles of her slender throat shivering down. Mangai had made eggs every morning for the pleasure of that throat.

The onions have almost burned. She must pay closer attention—nothing can be made perfect without the closest of attention. That is one of the first lessons. It is important to understand that onions cannot be allowed to burn for even five seconds—the slightest burn will coat the dish with an aftertaste that no amount of chili powder can disguise. Once things have started going bad, they are forever changed;

there is no going back to that perfect moment, the one that could have been. Although sometimes, there may be a going forward. Burnt food has its own flavor, and sometimes, you can work with it, make it into something else that is, at least, interesting. But that is not her current goal. Today she is creating perfection, and the memory of it to savor. She pours cold water over the cooked eggs; she cracks their shells, slices them into the yellow sauce. She scatters golden sultanas over the top, and slivered almonds. This dish will keep well; she turns a plate over it and sets it aside.

She stirs the potatoes. They are half done, and so is she.

Mangai's hands move to the front of her sari blouse. She undoes the hooks one by one, working from bottom to top. When it is entirely undone, she slips out of it, folds it neatly, sets it on a corner stool. Her breasts had always been small; now they are further shrunken. The cold still makes her nipples harden, and she can hear the children's sudden whispering. There are no boys outside, only girls. That is one of the rules, strictly enforced, imposed by the parents, not by Mangai. Only girls outside, to see what they will become in time. They have seen this before—still they whisper, every time. They enjoy whispering, as do their parents. That is one reason why Mangai can live in peace in this village; she brings her neighbors more pleasure as present scandal than she ever could as past expulsion. It is at times like these that they have an excuse to tell her story again, what they know and what they guess. It will give them something to talk about for days, something other than the war. In a way, it's almost a gift she gives them. Perhaps they know it. But she does not do it for them.

She takes a bundle of leeks in her hands, four thick stalks. She cuts off the ends, then begins slicing them, again, paper-thin. The thinner they are, the better. Her mother loved saying that. When not a single family offered for Mangai, her mother insisted that it was because she wasn't thin, not like her brother, her sisters. Small and squat and dark. Like a potato. Mangai lived at home until she was almost forty; then her father died, and her mother became unbearable. Mangai left then, bought her own small house with her share of her father's money. Her mother had screamed her rage but had been too feeble to stop her. The house was many miles away, far enough that she never needed to see her mother again. She heard, years later, that the old woman had died.

Mangai finishes slicing and ends up with two large bowls full of leeks. She washes them in cold water, sluicing off all the dirt that had lain hidden under the skin. It takes some time. This is the simplest dish; four ingredients are enough. When she is done washing, she fries the leeks briefly in ghee, then adds turmeric and salt. She covers the pan and lets them cook on a low flame.

The leeks will take half an hour to soften, and all she has left to make is the fish, which will not take so long. But it takes time to unwind her sari from around her waist, pulling the fabric out of its tucks in front, spinning slowly as she unwraps each layer of fabric. She would like to dance, but her hip does not allow for quick movement. It aches in this weather, in the rain. The place where the bullet went into her skin, grazing the bone, feels twice as large, twice as sore, when the rain is pounding down, thumping against the ceiling, the ground outside. In America, it wouldn't have been a serious wound. Sundar, or his wife, would have been treated at a white-walled hospital, half an hour and out again, all patched up, good as new. Here, she had lain on her dirt floor, bleeding until she lost the world and faded into darkness. Her servant woman away, visiting relatives—Mangai had been left alone, unprotected in that house. She will never know if her neighbors waited at all when they found her. Did they run for help right away, for Pettiah's son, who was studying to go to medical school in India? Or did they wait, deliberate? A chance to be rid of the scandal in their midst. The woman who had lived with her servant, Daya, for decades, in a house with only one bed. A woman they had insulted, behind her back and to her face. Did they wait, or did they run?

It doesn't matter. Pettiah's son had bandaged her up, and she had healed. She had refused to tell them if the man with the rifle had been

Tamil or Sinhalese. They left her alone after that—her hip had, inexplicably, won her peace with her neighbors. It was not a small blessing, after all those years—it made days like today a little easier. She finishes her slow turning, the layers of fabric cradled in her arms. Mangai folds up the sari with care, not letting any of the wet white chiffon drag across the dirt floor, and places it on top of the folded blouse.

She stirs the potatoes one last time and then starts the rice, lacing the water with saffron threads, a sprinkle of salt, and a tablespoon of ghee. She cooks the last curry standing in only her underskirt, a straight shift of unbleached cotton from waist to ankles. This is the most difficult dish—not because it is so complex, but because fish is fragile. It must be handled with care, neither over- nor underdone. All the preparation must be done first, the sauce built carefully. Onions and ghee, cumin and mustard seed, fenugreek and cinnamon, cardamom pods and cloves, chili powder and a spoon of the dry-roasted spice mix. Salt. Tomatoes and vinegar and tamarind pulp, turning the sauce dark and tangy, so that already it smells of the sea. The rice is boiling; she pauses to turn down the rice to a simmer, to cover the pot with a lid. Then she returns to her sauce.

Add a little water, cook it down until it is almost ready—and then slide the cubed fish in, so gently. Make sure all the fish is covered with the sauce, then just let it simmer until it is done, without stirring at all. If you stir too hard, the fish will break apart, will dissolve into fragments. Her fish are soon simmering; she stirs the potatoes one final time; they have been cooking for an hour now and are meltingly soft. Mangai turns off the heat on the pot. The rice finishes, and she turns off that one as well. And then she is only waiting for the fish, counting the time in her head, watching seconds slide by.

When Daya died, Mangai went to the funeral. The priest had carefully not looked at her as he spoke the final words. She had not cried, not in front of the villagers. That night, she rowed her boat out into the merciless sea; she lay down in it and let the water carry her where it would. But when the sun rose, she found that she was not so far out that she could not row back. She returned to the barren shore. Mangai gave away all her saris and began dressing in white. At first the seconds, minutes, and hours had seemed unendurable, but eventually she began taking pleasure in them, in every second that slid by with her still in the world. It was a quiet pleasure, most days. Quiet was enough. Most days.

When the fish is ready, Mangai turns off the last burner. She takes a plate down from the shelf, battered tin. She fills a tin cup with cold water. She serves herself rice, fish, leeks, potatoes, eggs. There is enough on her plate to feed a man four times her size. She undoes the tie on her underskirt and lets it fall to the floor. Mangai carries the plate and cup over to the wall; she sits down, cross-legged on the dirt floor, with her naked back against the wall, with the water sliding down, running along her wrinkled skin, over her ribs, pooling in the hollows of her hips. She takes a drink from the cup, and a sharpened edge cuts the corner of her lip. She balances the plate on her bony right knee, and, shuddering with pleasure, she eats.

Acknowledgments

I must first offer grateful appreciation to the University of Utah's Steffenson-Canon and Neff Fellowships for essential financial assistance in writing the dissertation that became this book, and to several professors in my doctoral program who offered guidance and insight, sometimes at the most unexpected moments: Vincent Cheng, Francois Camoin, Robin Hemley, Kim Lau, Kathryn Stockton. Special thanks to my thesis advisor, Katharine Coles, who gives more useful critique in five minutes than most people can give in five months. For invaluable historical advice and assistance (all errors are emphatically my own), I am indebted to Professor Anand Yang (University of Washington), Professor Choudri M. Naim (University of Chicago), and Mythri Jegathesan, graduate student at Columbia, whose work on child and female soldiers among the LTTE (Liberation Tigers of Tamil Eelam) has proven invaluable. And from my MFA program at Mills College, thanks to El-maz Abinader, Ginu Kamani, and Julie Shigekuni, talented writers and wise professors all.

In New York, I send thanks to Duncan Bock, Andrea Hirsch, Charles Melcher, and the rest of the fabulous crew at Melcher Media, who invited me to edit *Aqua Erotica*, which led to my writing "Seven Cups of Water," which enticed me to write this book. Thanks as well to Bob Mecoy, my Crown editor on *AE*, and now my cherished agent.

And bright shiny new thanks to Marjorie Braman, my editor at HarperCollins, for having faith in me and my book—may that faith be richly rewarded.

Academics and editors offer skills, experience, and insight, but I have always relied at least as much on a community of friends and friendly acquaintances to guide my writing. When a writer works on a book for a decade, the list of those people she has to thank grows impossibly long. Undoubtedly, a few will be forgotten, and I can only hope they will forgive me. Remembering everyone I can, I send gratitude to my sisters, Mirna and Sharmila Mohanraj, to my parents, Dr. N. A. C. and Jacintha Mohanraj, to friends Todd Belton, Beth Bernobich, Lisette Bross, Kirsten Brumley, Shannon Clark, Marcia Dibble, Sapna Gupta, Nalo Hopkinson, Paul Ketzle, Debby Levinson, Michael Maltenfort, Elaine Martyn, Debbie Notkin, Karina Roberts, Shmuel Ross, and Aparna Sharma, all of whom have put up with endless ramblings from me about this book and have often given helpful words in response.

Thanks to my journal readers, to my Clarion class, to my colleagues in the Ph.D. program at Utah, to the members of SAWNET (the online South Asian Women's Network), and the members of Chicago's SAPAC (South Asian Progressive Action Collective), all of whom offered support, encouragement, and critique along the way. Extra-special thanks go to Kate Bachus, Jed Hartman, Karen Meisner, Dan Percival, and Benjamin Rosenbaum; you guys give great crit! And finally, much love and gratitude to David Horwich, who spent far too many hours helping me untangle an almost impossibly snarled web of family history and chronology; again, any remaining errors are my own.